GOLDSTONE INN

②

Marilyn White

GOLDSTONE INN
MARILYN WHITE

TATE PUBLISHING
AND ENTERPRISES, LLC

Published by Tate Publishing & Enterprises, LLC
127 E. Trade Center Terrace | Mustang, Oklahoma 73064 USA
1.888.361.9473 | www.tatepublishing.com

Tate Publishing is committed to excellence in the publishing industry. The company reflects the philosophy established by the founders, based on Psalm 68:11,
"The Lord gave the word and great was the company of those who published it."

Book design copyright © 2012 by Tate Publishing, LLC. All rights reserved.
Cover design by Kristen Verser
Interior design by Rodrigo Adolfo

Published in the United States of America

ISBN: 978-1-62147-451-7
FICTION / Christian / Romance
FICTION / Romance / General
12.08.20

DEDICATION

I dedicate this book to my family, especially my husband. Your love and support have helped me to be the woman I am today.

ACKNOWLEDGMENTS

This is a work of fiction. The characters are based upon people I have met and befriended during the years, as are the places similar to some that I've known. The 1885 stone barn truly does exist in my hometown of Waterville, Kansas—a charming little town upon which I have based my fictional town of Whitney. I have actually experienced adventures in the places I've written about, but the storyline is purely fictional. The Craigdarroch Castle and the Butchart Gardens in Victoria British Columbia are both amazing. I grew up in a small town in Kansas, and I can proudly say that most of my friends are Kansans—good, kind, and big-hearted people.

I must acknowledge my dear husband, Tim; he is the one who has traveled with me and given me the emotional support through the process of writing this novel. Without him, these words would probably never have made it to paper.

Throughout my years, my family has been the one steadfast, never-ending support for me, and it is to them that I dedicate this book. My parents were so very excited to hear that my book was going to be published, and I thank them for a stable background and Christian upbringing. I am who I am today because they have always been there for me. My six children are such wonderful young spirits, with hopes and dreams; from you I have gotten inspiration to keep striving and to never give up. I also include my siblings in this dedication. My brothers have such diverse individualities, and their devotion to family has given me insight into how to write a novel with a lot of male characters. And finally, to my sister, I especially want you to know that your perseverance and personality were the motivation to create my main character, Lucy. Our lives are stronger for the hardships we have endured, but overcoming and pressing on makes us winners in the book of life!

You, O Lord, keep my lamp burning;
My God turns my darkness into light.
With your help I can advance against a troop;
With my God I can scale a wall.
As for God, his way is perfect;
The word of the Lord is flawless;
He is a shield for all who take refuge in him.
For who is God besides the Lord?
And who is the Rock except our God?

Psalm 18:28-31

From the ends of the earth I call to you,
I call as my heart grows faint;
Lead me to the rock that is higher than I
For you have been my refuge,
A strong tower against the foe.

Psalm 61:2-3

JEDIDIAH

Simon was nearly a carbon copy of Charlie at that age. There were six of us eating burgers and fries, attempting conversation on the premise that we were all in the same boat together and we wanted to keep it afloat. Simon had very good table manners for a three-year-old boy. Very neatly and deliberately he ate the hamburger that his mother had cut into two halves. Then he deftly picked up one French fry at a time and dipped it in a tiny bowl of ketchup.

We had all gone to church together that Sunday morning in May. Actually, my sons, Charlie and Caleb, had also been with us in the Jordan family pew, but they had not arrived yet at the diner; they were in a separate vehicle and tardy. In fact, they were so tardy that I had suspicions that they were going to ditch us; that is why we were eating without them.

This simple meal was to have been a Thanksgiving of sort, even though it was springtime. It should have been the first time that all of my family was gathered together, including Lucy. Lucy and I had been high-school sweethearts and had only been reunited on Friday night. Coincidentally, we had only learned of Simon's existence on Saturday, when Bambi, Simon's mother, had announced to us that her son's biological father was Charlie. She and Charlie had what amounted to a one-night stand four years ago in Kent, Washington, and she claimed that Simon was the result of that night together.

My other daughter, Heather, is still living in Washington state with her mother. I have hope that she will soon move to Whitney, Kansas, to live with us and join us in the family business, Rocking J Construction and Ranch. It was because of Rocking J Construction that I had once again found Lucy. She had inherited the property next door and moved in about a month ago and subsequently had hired our little firm to build a large stone inn near her cottage. She'd hired my sons to tear down an 1800s-era stone barn, and the plan is to use the stones to construct a Tuscan style inn complete with turrets and an impressive garden. My architect sister Aggie (who now goes by her middle name Scarlett) drew up Lucy's blueprints for the inn, and another renowned architect, Fergus Finchman, is doing the planning for the pergolas, gazebos, and other stone structures that will be in Lucy's garden. Lucy wants to open a bed and breakfast in the inn and also have some parties like weddings and reunions at the inn.

You may have picked up on the time discrepancy. Lucy moved to Whitney a month ago, but I only discovered her two days ago. It had taken her a bit of time to figure out that my family was her general contracting firm and my sister was her architect. And once she discovered that it was I, old Jedidiah, living next door to her, she quite innocently came up with a scheme to reunite with me in a special way. She had picked me up in a limousine, cooked me a wonderful meal, and before I left her house Friday night, my fate was sealed. I knew that I was falling in love with her all over again, and maybe, if I have to be truthful to myself, I must admit that I probably have always loved her, even though it had been nearly thirty years ago that I had lost track of her when I moved away from Kansas to the Seattle area.

But there is one more bit of this plot that has my mind wandering; Lucy is a very wealthy woman and is also the holder of my contract-to-purchase my 175-acre ranch, including my home and office. She had inherited it all from her ex-husband, and by her unexpected twist of fate, I have to settle in my mind that my love for her is totally separate from my desire to keep my ranch. I don't want anyone to get the idea that I'm cozying up to Lucy just to protect my financial interests. I've got three brothers who will no doubt make some derogatory comments about my love interest. They met Lucy's ex-husband when I bought the ranch and were present when I made the deal with him to buy it on contract. So it won't be too farfetched for them to figure out that Lucy is now my landholder, as well as the love of my life. And if Josiah, Elijah, and Darwin make the connection, the rest of the small town of Whitney will also figure it out. I'm a pretty old-fashioned guy—maybe you could even call me a bit chauvinistic, I guess—but it will probably take me a while to settle in my mind whether or not I'm way out-classed by Lucy's wealth. Not that it probably would ever bother her; she's a very laid-back, conservative woman, so I'm sure she won't flaunt her wealth or her superiority. Nevertheless, my heart and brain are battling it out a bit. Put that together with the fact that I now have an illegitimate grandson and my sons are not very accepting of his presence just yet, I'm feeling a bit of stress today.

Sitting in the restaurant, trying to enjoy my burger, I'm feeling a bit surreal as I'm taking in my dinner companions, all women except for my new three-year-old grandson. Simon is full of energy, happy, and very cute. He looks so much like Charlie had at that age, I'm dumbstruck and awestruck. He has a well-developed vocabulary for a three-year-old, and he isn't shy of any of us. I give Bambi credit, though, when she introduced us to Simon; she just said we were friends. There was no mention made of any possible family connection. I had introduced Lucy to Bambi, Dee, and Simon, saying she was an old friend that I had just become reacquainted with.

Simon, Bambi, and Dee Dee sat together on one side of the Formica-topped table, eating their burgers and fries. Simon looked up, grinning, and said, "Yummy, good French fries. Would you like one?" He proffered the packet of fries to Hannah.

Captivated now, Hannah accepted the potato stick that Simon held out to her. She popped it in her mouth and said, "Simon, I think you are right. These are good fries. Do you suppose they are the best in the world?"

"I don't know," he answered shyly. "The world is gigantic."

Conversation was light, mostly centered around the food. Charlie and Caleb still had not arrived when we had finished off all of our fries and burgers and were just sipping on the shakes. To make conversation, I asked Bambi, "So, how are you and Dee Dee related?"

She answered, "Our moms are twin sisters. They grew up here in Whitney, and my mom married my dad after meeting him at college. Willow, Dee Dee's mom, lives in Manhattan; she is an ER nurse at Mid-Town Hospital. In fact, Aunt Willow is trying to get me an interview at the hospital for tomorrow or the next day. I have my LPN license; of course, I'd have to take the Kansas exam to be legal here, but Aunt Willow says that they have an excellent continuing education program at Mid-Town and that most LPNs and CNAs have the opportunity to get their RN degrees while they work there. Mid-Town pays for the classes."

"So you are considering staying here?" I asked.

"It is a possibility. I just finished up with my LPN program last month, and I don't have a job yet. My parents have been great helping me out, but it might be time for me to broaden my horizons. And Aunt Willow has offered to let Simon and me live with her in the apartment over her garage. Since she's Mom's identical twin, I think that Simon would love her instantly and be comfortable staying with her alone while I work. Willow works the day shift, and I'd probably have to start working nights if they hired me."

Hannah commented, "I like the name Willow. What's your mom's name? Does it rhyme with Willow?"

"No, her name is Cherry; their maiden name is Wood. My grandma, Rose, was kind of a forward thinker or something, naming her children Willow, Cherry, Ash, Alder, and Aspen. Grandpa was plain old John Wood."

"That's cool," was Hannah's remark. "How did you come up with the name Simon?"

"I was trying to come up with something that was in the Bible but not common, like Matthew or Luke. And Mom used to play lots of Simon and Garfunkel music. You know the song *Bridge Over Troubled Water*? I listened to it over and over when I was pregnant, so the name Simon just kind of became my obvious choice. Some of the words in the lyrics just seemed to parallel my situation so much that it comforted me in a way."

At that point she stopped talking and abruptly stood up. "Actually, I noticed earlier that they have that song on that old jukebox over there." She quickly left the table and stuffed some coins in the machine, and after pushing the correct button combination, she returned to the table just in time to hear the song begin. The old song from the seventies filled the diner with sound. Bambi quietly sang along in a clear, perfectly pitched voice.

Her voice cracked with emotion a couple of times, and there were tears welling in her eyes, but she continued on. The lyrics did indeed have a lot of meaning to everyone present; pain, tears, and friendship were components of everybody's life. She sang all of the song without pause, and when the song ended the silence was heavy but comforting to all of us momentarily. Lucy was the one who broke the stillness, saying, "That was beautiful, Bambi. You have a very nice singing voice. Have you had training?"

Shyly, she replied, "I enjoyed music when I was in high school; I sang with a couple small choral groups and went to some music contests. I had kind of thought about pursuing a career in music, but when I got pregnant I decided that I had better make a more practical choice. I knew that Aunt Willow loved nursing; I used to spend a month every summer staying with her, and it had always been my second choice for a career.

"Besides, I can always sing for enjoyment, and one of my music teachers once told me that a career in music is very hard to break into. He compared it to sports, saying that there are some wonderful quarterbacks, but only a few that are really so well known that they can pretty much work wherever they want. Musicians have it tough because if they want to make a living at it they often have to sing the songs, or in a style, that satisfies an audience, an agent, or a customer, not really getting to just choose what makes you feel good."

This girl seemed very mature, with a lot of depth—not the immature waif that her appearance first suggested. I was a little concerned, though, that her appearance was going to be too wild for a small-town Kansas hospital. Bambi had several holes pierced in each ear, as well as her eyebrow, and there were tattoos on both of her forearms. "Bambi, I don't want to seem nosy or too old-fashioned, but have you considered that your piercings and tattoos might be a hindrance to a career in nursing? Don't hospitals usually have dress codes or something that might be contrary to allowing a tattoo or lots of holes in your ears?"

"Daa-aad!," Hannah whined. "Don't you think that is kind of personal?"

"Sorry, Bambi," I said. "You don't have to answer that, but I've lived in both Washington and Kansas for a good many years and I can definitely tell you that Kansans are a lot more conservative than Washingtonians."

Bambi smiled and said, "It's okay. Actually, I'm happy that you feel comfortable enough with me to ask and give me advice. I can take out most of my earrings for the interview and wear a Band-Aid or a long-sleeved shirt to cover the cat and mouse tattoo. The broken heart one is just henna, so it will wash off in a couple of days. Oh, and I know my hair is a little shocking, but I can make it look pretty normal if I don't spike it. I think I really want to work in the Manhattan hospital, so I can tone things down in order to get a job. After all, I have a child to support."

Dee Dee, who had been quiet throughout the visit, spoke up and made a comment that made the rest of us wince. "Now that you know where Charlie is, you can get some child support, don't you suppose?"

"I never had money in mind as a motive for finding Charlie. I never knew my real father, and I wanted better for my son." Bambi paused and continued with melancholy in her voice, "You see, my father left us when I was only two; my sister Ariel was just a couple months old. My dad, or I guess he is really my stepdad, has been the only dad I've known. Ariel had her second birthday on the day before Mom married Bob Bellingham. Bob was a widower with a sixteen-year-old son, Rueben. Bob has been very good to all of us, adopting Arial and me so that we all had the same last name. My biological dad's name is Winston Presley, and none of us have heard from him since he left. And even though Bob is wonderful, there has always been a part of me that feels cheated or something because I don't know my real dad.

"Anyway, long story short, I don't want Charlie's money. I just thought it was important for Simon to know his father, if possible, and to have a relationship. So when I discovered that Charlie was living here and Dee Dee actually knew him, I took it as a sign from God that I should bring Simon here to meet him. Do you know if he is going to be coming soon?"

"Sorry, Bambi," I answered. "I thought he and Caleb were right behind us. I cannot speak for him, but I thought he was planning to be here with us. I'll try to convince him that giving Simon a chance is the right thing to do. But he is of legal age, so I don't really have a lot of control over what he does and does not do, even though he is still living under my roof. You can bet that I will be discussing this situation with him, though.

"Whatever he chooses to do, I want you to know that I am happy to have a grandson, and you and Simon are welcome in our home, in our family. Simon actually looks so much like Charlie did at the same age I'm convinced that you are telling us the truth.

Let me know if I can do anything for you. And that is not just an empty promise—I mean it. In my world, God is number one, family is number two. So you have just joined into that number two spot in my life."

"Bambi, I'm with Dad. Simon's a real cutie, and I can see a lot of Charlie in him. I'm sorry he didn't come with us, but I'm standing by with what my dad said; you are family now," Hannah said.

"That means a lot to me," Bambi said. Unshed tears were glazing her eyes. "Truly, I never wanted anything other than that; I just want Simon to know his father's family. Well, his father too, but I know it has been a great big shock to Charlie. I've had almost four years to get used to the idea of parenthood. Don't push him; he'll come around when he is ready."

"You seem very mature, Bambi. Simon is lucky to have you for his mother," said Lucy.

"Thank you," she said. "I had a great role model. My mom is great. In fact, would it be okay if she calls you, Mr. Jordan? I know she is anxious to get to know you too."

I told her I'd be happy to talk with her mother, made sure she had both my home number and cell numbers, and told her again to call anytime. "Thank you for letting us meet Simon, and trust me, we will make it all work out. It might take time, but I am pleased that you found us."

We discussed plans to meet up again in a day or two, depending upon her interview at the hospital. When leaving a short time later Hannah asked her, "So what is Simon's middle name?"

"Charles," replied Simon's young mother. "I thought it only right. Simon couldn't have his father's last name, but at least he has part of his name as his own."

JEDIDIAH

I dropped Lucy at her door, promised to call her later, and gave her a big hug. Hannah was watching from the vehicle, so I didn't give Lucy the kiss I really would rather have shared with her.

I expected to find Charlie and Caleb at home when Hannah and I arrived, but they weren't to be found. I called their cell phones, and both went to voice mail immediately. Strange, very strange! What was even stranger was that neither of the boys came home the rest of Sunday.

When I got up Monday morning I discovered only my daughter in the kitchen. "They aren't home yet," she volunteered.

Still somewhat groggy without my morning coffee, I asked her what she was talking about.

She clarified, "Charlie and Caleb still aren't home. They never came home all night."

I was starting to get really mad; it wasn't like either of them to run from a fight, not that this Simon situation had to be a fight. But the boys were making it into a conflict that I could not sanction. It was six thirty, and we were due at the doctor's clinic in two and a half hours. On Saturday, shortly after Bambi had left our home, I had called Dr. Lovelace, asking if she could perform a paternity test so we could get a definitive answer to Charlie's paternity. But I had a feeling that Charlie would not return by then.

Considering that they were supposed to be on the job at Lucy's by seven o'clock, I was wondering if they were going to ditch the job today too. We were supposed to be digging the footings for Lucy's inn, and there would be a lot of manual labor involved, even though the excavators did the heaviest digging. I had my coffee, a bowl of cereal with a banana, and was out the door at five minutes to seven. As I neared my neighbor's building site, I saw Caleb's Nissan truck, and there was a crew starting to work on the footings. We had broken ground the previous week, and the clearing and excavation had been completed, taking care to preserve the large willow and oak trees that would be at the edge of the building site.

I parked and went to find my boys. I found Caleb talking to Mortimer Fredricks, the owner of the foundation company we had subbed the job to. Freddie's Foundations had done several of our projects for us, and we found them to be fair, competent, and always right on schedule. I said my hello to Mort, thanked him for being right on time, and asked Caleb if I could talk to him alone. Reluctantly, he agreed, and we walked toward a large willow tree. Out of earshot from the crew, Caleb turned and looked at me with an angry stance and said through clenched teeth, "You've really done it this time, Dad. You had no right agreeing to see that girl and her boy. Charlie doesn't want anything to do with them, and I agree with him. She's just some little tramp that is trying to throw Charlie under the bus, and trying to ruin his life."

"Whoa, wait a minute, young man. First of all, Charlie told Hannah it was fine to have them join us at church and told me he wanted to have lunch together with Simon after church. He never said a word about any of this to me; I'm wondering where he turned direction. What did you say to him?"

"It wasn't me, Dad. It was God."

"God?" I asked incredulously. "What do you mean it was God?"

"When we were in church, Charlie said that with every blare of that organ and trumpet he heard God tell him to run, run away. Don't get involved with this girl and her son. He told me that he couldn't even pay attention in church because God's voice was loudly telling him to bug out."

"Now, Caleb, I know I probably didn't do a very good job of teaching you kids about the Bible and getting you to church very faithfully, but this just doesn't sound right. God wouldn't tell a father to run from his child. There are a lot of verses in the Bible teaching a father how to take care of and teach his son; there is nothing about running from a son. Besides, God talks to us in whispers in quiet places, not shouting over organ or trumpet music. Where is he? Where has Charlie gone?"

"I don't know, Dad. He had me bring him home earlier and he got his van. He snuck into the house and packed up a bunch of clothes and stuff. I don't know where he went, but I don't think he'll be back until after that girl leaves."

"Well, son, there is a possibility that she isn't leaving. At least not for good. She is hoping to get a nursing job at the hospital in Manhattan and live with her aunt down there. He's going to have to face up to this young lady and her son sometime. He'll have to figure out sooner or later that you can't run from your problems. Nothing is solved that way. I'll give Doctor Lovelace a call; we were supposed to be in her office at nine o'clock for the DNA testing. Please let me know if you hear from your brother."

"Okay," Caleb muttered, and he started to walk away.

"Oh, and because he isn't here to work, it looks like you are going to have to work twice as hard. Sorry, but I had already told Mort that you two would help his crew out with the footings and foundation."

Caleb kicked his boot into the loose dirt and cursed. "Dad, for what it's worth, I still agree with my brother; I would have done the same thing." He turned and walked rapidly back toward Mort. He picked up a shovel and marched toward the crew, already marking out the plot for the footings.

JEDIDIAH

Charlie did not come back until the following Monday morning at six o'clock. He was tanned and unshaven. He shuffled in through the backdoor, tossed a duffel bag into the laundry room, and shot me a sullen look before brushing past to go up the stairs. He grabbed two bagels from the breadbox as he hurried by.

"Wait right there, Charles. Do you think you can just take off for a week, drop your laundry off to be cleaned, and return without any explanation? Where the hell have you been?" I boomed in my most angry, disciplinarian voice.

"The lake," Charlie said defiantly, still looking up the stairs and not looking me in the eye.

"Look at me! What gives you the right to take off and not say a word to me? You walked out on the family, walked away from your job, and above all, we need to talk about your attitude toward your son."

"I don't have a son! I never wanted to have a son with that girl; I barely know her. She should have given him up for adoption. I don't want to be involved with him, and I don't like it that you don't respect me. Caleb says you went and met with them; how dare you? I'm relinquishing my rights to the boy, and because of that, you won't be able to have anything to do with him either."

"Charlie, you can't relinquish your rights. That's not even a possibility. Who put such a ridiculous idea into your head? And the fact is that Bambi did not put him up for adoption, so he is here and in need of a father. I'm his grandfather; if you would get to know him, you would see he is definitely a Jordan. He looks exactly like you did at his age. I'm not walking away from him." My voice was rising, and I continued, backing Charlie into a corner of the kitchen. "You don't have any right to tell me that I can't be involved in his life. As far as respect, no, I do not respect your decision. It is wrong, and as your father, I don't have to follow your lead. My job as a parent is to lead you in the right direction, to advise you and to help you, but there is no commandment that says I have to respect you when you make mistakes."

"It doesn't matter now anyway. They are gone, and hopefully they will never return to Kansas."

"Sorry, Charlie, but they aren't gone. Bambi got a job as a nurse in Mid-Town Hospital in Manhattan, and she is living with her aunt Willow. She and Simon are staying in Kansas, and you need to face the fact that you are most likely the boy's father. I agree that it is an extraordinary and challenging situation, but you are the one that made the choice about four years ago to have sex with the girl. First of all, we need to reschedule you for the paternity test, and then I'll help you to decide what to do from there."

"Dad, you aren't listening!" Charlie's voice raised a few decibels. "I am relinquishing my rights to that boy, and I won't be having any paternity test. No matter what you say, I'm not changing my mind. I heard God tell me to run away from him, and that is what I've done. Now, do I still have a job, or am I fired?"

I stared at him for a few seconds, standing defiantly, looking downward, with his hands shoved into his pockets. Reluctantly, I answered his question. "You still have a job, but Caleb has been pulling extra hours to make up for your absence. This week, you have double the work to do, so you'd better get over to the job site early and plan to stay until dark. We are roughing in all of the plumbing this week, so there will be a lot of manual labor." With a scowl but no more battling words, Charlie tore up the stairs to the second story of our old farmhouse.

I heard rebellious boots stomping overhead, and minutes later, Charlie descended the stairs, and without a word to me he slammed the door on his way out.

Minutes later Hannah eased into the kitchen, wordlessly taking a skillet out of the cupboard and the egg carton out of the refrigerator. "Can I make you an omelet, Dad?" she asked.

"Thanks, sweetheart, but I'm not really hungry now. I'm just going to finish my coffee."

"How about I make you an egg sandwich to go, that way you can eat it when you do get hungry," she offered.

"All right, that would be good," I agreed.

Hannah was always the peacekeeper, and I could see she was trying to diffuse the heated tension that lingered in the room.

Silently she set about with the cooking task, not saying a word about the return of her brother, whom, no doubt, she had heard.

LUCY

As the self-appointed decorator of my new inn/wedding retreat, I have a lot of shopping to do to get all of the products in place so that I don't hold up the workmen when they get to the point of installation. Scarlett Stockton, Jedidiah's sister and my architect, and I had decided to add a stone summerhouse that would have multiple purposes, initially, to be used as storage. The summerhouse was situated perpendicular to the inn in the backyard, along the east fence line, and would be faced with the gold stone, shingled with the same metal tiles that mimicked clay tiles that would be on the inn and accented with wrought-iron work window grills.

The summerhouse would have a kitchen and small bathroom so that in the future it could be used by the caterer to stage the food for the weddings and other parties that I hoped to host in the large backyard. There would be a six-foot French door opening into the yard and a smaller door to exit to the parking lot in the rear so that the caterer would have easy access.

The kitchen countertops and open shelving would all be industrial stainless steel. The bathroom would be equally utilitarian with a white porcelain sink, toilet, and subway tiles, plus a small tub/shower combo unit. Scarlett had designed it with a full basement to be used as storage for the tables and chairs that would be used for garden weddings. She'd also suggested that we add on a couple more restrooms with doors opening to the exterior so that the guests in the garden would have easy access to toilet facilities.

All of the major building products were either already delivered or on their way to the building site—the shingles, trusses, studs, sheeting, nails, and screws. But the interior products, cabinets, tiles, and flooring—were up to the designer, me!

Originally, I had envisioned having the lap pool in the basement, but the architect and pool designers had agreed that it would be best if it was housed in a wing off the side of the house. I wanted the pool house to be tiled in aqua and sand colors. The floor and lower half of the walls of the pool room itself would be four-by-four-inch, glazed, light aqua-colored tiles, and the rest of the floors in the pool house would be twelve-by-twelve, sand-colored stone or ceramic. The open beams and upper walls would need to be painted in the same colors. The pool itself would be cement, with ceramic tile accents on the steps.

Durability and energy savings were my prime concerns in the wet environment of the pool, so I opted for insulated steel doors, triple-paned windows, and as much solar energy as possible. I wanted the solar panels to keep the water heated, and my pool contractor assured me it was feasible. The solar system was kind of pricey up front, but it would pay for itself in less than a decade with the savings by using the sun as the energy source.

There was space to have two large restrooms, complete with showers and lockers, a couple of closets for towels, a small sauna, a large storage space to house all of the pool chemicals and cleaning paraphernalia, and a fairly large room remaining to be used as a gym.

The pool house would be connected to the inn via a long, enclosed loggia, with doors opening to both the parking lot and the backyard. The restrooms could be utilized during wedding receptions, with the inner doors to the pool itself locked for safety. Scarlett had included a sunroom and greenhouse on the far west end of the pool house. I would eventually plant a vegetable garden beyond the greenhouse, but my dream seemed to be daunting at times, overwhelming me with way too many plans for the future.

The future was a topic that was in itself daunting. Now that I had Jedidiah back in my life, I had difficulty focusing exactly on where I'd be when the inn was completed. It was wonderful having him geographically close, and it seemed we were drawing together emotionally very quickly. I wasn't sure if that was what I wanted, but it seemed to be God's plan for us. I had two failed marriages, and before meeting up again with Jedidiah, I had been content to be single the rest of my days. Because of my new wealth, I had a lot of things on my mind. The first day that I had visited my cottage in Whitney with my parents, I had a sneaking suspicion that Jedidiah was nearby. It was really even less than a suspicion, just a feeling. A cowboy had come to the door looking for some lost cattle, and as he was leaving, I heard his companion talking and I had memories stirring of that voice; it had sounded so much like the voice of my high-school sweetheart, Jedidiah Jordan. I hadn't seen the cowboy's companion, and everything moved so fast, and before I knew it, I had moved smack dab next door to where Jedidiah was living. My only explanation was that God had plans all along to join us together again.

My days were occupied planning or drawing the interior design for my new inn, making lists and planning shopping excursions. I didn't find much time to sleep, and my old bossy cat, Jethro was often the only reason I eventually crawled into bed. If I was at my computer or curled up in my reading chair late at night, he grew impatient and would stand on his hind legs, swatting me with his forepaws until I would ultimately turn off either the light or the computer and carry him to bed.

And in the mornings if I slept too long, Jethro again played the part of my timekeeper by marching across my chest, back and forth until I opened my eyes and discovered the reason for my discomfort. That old cat was so used to taking care of me, that at times I truly believed I was his pet, not the other way around. Now if he could only do the food shopping, we'd be set.

On Thursday morning, four days after the day that I'd spent with Jedidiah and his family, including the visit with Bambi and Simon, I received a phone call from my old friend. He had been absent for several days, and since I had plenty to keep me busy, I had not made contact with him either. I knew he had a lot on his mind, and I did not want to be a source of any more anguish or distress. When he'd dropped me off on Sunday afternoon, he had given me a long hug and thanked me for being with him. He had said, "Lucy, I'm so thankful that God has brought you back into my life. I hope you understand that I have a little family situation that might occupy my time for the next few days. I'll give you a call in a few days, okay?"

I had relished the hug and kind words and said, "I'll be patiently waiting for your call."

So when I answered the phone at nine o'clock Thursday morning, I was very pleased to hear his husky voice say my name. "Lucy, I've missed you, but this has been quite a week. Charlie has not come home yet. Caleb and I have been working extra hours at the building site. On a bright note, Bambi has accepted a job offer to work in the Mid-Town Hospital and she and Simon will be living in Manhattan with her aunt."

"It sounds like it has been a very eventful week for you, and I think it's good news that Bambi and Simon will be staying on here in Kansas. How are you doing, Jedidiah?" I asked.

"I'm holding up. It will be good to have Simon so near. Please say some prayers for Charlie that he would do the right thing," Jedidiah said. We chatted a short time and made plans to go to Mass together on Saturday night and out to dinner afterward.

Energized from the phone call, I decided it was time to purchase tile and make final cabinet arrangements. Kermie Weed had built the beautiful cabinets in my cottage, and I had already spoken with him, asking him to construct those for the inn. He already had the sizes and layout blueprints, and he was working on the boxes, building everything out of oak. I had yet to give him my final decision for the doors and fronts. I had concluded that I wanted all of the woodwork on the first floor of the inn to be stained a driftwood tone and the cabinetry to be faced with pecky cypress. I knew it was kind of pricey and rare, and I prayed that he could come up with a source for it. I had several photos of pecky cypress cabinetry that I had printed off to show him what I had in mind.

I phoned Kermie, asking if I could stop by, and he was eager to have me come over to see what he had built so far. After feeding the cat and taking care to stuff all the necessary photos, color swatches, and drawings into my briefcase, I drove across town to Kermie's.

He had a large metal building behind his house that he called his woodshop. I had visited one other time and had been impressed with the quality of his work, as well as the infinite number of woodworking tools that the man had neatly arranged in the large workspace. It was well lit and very clean, considering the quantity of sawdust that he must generate each day.

I stopped my VW in the driveway, and Kermie came out to greet me. "Miss Lucy! Great to see you!" he said with a huge grin and welcome, widespread arms. The hands at the ends of his long, wrinkled, age-spotted arms were large and weathered. The knuckles were dry and cracked, and the nails looked as though he'd torn them rather than cut them with nail clippers. But regardless of the care he took with his hands, I knew that they could create magnificent cabinets.

"Good morning, Mr. Weed. It was nice of you to allow me to drop by at such short notice."

"Nonsense, you are welcome any time, and stop with the Mr. stuff; remember, call me Kermie. Everyone does."

From the kitchen door I heard a woman's voice say, "Oh, goodness! You must be that Lucy Golden I've heard so much about."

Turning, I saw that she was in a wheelchair, coming through the backdoor. I went toward the cheerful woman with the pink, rosy cheeks. She looked like my image of Old Mother Hubbard, wearing a white ruffled apron over her yellow-print dress. She even had an old-fashioned, crocheted snood that covered and contained the back of her hair, which appeared to be quite long. On her tiny feet were white sneakers with images of Hello Kitty stamped on the sides and toes. She was such a cheerful, robust-looking woman, and it was easy to focus on her, not her wheelchair.

I walked toward her and greeted her as she wheeled herself carefully down the angled, wooden ramp. At the end of the ramp I reached out to shake her hand, but she reached higher with both hands, and I bent down to meet up with her proffered hug. Mrs. Weed was short with tiny features—a cute, pert nose, blue eyes close together on her small head, and tiny hands. She said, "I'm so happy to finally meet you; I'm Kitty Weed." I couldn't help myself. I glanced at her shoes. Catching the movement of my eyes, she grinned and said, "When you have tiny feet, it is hard to find shoes, so I often have to shop in the children's section. So when I found these with Hello Kitty on them, I thought they were just perfect." She sashayed her right foot, stretching it out for me to see.

"Very cute. I have size-nine feet, so I often have the opposite problem and have even resorted to wearing men's shoes at times to find something that is comfortable," I admitted to the endearing woman I'd just met.

"You're such a beautiful gal," Kitty said. "Now, you run along with Kermie, and when you are done, come into the kitchen and have a fresh apple cinnamon muffin and some coffee. I'll be right in the kitchen doing a little cleanup."

After assisting his wife back up the ramp, Kermie led me into the workshop, saying, "My little wife makes wonderful muffins. She takes such good care of me."

Once inside, I relished in the aroma of fresh-sawn wood. It had always been one of my favorite scents. I could probably call it number three on my list, right behind fresh rain and honeysuckle blossoms. Kermie was chattering, explaining which cabinet he was working on. He had numbered his blueprint copy, showing cabinets one through forty that he would be building for my inn. His numbering sequence was not sequential as they were laid out, but instead, they were laid out according to size. All of those that were of identical size he had sequenced to make in succession. He led me to the storage room, turned on the light, and my eyes nearly popped out of my head; I was amazed. His workmanship was remarkable, and the speed at which he worked was no less than miraculous as well. He said, "I'm working on the upper cabinets twenty-one, twenty-two, and twenty-three and should be finished with them by the end of the day. I've also nearly finished the cabinets for your cottage sunroom."

I complimented him on his workmanship, thanking him for building them so quickly. I said, "You are probably anxious to see the front and the doors that I have decided upon for the inn cabinets, right? I've brought some photos to show you."

"Oh, yes. Let's go into the workshop so we can lay out your pictures."

I followed him, and he turned on a bank of overhead lights, illuminating a large workbench. I unzipped the case and pulled out the pictures.

"I don't know if you've ever heard of this before—I know I hadn't—but I found these photos of pecky cypress that I just fell in love with. I love the mottles and dapples, showing the character of the wood. It says here that it is very durable and resistant to insects." I continued to spread out the photos that I had printed off of the Internet, and he was silently picking up each one and examining it, stacking it up, and when he finished he handed the stack to me.

Finally he spoke, but I was a little disappointed that he did not comment about the wood. He said, "I believe that I heard the timer go off on the oven, so we need to go in for our muffin and coffee."

He turned off the bench light and turned to go. Not knowing what else to do, I followed him, stuffing the photos back into the pouch.

There was a tiny porcelain sink right inside the back door where he stopped and washed his hands, drying them on a faded towel. I stood sheepishly in the corner, waiting for his direction, too timid to proceed into the kitchen. He noticed me standing there and said, "I hear those muffins calling our name. Shall we?" He placed his fist at his waist, creating a triangle for me to place my arm through as if he were escorting me down an aisle. I followed his lead, allowing him to pull my hand through his crooked arm. As we entered the kitchen I saw an amazing sight.

Pecky cypress cabinets! They were magnificent, even more beautiful than I had imagined and had seen on my computer monitor. I looked up at the cabinets and then at his beaming face. He stood proudly, letting me marvel at the vision of the cabinetry that he had built for his own home, the same that I had just pronounced to him that I wanted him to build for me. They were even stained the same driftwood color I had in mind. I stood with my mouth agape, and when Kitty rolled into the room, saying, "I thought I heard you come in..." she stopped in midsentence, probably wondering why we were standing there awkwardly gazing at her lovely cabinets.

"Pretty, aren't they?" the little woman asked. "Kermie built those for me the year we got married and moved into this house, forty-five years ago."

"Yes, indeed they are pretty," I agreed.

"Kitty, Lucy here just told me she wanted me to build her pecky cypress cabinet fronts. Isn't that something else?"

"Well, I'd say that's quite a coincidence. Come in, sit down, and enjoy a little snack with us. Please try to overlook the peeling paint on the walls, and have a muffin."

"Kitty has been harping at me to paint the walls for years now, but I just don't seem to get around to it. I have plenty to do, and I don't think they look so bad." Kermie said this with kindness, but I could tell he was saddened that he hadn't been able to provide perfection to his wife.

I spent a couple hours there with the Weeds, enjoying her muffin, listening to their tales. It was a relaxing morning, and I unexpectedly remembered the charm of a small town. The people are what make small towns alluring—their kindness and simple pleasures. Nothing was said about her disability, but truthfully, the fact that Mrs. Weed was in a wheelchair didn't seem like a disability for her. She was full of energy and had a bubbly personality that revealed her vivacity for life. Kitty Weed shared photos of their three grandchildren and their one great-grandson. There was distinct pride showing as she relayed stories about each of her offspring.

They gave me a tour of their cozy home, neat and clean, but the walls did need to be painted. When I saw the aqua-colored tiles in the guest bathroom, I remembered that I had other places I needed to go. I thanked them for the wonderful morning, and Kermie assured me he knew of a source for pecky cypress. As I left them, I saw that together they went to gather the sheets off of the clothesline. She held the laundry basket in her lap as her husband pushed her across the patio to where the clothesline started.

LUCY

I had written down several addresses of tile and stone sources in Manhattan and Topeka, hoping to find the tiles that I had in mind for the pool house. I was still undecided about the countertops and backsplash for the kitchen in the inn, so I had it on my list to investigate possibilities. I knew that traditionally, Tuscan-styled homes utilized marble on the countertops, but I wasn't sure if that was the way I wanted to go in my kitchen. Maybe some kind of surface that looked like marble would be better and easier to care for.

I was hoping that I would not have to go all the way to Topeka, especially since I had spent the entire morning at the Weeds' home. The first place I went to was called Tile Style, and it was obvious the moment that I walked in the door that their specialty was high-end *designer* fashion tiles. They showed me a lot of glass tiles and patterned tiles. When I mentioned to Gregoire (whom I suspected was just simply Greg from a farm family nearby, with a fake French accent) that I had a Tuscan theme in mind, he took me to a special room that showed me all of their Tuscan styles. He had samples of travertine cobblestones, Terrazzo floor tiles, murals created from mosaic tiles, and even some that he said were genuine eighteenth-century reclaimed tiles from an Italian monastery.

He looked heartbroken when I told him I didn't think that his idea of Tuscan was the same as mine. "I'm looking for aqua and sand colors for the pool house."

He gave me a snobbish, quizzical look and said in his uppity, fake accent, "But those are not genuine Tuscan colors."

I thanked him and said that it was my idea of a modern Tuscany. I would keep his shop in mind, and I got out of there immediately. I did like the murals and the glass tiles. I might go back later, but today I needed to focus upon the pool house tiles.

The next place on my list was actually a small factory that made custom tiles, specializing in patio tiles. I spent just a few minutes looking at their samples, but the salesperson, Doris, was the direct opposite of Gregoire—very aloof and making only a cursory attempt to help me find a few samples to show me.

Doris, a bubblegum-popping girl of about twenty-five with a green stripe in her blonde hair swept aside a stack of papers from the counter, which fell to the floor. Not making any attempt to retrieve the fallen papers, she plopped an old Hush Puppies shoebox on the counter and told me to feel free to look at the samples. The samples were dusty, cracked, and nothing close to what I had in mind. Ignoring me, Doris had picked up the phone to dial out, and I gave her a little wave as I left.

I bypassed the big super building store, hoping that I wouldn't have to come back to it. I try to avoid those mega stores whenever possible, and I make great efforts to do business with the smaller guys. The next on my list was a place called Tile-O-Rama, and I had a little difficulty locating it. The address was 1711 Sunset Street, but I must have driven right by the shop three times before I found 1711. The business actually opened onto the alley; it didn't look much more promising than the establishment where I had been attended to briefly by Doris.

But not to be discouraged, I pulled my Bug up close to the door in the alley, parked, and went in. There was a cowbell over the door that jangled loudly as I entered, and a perky African

American woman of about my age came out through a curtain of beads. I was a little doubtful, but I told her what I was looking for and she smiled, showing a large gold tooth. "Honey, I think you will be pleased. Come on back here with me. By the way, my name is Lila Penrose. Can I ask how you found us today?"

I followed her as she pulled back the beads, telling her my name and that I had found her ad in the Yellow Pages. We stopped in a large storeroom with low ceilings; it was well lit and neatly arranged. The room was lined with shelves, which were full of boxes of tiles. Lila led me straight to the four-by-four-inch aqua tiles that I had asked about, gingerly lifting one out of a box for me to see. I told her, "These are exactly what I wanted."

When I gave her the estimated number that we would need, she said she didn't think that would be a problem. She went to a centrally located file cabinet and pulled out a file, running a finger down a chart until she found what she was looking for.

"Yes, I have that many. Actually, we have nearly twice that amount of that one tile with the same batch number. We have several boxes of the bullnose and endcaps in that color as well. Would you like to take them with you today, or do you want them delivered?" We discussed the delivery arrangements and payment. I then moved on to ask about the twelve-by-twelve, sand-colored tile, but Lila Penrose regretfully told me that they only dealt in four-by-fours. She suggested the big-box store that I had bypassed, saying she thought they had those on sale this week. She asked, "What sort of project are you building?"

"It's going to be an inn with a pool and wedding retreat."

"Tell me more about the wedding retreat. I just got engaged last week, and my fiancé and I are looking for someplace unique to get married," Lila explained with a huge smile on her friendly face.

"We are hoping to be open for business by Thanksgiving, and I would love to have your wedding in my inn." I gave her a couple of my business cards and told her to keep us in mind.

"Could I have another card?" she asked. "My cousin also just got an engagement ring, and she might be interested too."

Feeling very contented with the aqua tile purchase, and the contacts I made regarding a possible wedding or two, I stopped at Home Depot, deciding the day was drawing to an end and if I could find the right twelve-by-twelve tile there, I could satisfy the tile list.

The tile I found at Home Depot was perfect, just what I had in mind, and much cheaper than I thought it was going to be. The only problem was that it was on sale this week only, so if I wanted it at that price I would have to take it soon, and since the summerhouse wasn't finished yet, I couldn't store them there. Not really a problem, just a little outside of the plan. I arranged for delivery of the tiles; I could store them in my double garage at the cottage.

I went in search of kitchen displays. I found several mock-ups of cabinets, backsplashes, and countertops. I decided to wait until I had an actual sample of the pecky cypress cabinet doors, and then I'd come back again to see if I liked any of the color combos.

I strolled down the floor-covering aisle and browsed the hardwood flooring, but I was a little overwhelmed. I decided to try to get Jedidiah to help me out with that decision.

Before leaving town I got several bags of groceries at the big supermarket nearby and headed home. It was after seven o'clock by the time I arrived, tired and hungry. I unloaded my purchases, fed the cat again, and put a frozen lasagna in the oven to bake while I soaked in a hot bubble bath.

LUCY

On Friday I returned to Manhattan with the truck to do some furniture shopping for the inn. Since the largest room on the main floor would be the party room, I really didn't want much traditional living room furniture in it like couches and recliners. It would only be in the way and need to be moved when we set up for a party. I'd need to have lots of tables and chairs, though, and hopefully, a wonderful bar or low cabinet to use as a reception desk, which could double as a bar during wedding receptions.

I was also in need of several small dinette sets. I would be serving breakfast in my dining room and turret, and the plan was to have fifteen matching dinettes. Considering that I was only planning on nine guest rooms, fifteen was probably overdoing it, but I was thinking that with the wedding theme I could do smaller parties like showers in the dining/turret rooms. The stone inn was going to have two large turrets on either end of the building. I always liked the majestic feel of those large, tower-like rooms, and my dream was that with them built of stone, that they would be cool inside, even on the hottest of Kansas days.

The other major room on the main floor would be the dancing circle—the turret on the west side of the house. I planned to have at least one window seat, cushioned with a fabric that coordinated with heavy draperies. The Kansas sun could be relentless, and that room would get the afternoon sun. I wasn't planning on furniture for that room; I wanted to keep it open so that the guests at my parties would have a great place for dancing. We'd pull back the heavy draperies and have twinkling fairy lights illuminating the dance floor in the evenings.

Until the summer home was ready I didn't want to get too far ahead of myself, but I knew that reputable furniture stores would hold my purchases for a couple of months for me, and I would perhaps need to order duplicates if I wanted matching pieces.

I spent a couple of hours driving from one furniture store to another, but I was disappointed in the end. I stopped at the salon where I'd had a manicure before my first date with Jedidiah and treated myself to a mani/pedi. The salon had a new professional on staff that gave massages; I considered a massage, but decided it would be best to wait until I had worked harder and really needed to work out some sore muscles. I had had a pretty easy week, just shopping and finishing the interior design on paper.

My architects, Scarlett Stockton and Fergus Finchman, were to come to the site on Saturday morning to review the final pergola and backyard designs with me. I had talked several times on the phone with both of them, making adjustments and listening to exciting new ideas. I was eager to hear what the final plan was.

When I arrived home, after the manicure and pedicure, I pulled the truck into the big shed. I didn't have anything to unload—it had been a rather disappointing day of shopping. I ate leftover lasagna and held my big cat on my lap while I read my Bible. I took a quick shower and was in bed by nine o'clock.

I was awake to see the dawn on Saturday morning. The sun shone brightly through my bedroom window as I sat relishing in the new day. Jethro was still sleeping on the foot of my bed; he had not stirred when I got up to make myself a cup of tea and a bagel. I was quietly breakfasting at the little iron ice-cream table that I had positioned in the big east window of my bedroom, dreaming about my date tonight. It had been nearly an entire week since I'd seen Jedidiah, and I was missing him very much. It was a little hard to comprehend since we had just found each other only a couple weeks ago, but being without him now was very difficult. I hoped he would open up to me and tell me what was going on with his family. I knew some of the story regarding Simon, but Jedidiah had only told me a little regarding Charlie's disappearance. I could tell he was hurting, and I just wanted to help.

When I finished my meager breakfast, I dressed in old jeans and a paint-spattered T-shirt. It was still about three hours until my architect team was due to arrive, and I wanted to paint a little artwork while the hour was early. I had set up my studio in a cursory fashion in the sunroom, but I had not yet done any painting. Kermie would probably be installing the cabinets in the sunroom sometime during the next week.

I had a sunrise painting in mind, with muted tones of pinks, yellows, and lavenders, and maybe even a little aqua-colored water—perhaps a lake or an ocean scene. When I painted, I usually did not have a complete plan when I started; I would usually start mixing colors and putting the brush to canvas. The paintings took on whatever they were meant to be.

At times I would try to copy a photo or have a specific idea in mind, but most of my favorites were those that were unplanned. I started with a small eight-by-twenty-four horizontal canvas. On my pallet I had small dabs of acrylic paints from the tubes—red, white, yellow, and blue. From these I mixed a few different hues of pastels before I started stroking the colors onto the canvas.

Jethro momentarily interrupted me, begging for kibble, so I stopped for a few minutes to feed him and to make myself a second cup of tea. I also turned on the stereo, choosing an Andrea Bocelli CD. I continued painting until the CD finished, and when I noted the time I saw that I had just enough time to clean my brushes and make a quick wardrobe change before my guests would be arriving. The painting was nearly finished, needing only a little fine-tuning, which could be finished later.

Scarlett was the first to arrive, perky as usual. Fergus rang the bell at precisely nine-thirty, and when I opened the door to greet him, I was surprised to see that he was looking very spiffy. He had on a cream-colored, linen blazer, khaki slacks, and loafers. His gray hair was newly cut, and he was walking more upright than when I had first met him. I had merely spoken over the phone with him since our first meeting, so this was only our second face-to-face meeting, but I'd been expecting the dreary, washed-out old man I had met a few weeks ago.

When I offered him a cup of tea, he said, "Deary, that sounds good, but what I really am craving is a cola. Do you have a cold one?"

"I do. Would you like a bagel or some toast too?" I offered.

"Oh, no. I'm much too excited to eat," he said.

I got him his Pepsi, pouring it into a glass with some crushed ice. I set it on the dining room table on a coaster, and after turning on the chandelier, I asked if that was enough light.

Both Fergus and Scarlett complimented the good light and the beautiful oak table. They spread out their collaborated design sketches for an amazing plan for my backyard. Scarlett began describing their plan. "Starting from the large sunroom at the rear of the inn, we have planned a covered arbor that is six feet wide, the path laid with native stone, and the iron-work posts twined with vines. The arbor bisects completely through the center of the backyard, leading toward an amazing Grand Pavilion at the other end of the large yard. It'll have a ten-foot ceiling, with three steps up to the platform. There is to be intricate, scrolled, wrought-iron grillwork columns and stone balustrades, which you can further decorate on special occasions with scarves and floral garlands." She paused, and said, "But I'm sorry. I really should let Fergus describe this all to you; it's mostly his design."

With a silly, excited grin, Fergus took up where she'd left off. "The pergola platform is twenty feet square, plenty of room for an entire wedding party or subsequent dancing after the pronouncement of wedding vows. Beyond the pergola is the stone wall, but between the pergola and the wall is a six-foot *beach* made of patterned concrete. We propose to create a painted mural depicting an ocean scene on the whitewashed stone wall. The mural will be thirty feet long and I'd like to see white iron fencing finishing off the enclosure. On both sides of the yard will be another pergola, smaller but identical in design to the larger Grand Pavilion. One could be for the wedding cake to be displayed and the other for the musicians."

"We have also drawn in ten gazebo-like structures." Looking up from their drawings, Scarlett said, "We know how brutal the Kansas sun and wind can be, so we thought you might like these to shelter your guests. Each gazebo would be large enough to seat ten people around a six-foot round table."

Fergus took up the cause. "The gazebo structure is made of the same ironwork that we have on the pergolas and the arbor, but the roof of each would be either copper or perhaps the same roof tiles you have on the inn. There could be some stone benches near the entrance of each gazebo too."

"I like that," I said.

"All of the iron work will be painted white, and with small openings so that small children and animals could not get through or get caught. The stone walls would be your beautiful gold stone that you salvaged from the barn. It will be a fortress, and a wonderful venue for garden weddings." Fergus's excitement explaining the details of his plan was endearing.

"Or the stone for the arbor path and stone walls could be quarried from your acreage; Jedidiah told me that he has made preliminary digs and that you have quite a treasure out there," Scarlett interjected. "I know we aren't using all of the barn stone in the house, but if you don't have enough from the salvage, Jedidiah has assured me that there is a lot more just waiting to be quarried."

"Stone walls?" I asked. I was getting a little confused. I hadn't thought about stone walls around the backyard.

"Oh yes," said Fergus. He pointed out the stone walls on the drawings. "We thought that we would break up the iron fencing periodically with a stone wall. That way if the Kansas wind was particularly strong, the stone walls would again shelter your guests somewhat. But you wouldn't want to have a complete stone fortress, we didn't think, because then you wouldn't get any air flow on hot days."

It was obvious that the two had done a great deal of collaboration on this plan. "I'm very impressed. I had really only thought as far ahead as having a pavilion, a tall fence, and grass with some trees. I can see that my simple plan was far out-classed, and I'm so very pleased that I have enlisted the assistance of two extremely talented people. I love the entire plan!"

Scarlett said, "We have left the particulars of the plants and trees to you, but we have drawn a layer over the blueprint showing proposed placement of plant materials." She spread out a layer of parchment over their drawings, on which were noted trees and shrubs. "We have incorporated into the design enough structural enhancements so that you could add large sheets of canvas tenting overhead to act as shade, at least until your trees have a few years to reach maturity. There will be several twelve-foot poles placed strategically that have iron loops to fasten the tenting sheets to."

Fergus added excitedly, "I actually have an acquaintance in Manhattan who has used a similar shading technique over her strawberry patch. She does some commercial sewing, and I'm sure we could enlist her to make the large canvasses with grommets at the corners. You could also consider having her make canvases that are the size of the gazebo walls, and you could clip them on with carabineers to make the gazebos slightly protected from the weather.

"Also there will be electrical power in all of the pergolas and gazebos so that you can have your receptions and parties after dark, and a ceiling fan with a light in each. Oh, and we nearly forgot to point this out." He shifted the drawings and pointed toward the area in front of the summerhouse. "We have designed a second, long-covered arbor here, parallel to and near the summerhouse so that a banquet could be laid out on long tables. You could also enclose the arbor on the open side with the draperies or canvasses, thereby giving a protected spot for the caterer to do all of their set up in private, and then pull back the draperies to reveal the commencement of the banquet."

Scarlett pointed out, "Fergus also added copper cupolas on each of the pergola roofs; he said that you'd spent several years in Maine and copper cupolas are quite popular back there. We thought perhaps you could find designs that were wedding-themed like a bell tower on one, and perhaps hearts or double wedding rings on the others."

As the meeting drew to an end, I told them both that I was pleased with everything they had shown me. I sensed that they were both as excited as I was to get started. I told them I would be honored to have them both come to the first wedding that I held at the retreat as my special guests so that they could see how wonderful their designs would be once we had an actual party in the backyard.

We walked over to the building site, and together we discussed the placement of each pergola, the gazebos, and the covered arbor/aisle. Jedidiah was at the site, and he joined us, listening to the plan as the three of us explained it to him. Scarlett assured him that his sets of blueprints for the construction were in her car and she would be sure he had them before she left. He said he was surprised that she was in town and apologized for not returning her phone calls when she scolded him. He merely said that he had had a busy week. Before he was called away he asked if I was available for dinner that evening. I happily replied in the affirmative, and after setting a time to meet up, he wandered toward a large backhoe that was making a huge hole in the earth.

LUCY

Jedidiah and I went to dinner in a unique restaurant about a half hour from home, in a large, old Victorian mansion painted lavender, with multitudes of white gingerbread accents. The entry door was oversized and intricately hand-carved—a very heavy, walnut piece of art. The flower arrangements and woodwork were ornate, and on the glistening hardwood floor were antique oriental rugs in tones of red, plum, and forest green. We were greeted by a young, cheerful blonde wearing a short, black dress and tall, high-heeled sandals—her nametag read Gretel. She took us through one large, open dining room to a smaller one and then gave us a table in a bay window with a view of the rose garden.

She handed us large leather binders that opened to the menu; the menu had sophisticated choices, surprisingly elaborate for a small town in Kansas. Our waiter, who introduced himself as Karl, arrived shortly after we were seated and abruptly asked, "What do you want to drink?"

Jedidiah answered, "Water to begin with please, and could we see the wine list?" Without answering, Karl left our table, and we studied the menus. Jedidiah and I decided upon the Chateaubriand with baked potatoes, starting with spinach and strawberry salads and cold cucumber soup. When Karl finally returned about five minutes later, he sloppily set down tall glasses of ice water in front of each of us and shoved a red leather folder toward my date; he marched away without speaking.

Jedidiah and I made small talk, comparing this restaurant to the pizza place we had enjoyed twenty-five years ago called the Establishment. We were interrupted by Karl after another five or six minutes passed, asking, "Would you like an appetizer?"

Jedidiah answered, "No, I don't think so."

Karl started to walk away again, but Jedidiah reached out and caught the young man by the arm and said, "But we are ready to order."

Karl stood stone-faced listening to Jedidiah's description of our preferences, not writing anything down. When Jedidiah finished, Karl said a curt, "Thank you, sir," and left.

As he walked away, my lavender eyes met with Jedidiah's green ones and we shared an eye roll; then we both giggled. It felt so good to be laughing with him again. He asked me about my children and Jethro. I asked him about his goat and he said that she was doing fine, performing her lawn-mowing tasks to a tee! Jedidiah's goat, Hesper Jane, was the cause of one of our misfortunate failures to meet up sooner. Jedidiah's youngest daughter, Heather, had expressed desire to have a goat, so in order to lure her to Kansas, he had driven all the way to Wichita one rainy Sunday to purchase the goat. He'd had car trouble and wasn't able to get repairs until the following day and consequently had missed a meeting on Monday morning, when I had thought we would actually first meet up face-to-face.

Then he explained all about Simon and Bambi, and he said that Charlie had come home, angry, but at least he was home and back to work anyway. The situation was tense, but Jedidiah was standing firm on his faith. He said, "All children are gifts from God, and Simon is no different. Even if a paternity test proves that Charlie is not his biological father, knowing Simon has been a gift."

The wine, soup, and salad were served by Gretel. She was very sweet, and the food was delicious. We were finished with the salad for several minutes when Karl delivered the steaks and potatoes. His presentation had something to be desired, but the food was excellent.

Later, Karl had cleared away our empty plates and we were enjoying a moment of intimacy. Jedidiah was looking across the small, linen-covered table into my eyes and said, "Lucy, I've always wondered what it would have been like to have children with you, and in some way, I just know that God has plans for us to have a future together. Obviously we have reached an age where having a baby together probably won't be in the cards, but we have come together perhaps just in time to have grandchildren together!"

"Jedidiah," I said, "I'm so happy to have found you again! I've missed you so much. I never forgot my love for you, never forgot your voice or your gentle manner."

Before I could say more we were interrupted by Karl. He clumsily moved our glassware and set our dessert in the center of the table. We had ordered one piece of coconut-cream pie to share. He abruptly said, "Here's your pie."

Karl's interruption had required us to break our handhold, and the intimate moment had been disrupted. Silently, we lifted the forkfuls of pie to our mouths, sharing and enjoying the sweet creamy pie. As we took the last bit of pie, once again Karl bound upon us, saying loudly, "Here is the check, and I hope that your visit to the Manor House Restaurant has been pleasant." This sounded rehearsed and scripted, not at all sincere. Jedidiah set down his fork, pushed back his chair, and retrieved cash from his wallet. Ignoring the waiter, he looked at me and asked, "Are you ready to go?"

As we were leaving, a tall, sophisticated, older gentleman met us at the door and thanked us for dining at his restaurant. He introduced himself, saying, "I am Heinrich Schmidt, the proprietor of the Manor House. I hope you had a pleasant evening with us." The man had a bit of a German accent.

Jedidiah shook the man's hand as it was offered, smiled, and replied, "Mr. Schmidt, the food was delicious and your establishment is amazing. We truly enjoyed ourselves. However…" he paused and nervously looked at me before continuing. "However, I don't like to complain, but the waiter Karl could use a few lessons on decorum and finesse. He seems a bit too abrupt and not in tune with the elegance of the surroundings."

"Oh sir, I'm sorry. I assure you I have tried to give Karl chances and guidance, but he just doesn't seem to understand. You see, he is my youngest son and he has something of a bad attitude. Gretel is his sister, and we are very proud of her. She seems to do a fabulous job as a hostess, but wherever we place Karl he just doesn't seem to fit. Gretel's twin brother, Hans, is our chef assistant, and my wife is the head chef. You see, we've tried to keep this a family business, but Karl has made it quite challenging sometimes."

Jedidiah chuckled. "Mr. Schmidt, I totally understand your anxiety. You see, I too have a family business, and my youngest son has become rebellious and uncooperative lately. I know we try to give them every opportunity, but sometimes we just don't know how to make it work."

"I think it is probably time for Karl to go back to dishwashing and other janitorial duties, and keep him away from my customers. You see…you are not the first to complain about him. Thank you for being so candid with me and I hope to see you again soon. May I ask what family business you have engaged in?"

Jedidiah gave him a business card and told him about his construction and ranching enterprises, and then he also told him that he was building an inn close to his ranch. And drawing me nearer, he introduced me, saying, "Let me introduce you to Lucy Golden. She is the proprietress of the Goldstone Inn and Wedding Retreat that my family is building for her. Perhaps you will join us at the inn near Whitney sometime; it should be completed by Thanksgiving."

He reached out and shook my hand warmly and earnestly said that he was happy to make my acquaintance. I fished out a card from my purse and handed it to him. "Yes, please keep us in mind should you or your family want to get away for a while. Or if you want a special place for a wedding."

"That's quite coincidental, in fact," he replied. "Gretel has just become engaged to a wonderful young man from near there; her fiancé lives in Express. Perhaps your inn would be a good fit for their wedding. I will be sure to keep it in mind and tell Gretel about it." Then, rather sheepishly, he added, "Karl tells me that his passion is building; he wants to work with tools and construct things, not a plate of food that is gone with one sitting. Perhaps someday you could let my Karl work with you. Maybe it is time for me to let him go out and seek his true calling."

Jedidiah told him to have Karl come see him and he'd see about putting him to work. "We are building Lucy's inn, so we are pretty busy right now and could use an extra pair of hands."

The ornate front door opened and a large group of people wearing western attire started filling the small vestibule. We waved our good-byes to the tall German man and retreated out the open door. We were swinging our hands, clutched happily together, as we walked toward his pickup truck. He opened the door for me and waited as I climbed up into the seat.

On the long drive home I sat close to Jedidiah, just as I had when we were young in his parents' 1974 Buick. We were silent for the first ten minutes or so, listening to the radio playing oldies from the seventies. But when he came to a stop sign to turn onto Highway 77 North, he pulled me close, gave me a kiss, and said, "Thank you, Lucy. You are a very special woman."

I echoed his compliment, telling him he was a very special man. A car pulled up behind us and tooted the horn, so he again tended to the driving. We spent the rest of the drive discussing the building project. He told me about the progress they were making on the foundation and rough plumbing-in. I told him about the tiles I had found for the pool house. He told me that they had finished the basement for the summerhouse and they would be getting the structure up the following week. They had subbed out the foundation and plumbing work for the inn, and while that crew worked on the grading and preparations, he and his boys would construct the smaller building.

When we got to my house, he got out of the truck and was around to my door to open it very quickly. I handed him my door key and asked if he wanted to come in. His answer was, "Lucy, I very much want to come in, but I'm afraid I wouldn't be able to leave. Maybe I should just go home."

Reluctantly, I agreed, and after a long kiss on the doorstep, we said good night. I went inside as he returned to his truck to drive to his home just down the road. I had locked up and went upstairs to my bedroom, carrying a bottle of water and my big cat. After I settled the cat comfortably in his spot at the foot of the bed, the phone rang. Jedidiah said he wasn't ready for the night to end and asked if it'd be okay if we talked a while longer. We talked for another two hours before we said our final good nights.

I slept a very peaceful, but dreamy sleep that night. When I woke early the next morning, I remembered my dream. My inn was an all-inclusive wedding retreat, complete with a florist, photographer, wedding cake baker, and a wedding planner. The calendar was booked months in advance, and it had become the preferred wedding venue for hundreds of miles. Waking, I continued to daydream about the possibility of living that dream, musing on the possible outcomes. What if I did make it more than just a place to have a wedding? What if it was the place to go to for a very special wedding, one that my staff planned and executed in its entirety?

As I ate my breakfast I made notes, trying to figure out how large of a staff I would need if I were to expand my plans to include a full-fledged wedding business. I would need a florist, and since I already had a greenhouse in the plans, we could grow some of our own flowers. In addition to a florist, I'd need to hire someone to bake wedding cakes, a caterer, and hopefully a wedding planner. And to keep it all together, I'd need a housekeeper and an accountant.

My next list was compiling things I would need to change, enlarge, or add on to the existing blueprints of the inn. If I added a second kitchen to the summerhouse, the wedding cakes could be baked in there. The basement of the inn could be finished to include probably four or five more guest rooms, and maybe the groom and his entourage could inhabit the lower-level rooms the night before the wedding. I'd see if Scarlett could increase the size of the turrets by about five feet to be sure that they'd be large enough. The large party room would now be called the ballroom, and I wanted to have elegant chandeliers with dimmers on them to light both the ballroom and the dancing room. The sunroom would be perfect for showers, and maybe the rehearsal dinners. I thought that perhaps I should see if Scarlett could change the plans so that the ceilings on the main level would all be at least nine, maybe ten feet high.

On the second level, the room that I had already designated as the honeymoon suite would be the room where the bride would get dressed. The bed would be in the turret, and there would be a large antechamber for the bridal dressing and pre-wedding photography. Her bridesmaids could be in rooms close by, and there would also be room for the parents of the couple to stay at the inn.

Back on the main floor, on either side of the ballroom, I could bump out small office spaces for the wedding planner and another to be used as a conference room.

I was so very excited about my new plans that the morning quickly got away from me. I had only gotten dressed moments before Jedidiah arrived to take me to church. I was keyed up about my plans and was quite the chatterbox the whole of the drive to church. He seemed equally enthused about this new idea too. It was wonderful to have a cheerleader in my corner. It had been a long time since I'd had a man support my dreams and give me emotional support—truthfully, it was maybe the first time ever.

His brothers were at church with their wives. We slid quietly into the pew next to them, but each of his brothers crowded toward me and gave me a small hug, welcoming me. Their wives smiled and waved, and I felt truly received into his family. Jedidiah's children were absent, but I did not ask about that. I knew he would eventually share with me his concerns about their faith. We had become very close in a short time and were so in tune with each other, at times it was like we had never been apart for over a quarter of a century. During church I had a hard time following along with the service because my mind was still circling wildly with plans for my wedding business.

Jedidiah's parents joined us at brunch following Mass; they had gone to services the evening before. We met at the Hometown Café and ate heartily from a meal served buffet style. The joy and ease of family togetherness was very present at our large table, and I felt truly blessed to have been included in the day.

Following the brunch, we took a slow walk around the town, all the while holding hands and enjoying the lovely spring morning. Grudgingly, Jedidiah took me home at about two o'clock. He confessed that he had some work to attend to with his herd of Hereford bulls; I told him I had notes to write down and lots of things to work out. I also wanted to call his sister and run the changes by her. I'd already asked him his opinion regarding enlarging the summerhouse. I knew that the footings had already been poured, but he assured me that it was perfect timing. It would be easy to add on another kitchen at this point. There just wouldn't be any basement under the new kitchen space. We kissed good-bye again at my doorstep—a long, delicious, tingling kiss.

LUCY

On Monday, I had a productive afternoon and wrote down my ideas for each of the guestrooms—the styles and colors and all of the furniture that I would need to find for each. I numbered them Rooms 1 through 9, starting at the southeast corner. There would also be three guest rooms in the basement of the inn, and possibly room for a wedding photography studio.

I made the outline on my computer, and then, by cutting and pasting, I created a shopping list. I would need more tile, chandeliers and sconces, fans, and lots of shutters. The windows, doors, heaters/air conditioners, and plumbing fixtures were already ordered, thanks to my wonderful architect, Scarlett, and her dear brother. I also needed to shop for carpet, fabrics, and, of course, furniture—lots of furniture.

I did some online shopping to find pictures of wrought-iron chandeliers and sconces, but I wanted to try to purchase them locally if possible. I printed off a few of the ones that I liked to use for comparison.

I also shopped for the log furniture that I wanted to use in two of the rooms, and found the perfect pieces. I placed an order for two queen-sized beds, two sets of bunk beds (the lower bunk was a double-size bed in one of the sets), one twin-sized daybed with an accompanying trundle, ten nightstands, and one chandelier that was designed to look as if it were made from bentwood, with bark remaining on the arms of the five-light chandelier.

I was tempted to purchase a reproduction antler chandelier, but the prices were so high that I decided to wait for a sale price. I had checked the box indicating to ship all together, not piece by piece, and was delighted that I could choose an approximate shipping date in the future, so I asked to have the items shipped to me on October 30.

On Tuesday morning, I took my shopping list and set out in the pickup to begin my search for furnishings for my inn. I started at the Brown and Brown Furniture Barn by Moxford and was pleased to find Miles eager to help me when I walked in the door. Miles had previously helped me when I was desperate to find the perfect dining room table, the day before I planned my first date with Jedidiah. He remembered me too, asking me, "How is that beautiful dining set working out for you?"

I answered, "I'm thoroughly enjoying it and have had several compliments already on it. Today I'm here to see what you can do for me regarding furnishing my inn. I need to furnish twelve guest rooms and will be decorating each with its own unique style. First, let me say that I won't need anything for a few months, until it is much closer to completion. But I wanted to see what is available locally, and if I have to I can purchase now and store it if necessary. First, could you please show me the bedroom furniture you have in stock, especially the iron beds? I think I want most of the guest rooms to have ornate iron beds, but I don't want to limit my choices."

Miles showed me several basics, like well-made wooden beds—some with plain, nondescript headboards, and others with intricately carved, massive headboards. And even though the carved ones were marvelous, I wasn't prepared to spend the bucks for that much expression. I had a budget in mind for each room, and those beds alone were over my budget.

I saw one that had an old-fashioned style to it, with a feminine curve and a soft, mellow attitude. It reminded me greatly of the bed from my childhood, but again, not what I had in mind. Moving on, I walked past bookcase-style headboards and a couple that had a very modern and Oriental feel—ebony and glistening with clean lines.

The next bed was one that caught my eye; while not on my list, I fell in love with it. The headboard looked like it was made of old barn wood, a lovely weathered tone of gray. But rather than being dry and splintery, it was very smooth and brawny, a true masterpiece of craftsmanship. "Oh, this is an incredible bed, Miles."

"Yes," he answered. "That is a one-of-a-kind indeed. It was hand crafted by a local gentleman. He hand-hued the planks into that headboard and sanded it until it was absolutely smooth before he finished it with multiple layers of glossy polyurethane. The wood was reclaimed from his grandfather's barn, so it has a legacy too."

"I must have this bed," I said. I would use it in Room 7, the olive and navy room. I didn't care if I had to store it for months. I wasn't going to take a chance of losing this one. "Miles, put a sold tag on that one, I have to have it! Now, I'm looking for iron beds, hopefully with four-posters and canopies."

He showed me what he had in stock, and while they were well made, they weren't quite right for my design plan. He led me to an online catalog, showing other styles made by the same manufacturer. The bed on the showroom floor was very solidly constructed, sturdy welds and heavy iron, not hollow. Online, I found the iron beds that I wanted, all were four-poster, but with slightly different designs.

The one I chose for the rust room was a bronze metal canopy bed with elaborate scroll designs. It was available with an optional trundle, which I added to my order. That room could sleep a family of four with the addition of that trundle.

The bed I chose for the bridal suite was heavy, black-bronze iron with a boxy shape and somewhat modern ornamentation in square and rectangular geometric shapes. It too was a four-poster canopy bed.

The next two rooms for which I wanted an iron bed were the ones I'd designated as my lighthouse rooms. These beds were ordered in the snowy white option, but with antique pewter accents in wavy scrolls. The canopy frame was designed with both white and antique pewter inlaid scrolls. These beds also had an optional trundle, so I ordered one for each as well. Trundles would leave more open floor space instead of sleeper sofas.

For Room 7, I had the lovely barn-wood bed as the main bed. Rooms 8 and 9 were adjoining and would have the log furniture. I still needed beds for the two smaller rooms—Rooms 5 and 6. Looking through the website, I located a charming bed with a trundle in the antique pewter finish that would work well for my purposes, adding two to my order.

The rooms that would be in the lower level were still a bit undecided. I was thinking that I would put a Murphy bed in the groom's quarters in the lower turret, and maybe adult-sized bunk beds in the other guest rooms.

Miles had left me alone at his computer to do my searching while he helped other customers. I had written down the product numbers and colors for each on an order sheet, so upon finishing I went to the showroom to find him. He was showing a cute little elderly couple a living room set, so rather than interrupting him, I found a quiet corner to check my voice mail. My phone had vibrated in my pocket while I was looking for beds, but I hadn't wanted to disrupt my search. There was a message from the mayor of Whitney; he seemed very anxious for me to come into his office. I returned the call, but his secretary told me he had stepped out. I told her that my plans were to be shopping all day, but I made an appointment for first thing the next day for me to meet with Mayor Coldwater.

I eventually got Miles's attention again, and when he asked if I'd found everything I needed, I asked him if he had any ideas for the lower-level rooms. He told me that there was a bed on the floor that he thought might be what I was looking for. They had it set up in the display window on the opposite side of the building. I followed him through the maze of recliners, sofas, dinettes, and coffee tables. When we reached the window and he pulled aside the curtain so that I could see the bed, I knew instantly I had found the final beds for the guestrooms in the lower level.

It was a hand-carved, walnut, large bunk bed, and it made a very impressive statement. The lower bunk was queen-size and the top was a super twin. It was part of a featured group from Banjo Manufacturing and was on a ten percent off sale, so even though it was still a bit outside of my budget, I rationalized that I would put little else in those rooms. The rest of the pieces would just have to be rather generic because I wouldn't want to put anything else in the rooms that may try to compete; it would be too overwhelming.

I asked about a Murphy bed, and Miles hooked me up with that too. It was housed in a stunning mahogany wall shelf unit and would be perfect for the groom's room.

I finalized the sales of the beds, and Miles assured me that they would store the barn-wood bed for me safely in their storage area until I needed it in the fall. The other beds would take a couple months to build to my specifications, but they would also be ready for me by fall.

My next stop was the giant furniture mall in Lincoln. I started in the fabric gallery. Every one of my guestrooms would be unique, so I needed at least nine different palettes; the lower-level rooms were still a bit of a conundrum for me. The common denominator had to be that from the exterior all of the windows would look the same, so all of the draperies needed to be lined with the same fabric. The ivory lining was the easiest to locate.

I also decided to use matching matchstick, rollup shades in all the guestrooms behind the drapes. Both of the turrets would have lots of windows, so I'd upgrade those shades to room darkening ones by adding the optional privacy lining.

For Room 1, the rust room, I found coordinating stripes and paisleys, deciding to use the stripes for the draperies and a dramatic, large, paisley print for the bedspread. A third pattern, also coordinating, had the paisley pattern and a white lacy overlay design; I would use that for the canopy drapes and accent pillows.

For the honeymoon suite I wanted to use a leather and lace theme, but the fabrics had to be washable, comfortable, and sturdy. The first fabric I chose for the room was a Battenberg lace that I would use for the canopy. Then I found a black and white print microfiber bolt that simulated leather, and it satisfied all of my criteria. It was a zebra-striped pattern that would contrast nicely with the lacy canopy. That would be for the bed covering and the draperies. I decided on a red microfiber fabric for accent pillows and chair cushions. The room would also have an overstuffed sofa or loveseat, but I hoped to find that piece pre-made and not have to customize one.

For the portrait wall, I purchased twelve yards each of lightweight microfiber in solid tones of yellow, peach, pink, ecru, baby blue, navy, emerald green, lavender, black, white, burgundy, and Christmas red. I would have four lengths sewn together to create a wide panel, and all of them would be hung from a sturdy rod at the top of the wall. The photographer could pull the desired color over the wall to create a background for the bridal portraits taken in her room after she was dressed.

The lighthouse themed rooms, Rooms 3 and 4, called out for anything nautical. I had fun looking at all of the possibilities for these rooms. I decided on plain blue duck cotton for the windows. Room 3 would have a lot of windows, and I didn't want the curtains to dominate the room. For the bedcovers I decided on a bolt of fabric that had a queen-sized repeat that looked like a quilt. The quilt was patterned to look like it was hand-appliquéd of several fabrics: patterns of lighthouses, sea creatures, waves, and boats. For the canopy fabric I picked out a coordinating pattern that had an aqua background with the sea creatures on it—seahorses, starfish, clownfish, octopi, etc.

Room 7 was the one for which I had just found the amazing barn-wood bed, so I had to do a little rethinking for this room. I had wanted to have dark colors of olive and navy, but perhaps I should do a more country theme with red and white checks. I couldn't find a fabric yet to satisfy me, so I moved on to the hunter's rooms—Rooms 8 and 9—which would have the log furniture.

My idea for these rooms was that perhaps I would attract some hunters in the fall, maybe a family of father and sons, or brothers and cousins to all bunk out together in a room that would sleep four to seven comfortably. I had seen camouflage-patterned bed and drapery sets in catalogs in the past, but I wanted to have them customized to my room specs, the same as the others, so I was looking for a camo-patterned bolt of fabric. I was somewhat disappointed with the choices; this store did not have anything like I had in mind. But they did have a huge array of animal prints—giraffe, zebra, cheetah, and leopard—so I chose a variety of these and decided that the rooms would take on more of a big-game hunters look. It actually might appeal more to a woman as well, so I wouldn't be limiting the rooms' appeal to only hunters in the fall.

I also discovered a palette of coordinating prints that would work in Room 7. The bed cover would be a navy and olive, large plaid, with small rustic barns printed in ecru patches. I also purchased several yards of the coordinating, larger barn prints on ecru, which would make charming café curtains.

That only left Rooms 5 and 6. I discussed my dilemma with the sales clerk, Gayle. I'd planned one in lemon yellow and rose in the other. She made some suggestions: heavy silk with lemon trees, silkscreen with cherry trees, and a heavy cotton with cabbage roses. The trees intrigued me, but not cherry trees. I asked if there was perhaps a fabric she could show me with birch trees or willow, or even aspen. Wow, was I happy we went down that path!

She led me to a section of botanical prints, and I found the most lovely pieces. It was really hard to decide on only two; there were many that coordinated so I decided to make both the window and canopy drapes out of two fabrics: one had aspen trees, the other had birch; these were for Room 3. The fabrics were similar—both on a snowy background in yellow and lime green tones—but the tree bark was beautifully textured in white, gray, and tan. The bed covering would have a giant willow tree centered, and, hopefully, a good seamstress could customize the quilted top with fabrics in tones of ivory, yellow, lime green, and tan. For the art in the room I would simply frame pieces of the fabric, highlighting the beautiful botanical details of the different trees.

The tree prints were magnificent, so I changed my mind about the rose room. I chose a second botanical palette, this one with silver maples, depicting the four seasons of change for the maples. The colors ranged from a spring green with tiny new leaves to a darker green of summer with the tree fully foliaged. The fall show was a brilliant red, and the winter displayed silver limbs against a backdrop of snow-laden hills.

Finished with the fabric selection for the guestrooms, I needed fabric for the main floor draperies. Since the floor plan was very open to accommodate large parties, I wanted the window coverings to be simple and understated. I wouldn't want a bride to feel overwhelmed with one color covering my windows that wouldn't coordinate with her wedding colors. I planned to paint all of the walls a neutral tan with a yellow hue, but I didn't necessarily want the draperies to blend completely. Gayle, who was still helping me, realized my frustration and suggested that maybe I would rather just have either shutters or wooden shades.

I told her that there would be shutters on the outside, and wooden shades were a bit boring.

"Oh no, not boring!" She grabbed my arm, leading me to yet another room. "Look, just look! There are so many new, exciting patterns and materials being used. Some even have woven grasses, bamboo, and reeds accenting them."

What she showed me was indeed amazing. I was only familiar with plain slatted wooden shades, but the ones she showed me were elegant and multi-textured. I fell in love with the look of the shades and decided upon one pattern—the Malinas pattern with twisted bamboo and hemp, alternating with the wood slats. Gayle told me how they would fit, either inside the window frame or on top of it. I told her I would get her all of the measurements and she could order them all customized to fit.

But, not satisfied yet, I decided that I would need to dress up the windows just a bit more, so I returned to the laces and found a bolt of ivory lace that I could make simple curtains to cover each window. I wouldn't even need to employ a seamstress for that purpose. I could cut and hem each piece myself, and then if we wanted the sun to shine in, but be filtered somewhat, there would be lace to dress each window. I actually purchased the entire bolt of lace and took it with me. I would be able to work on the lace curtains in my free time; I had the measurements on the blueprints thanks to my very thorough architect, Scarlett.

The day was getting late, but I asked Gayle to show me carpeting before I left. I wasn't sure if I wanted to purchase that just yet, but I hoped to get a few swatches. I had collected a swatch of each of the fabrics as I had purchased them for the guestrooms. I'd put each inside a vinyl page-cover, and I had each organized in a three-ring binder according to the room. I also had a print out catalog photo of each of the beds that I had ordered for the rooms.

The carpeting swatches were in a basement showroom, so Gayle led me to the escalator that took us down in the huge store.

I had already told her that I was decorating an inn and that even though each room was decorated differently, I would love to find a carpet that could go throughout the entire second floor. She told me about a wonderful new commercial carpeting that they sold a lot of—Hi-Life. It came in several colors, of course, and was surprisingly plush. It had an amazing warranty and was stain resistant. Her description of the carpet called Hi-Life intrigued me, and when we stepped onto the floor of the carpet showroom, I saw that the floor was carpeted in beautiful tweed, gray-plush carpeting.

"Gayle," I said. She was a few steps ahead of me. She turned around and I said, "Gayle, the carpeting underfoot here, the one that they have used on the showroom floor, what is it? I love this."

With a little laugh, she said, "It is the Tuscan pattern of Hi-Life. Do you like it?"

"Oh yes," I agreed. "It would be perfect I think. Is there somewhere I can spread out my swatches and compare the color tones?"

She led me to a large design table that they had carpeted in the same carpeting and I laid out all of the fabrics, careful to keep them in rooms. The tweed had bits and pieces of all of my colors—rust, ivory, lime green, black, blue, forest-green, navy, and olive. Gayle was explaining all of the wonderful attributes of the carpeting, and I was marveling at how well it seemed to harmonize with all of my color palettes. "I'll take it," I said. I gave her the square footage and added on the recommended percentage, and she added it to my order. She also gave me a twelve-inch square remnant to take with me to help me when choosing my paint colors and accessories.

I checked over my list and found that a TV and stereo for my cottage were the only items left. I asked Gayle if they could hook me up and she helped me pick out a very nice compact stereo and a small flat-screen TV with a built-in DVD player.

I felt a small twinge of guilt when I paid for all of my purchases; perhaps I could have found everything in small, local mom-and-pop stores closer to home, but all in all, I was pleased with my day's purchases.

After all the arrangements were made for delivery, I headed toward home, the TV, stereo, swatches, and the bolt of lace fabric all tucked carefully into my backseat. Hungry, I stopped at a steakhouse and treated myself to a medium rare filet mignon. While dining I received a call on my cell phone from Jedidiah. I was happy to hear from him, and we chatted amiably while I ate my meal. He told me how much he missed me, and I agreed that I would rather be eating with him than alone. We made a date for the following evening. Somehow, the drive home skipped by quickly without incident, and before I knew it I was snuggled in my bed, Jethro purring quietly on my feet.

LUCY

The next morning I was seated across the desk from Mayor Harvey Coldwater. He had the Cheshire Cat look about him, or perhaps it was the cat who swallowed the canary. He started by telling me to call him Harvey, and I returned the favor by insisting he call me Lucy, not Miss Golden. Getting that formality out of the way, he dove right into his news, which I could see was very exciting to him.

"Lucy, you have definitely caught the attention of the locals. Everyone I talk to is excited about what you are doing for our community. In the age when the small town seems to be dying out, we are so happy to have one of our own return and start up new commerce, as well as new services for the community.

"In fact, I have the distinct pleasure to inform you that one of our distinguished local citizens is so pleased with your plans to build a pool and gym for the local citizens that, anonymously, this citizen has given me a check to contribute to you, no strings attached." And with a flourish, he pulled an oversized check out of a plain manila folder, handing it to me across his desk.

I was a little hesitant, since, in my experience, no strings attached usually meant there were consequences to deal with. But I cautiously took the check from him, and at once I saw a lot of zeros. In fact, it was a check for 500,000 dollars!

"Oh, my!" was all I could say.

Harvey was so excited that he jumped out of his chair, not an easy feat for the plump, short mayor. "Oh, my, indeed! Isn't that thrilling? Exhilarating even?"

"Oh, my!" I repeated. "I don't think I can accept this."

"Of course you can," he said, chuckling and kneading his hands as he walked around in his office. "Like I said, no strings attached. This anonymous donor wants you to double the size of your pool and gym so that more local citizens will be able to utilize it. The donor has said that it is of great concern how our country has become lazy and under-motivated to keep physically fit."

I said nothing, just held the check, my mouth agape.

"Lucy, you were planning to have some sort of a membership plan for the local population to use the facilities, weren't you? In addition to your bed and breakfast guests, of course. So why not make it larger, and then more people will be able to use it. What do you say?"

"But half a million dollars? Who has that kind of money? Who is this donor? Surely you can tell me who to thank. To say the least, I am flabbergasted!" I quickly stammered my response. "Mayor Coldwater, I've already purchased the ceramic tiles, and they've already started digging the foundation. It may be too late."

"Now Lucy, remember, call me Harvey. I bet you can find more matching tile. And I had breakfast only this morning at the café with Fred, the fellow who is digging your foundations. I hinted that I thought that there might be a change in the pool house, and he said that he was used to changes, and they had really only got the foundation dug for the inn and the summerhouse, and they would be working on the pool starting on Monday. So you see, that won't be a problem."

"Harvey, I don't know what to say. I love the idea of making it bigger so more people can use the pool and gym, but I think that 500,000 dollars is a bit extravagant. It could be done with a lot less."

"Yes, but this donor is aware that by making it twice as big that your expenses for water and utilities will also be twice as much, so the extra money will come in handy for that. The donor also wanted me to suggest something else, but mind you, this is only a suggestion. You may want to consider building in a few little rooms that could be used in the future if you choose to expand."

"I'm not sure what you mean. The plans are already quite extensive; I can't imagine expanding at this point."

I gave him a quizzical look, and he replied, "Perhaps something like a spa, a dance studio, or maybe even a small retail shop for formal wear. It's just a suggestion, but by expanding the pool, the building will undoubtedly have some vacant space."

Harvey was again seated, grinning widely. "I almost forgot the other part of what I wanted to tell you." He cleared his throat. "Ahem, the city council and the county commission are aware of the monumental distinctions that Goldstone Inn is set to achieve. I have the pleasure to notify you that you have been granted a tax holiday for ten years. That is, you will not be responsible to pay any property tax for the inn, the pool, or any of the other improvements on the Goldstone land for the first ten years. We want to give you every possible advantage to make this work. We know that by building your inn and gym, people will come to our town that would not have otherwise come here, and they will spend money with other merchants as well."

"That is too kind. Thank you! It looks like I really don't have a choice other than to accept the generosity of the town, and even the county. How can I ever thank you all?"

"Well, I guess, maybe you can throw some kind of kick-off shindig once it is finished and invite all of the town. How's that sound?"

"Not a problem. I will love to host a citywide party. We hope to be open by Thanksgiving, but I'll keep in touch with your office and we can work out details closer to the opening date. Thank you again, Harvey!"

"No, thank you for undertaking this enterprise in Whitney. New business is certainly welcome, and especially when it is one of our own citizens returning to start up something new."

More pleasantries were made as I left the mayoral office, and when I got to my car, I immediately phoned Jedidiah to find out if we could meet right away so that I could go over the new plan. Then I phoned Scarlett too, asking if she would be available for a phone conference when I got to Jedidiah's office.

JEDIDIAH

As if I didn't have enough to do, I was in the midst of organizing our annual Father's Day picnic at the ranch. It was usually a joy to plan and I generally looked forward to the day, but this year it was becoming tedious and I was trying hard to not lose my patience. Charlie was still being very obstinate, and even though he was continuing to work on our construction crew, he said very little to me and did his best to be on the opposite side of the property from me. I tried to visit with Simon at least once a week; he was such a joy to have in my life! But on the other hand, Charlie was doing his best to ignore Simon's existence.

And it was such a blessing to have Lucy back in my life. She was very understanding of my workload and the family situation as well, and even though I longed to see her daily, some days flew by with barely a quick phone call. I hated it, and I really would rather spend every evening with her, but she understood how much stress I was under with the huge construction project and the Charlie/Simon situation.

Lucy's inn was coming along nicely, right on schedule. In fact, the pool house was ahead of schedule and would probably be finished by the Fourth of July. The huge donation that she had received was incredible and everything fell into place remarkably.

The pool builder added on several hands to his crew, and they made very fast progress.

One Saturday morning in mid-June, I was sitting in my office, reviewing notes for the upcoming picnic. J.J., my ranch foreman, was in charge of mowing and trimming the yard, and his very capable wife, Lael, would do some of the cooking. My girls were shopping for all of the paper goods we'd need like plates, napkins, and cups. Heather had arrived on Memorial weekend, saying she would stay for two months and then decide if she would return to Washington. Caleb was to purchase the kegs of beer and cases of water and soda pop, and be sure to have enough ice on hand to cool it all down. I would buy all of the meat and buns, as well as the condiments. The rest of the food would be brought by the guests, potluck style.

Normally Charlie would be given the task of setting up the tables and chairs, but he hadn't been available for any of our family meetings, so this year I would be doing the setup, with the help of Lucy and J.J. Kermie Weed would be on hand for the setup too. I had my hand on my cell phone to call Lucy, when it rang. "Hello," I said into the phone.

"Hello, Mr. Jordan. This is Bambi."

I had unsuccessfully tried to get her to call me Jedidiah.

"Well, hello, Bambi. How are you and that sweet little boy today?"

I had talked to her on Thursday evening during her break at the hospital. She was working hard, and living with her aunt had been a great plan. So far, her aunt had been able to keep Simon when Bambi had to go to work, and Simon loved his Auntie Willow.

"We are fine. Simon got to go swimming today at the city pool, actually, in the kiddie pool, but he wants to take swimming lessons, so I've got him enrolled in the second session that starts right after the fourth."

"That's wonderful. He should definitely know how to swim, and I'm sure he'll learn quickly."

"Yes, I think so too. Mr. Jordan, I thought I should let you know that I got a letter today from the state of Kansas."

"Oh?" I said, simply.

"Yes, I was very surprised when I read it. It seems that Charlie had the DNA test done, and the results prove that he is indeed Simon's father."

"Oh my God! That's wonderful," I exclaimed. I jumped out of my chair and was dancing around my office. "Wow, when did that happen?" I asked stupidly.

"I don't know. The letter just says that he had the test done, and the results are that Simon is his biological son."

"I didn't have any doubt that he was, Bambi, but it is fantastic to have legal confirmation of the fact. I wonder if Charlie has been notified. He hasn't said anything to me."

"I received my letter just today, so maybe he will get his today too. I just wanted you to know. I don't really know what this means for Charlie, but Mr. Jordan, I don't want him to think he is obligated in any way. I never wanted that; I just wanted Simon to know his father and his family. I never wanted to cause any trouble." Bambi sounded so young and meek.

"Bambi, no worries. I am very happy that you found us. I pray every day that Charlie will realize that Simon is a blessing, not a problem. And until he does, I don't want you to ever be concerned that you are causing any trouble. Growing up and life in general brings change every day, and sometimes those changes are hard to accept. That doesn't mean that change is bad, but every one of us has a different timetable when it comes to accepting modifications to our life. Now, are we still on for that picnic tomorrow afternoon? Lucy and I will be in the Manhattan City Park at twelve thirty with a bucket of fried chicken, baked beans, and potato salad. Will you and my grandson be ready to dig in?"

"Oh, yes, we will be there. Simon is excited to see you. I am too. Thank you, Mr. Jordan."

"Bambi, come on now, don't you think it is time to drop the mister stuff. Call me Jedidiah."

"Okay, I guess it is official now, you are most definitely Grandpa Jedidiah. I'll call you Jedidiah from now on. See you tomorrow."

As soon as I hung up, I dialed Lucy's number. I was so excited; I had to tell someone! But Lucy's phone went to voice mail. I left her a cryptic message, hoping she would return my call soon. Poised to call, I realized my next instinct was to call my children. But I couldn't call Charlie, and most likely I shouldn't expect Caleb to share my joy. My daughters would probably be more receptive to the knowledge that Simon truly was their nephew, but still, I was reluctant to tell them over the phone.

I suddenly felt very alone in the world. I had this wonderful information to share, and other than Lucy, I didn't feel I had anyone to tell. I didn't even have a dog. I could tell the goat, but she wouldn't share my enthusiasm. There was an old yellow tomcat that wandered around the barn, but he was pretty elusive too. I decided that my mother would be the next likely choice to share my grandfatherly knowledge with, so I called her.

"Hello, son!" She had a caller ID feature that flashed my name on her TV set when I called. The TV rarely was shut off in her house.

"Hi, Mom. I'm not interrupting anything am I?"

"Oh, no! Nancy Grace's show is on, but there is a commercial on at the moment. How are you, dear?"

"I'm wonderful, actually. You remember I told you about the boy named Simon that is my grandson? Well, his mother just called me and told me that she got results in the mail today that proves he is truly Charlie's biological son, so I am really a grandpa! And I guess that makes you a great-grandma! What do you think of that?"

"That's nice, son. What does Charlie think of it?"

"Mother, I haven't spoke to Charlie about it yet. In fact, I'm not sure if I'll get to talk to him about it any time soon. He may receive a letter today in the mail too, but we aren't exactly on good terms right now, so he might not be very forthcoming with conversation with me when he reads it."

"I was afraid that was the case," my mother said. "You should probably see about healing that wound somehow. I'm happy that the child is truly a Jordan, though. When do I get to meet him?"

"Maybe next Sunday at the Father's Day picnic; I hope they come to it. That gives me a week to iron out the wrinkles with Charlie. Any suggestions, Mom?"

With a chuckle, she answered, "You will most likely need a lot of steam in the iron that smoothes that boy's misgivings. I would imagine he is afraid that his days of being footloose and fancy-free are over. You've been very good to your children, Jedidiah. But it may be time to let God take over and not push him too hard. He'll come around with time. You wait and see. In the meantime, why don't you see if you can get him to come visit with me? Maybe your daddy and I can help him to see the light."

"Mom, maybe you should call him and invite him to Sunday dinner. I'm afraid if I ask him to call you he'll only do the opposite since that seems to be his pattern of late."

"I'll do just that. Now, how are you and Lucy doing? Are you getting any closer to asking her to marry you?"

"Mother," I said with shock in my voice. "We've only been seeing each other for a few weeks. Don't you think that would be a little soon for a proposal?"

"Son, I've seen how you look at her, and when you talk to her it is obvious that you are in love. You know, your father asked for my hand after only our third date. And we've been married now for over fifty years. I think it worked out okay."

"I know, Mom, but I think Lucy and I both want to take this a little slow. We don't have a war pushing us together, and we both have a lot going on in our lives right now. Maybe after things with Simon and Charlie get settled a little, and maybe after we get Lucy's inn built, then we will think about a marriage, but for now, we are both pretty busy."

"Oh, that's a bunch of hooey, and you know it. You could get married and still do all those things, but you two do what you want. Don't listen to an old lady, no matter how wise I am," she cajoled playfully.

"I got to go, Mom. Tell Dad hello. And I pray that you can talk some sense into Charlie tomorrow."

JEDIDIAH

At the park the next afternoon, Lucy, Simon, Bambi, and I had an enjoyable picnic. The weather was cool and threatening rain, so we had our picnic in the shelter at a rustic, weathered, wooden picnic table. At one time it must have been painted red, but there was very little paint remaining on the surface. Simon ate heartily, talking excitedly about his upcoming swimming lessons, the new kitten that his Aunt Willow had, and the neighbor girl named Veronica, whose name sounded more like Vonka when Simon said it. He was a joy to be with, never showing any shyness or inhibitions. He very easily called me Grandpa, but when he struggled with my name, I told him that my sons often called me Diddy, so he started calling me Grandpa Diddy. Simon's joy and glee were infectious. He made me laugh!

He asked Lucy if she was his Grandma, but she straightforwardly told the little boy that she wasn't really his Grandma, but since she was Grandpa's girlfriend, he could call her Granny Lucy. Simon's interpretation of that was one word, Grannyloo, so Lucy became Grannyloo to Simon.

Bambi had already told us that she hoped to get Simon down for his nap by two thirty, so we had less than two hours with him, but it was a fun-filled, joyous two hours. And shortly before it was time for him to leave with his mother, the skies became dark with clouds, rumbling with thunder and occasional lightening, and the rain started to sprinkle down. Reluctantly, Simon agreed to make a dash for the car before it poured, so with a quick hug to both Lucy and me, they left our little picnic.

Lucy and I rapidly put our picnic remnants back into the basket she had brought, and, holding it in one hand and her hand in my other, we also exited the park before the downpour let loose. Safely back in the truck, we hugged and kissed, agreeing that the picnic had been a success. Not wanting to go directly home, I asked her if she had any place else she wanted to go in Manhattan.

"I do have a suggestion," she answered hesitantly. "But I don't want you to think I am crossing over work with a Sunday outing. Could we go to the big lumber and home store on Anderson Street? I need to pick out a style of moldings and doors, and I kind of would like your assistance. Would that be okay?"

"Of course, anything you want to do is fine, as long as I get to spend more time with you. How can I go wrong?"

I've never really enjoyed shopping, but spending two hours with Lucy in a lumber store was a pleasant way to spend a rainy Sunday afternoon. I helped her pick out some paint samples, molding, patio flagstones, shutters, hardwood flooring, chandeliers and sconces, and finally, doors. She had her little notebook and digital camera in her purse, so she was recording our choices as we shopped.

We were in the aisle looking at the exterior doors when she got very excited, declaring, "Oh, my, Jedidiah, I nearly forgot. I wanted a Dutch door at the kitchen in the inn. I don't think I have that noted anywhere; I know I forgot to tell Scarlett. Will that be a problem?"

"No, I'm sure a Dutch door won't be a problem to work in at this stage of the build. And even if it were, I'd make it work; I'll do anything to make you happy, Lucy."

"Anything?" she asked coyly.

"Yes, anything," I answered earnestly. Looking her straight in the eye and holding both of her hands, I declared to her, "Lucy, I think I have fallen in love with you all over again. Maybe I've always loved you. You are the best thing that has happened to me in all of my life." I kissed her then, a deep, passionate kiss. And when we came up for air, there was a small crowd that was watching us at the end of the aisle.

A tall guy wearing striped overalls ventured the question, "Hey, did we just witness a proposal, or what?"

Blushing, I gave him a shrug, and said, "No, but if I do propose to her at the Home Store I'll send out invitations so you can all see that too."

I grinned, gave her a small kiss, and whispered in her ear, asking if she was ready to go.

As we brushed past the audience, the fellow in the overalls was humming an off-key rendition of the wedding march, and the others were singing, "Here comes the bride."

Running through the rain, we got to the privacy of my pickup truck, and after I had the heat turned up full blast to ward away the chilly dampness, I asked her if she was all right. "Of course I'm all right. But, Jedidiah, I didn't get a chance to respond to your declaration of love." And turning in her seat so that she faced me, she took my hand, and said, "I love you too, Jedidiah. I've never stopped loving you; you have always been the man I tried to find. I married twice, to men I hoped would become the man of my dreams, but it has always been you. Nobody else could ever live up to the remembrance of what I had of you. And now that I know you as a man, not just a boy, I am so happy to have found you again, and I love the man you have become."

We shared an extraordinary passionate kiss, and after staring into each other's eyes, she said, "Now, why don't you take me home. I think the weather is only going to get worse and my silly cat gets scared in thunderstorms, so he may be tearing up my house in terror."

JEDIDIAH

That evening I received a phone call from my mother. Charlie had spent the day with them, and she was calling to report progress. "I came right out and told him that I knew that he was a father, and I thought it was time that we talked about it."

"That was pretty bold, Mom. Did he get angry and storm out?"

"No, interestingly, he was silent and sullen. I just continued to talk. Your dad didn't have much to say either, so I was in my element. I told Charlie that even though I wasn't happy about the circumstances, it was about time that I had a great-grandchild. Then I told him that I didn't see the problem; why wasn't he happy about the child?"

"Did you get a response to that?"

"You better believe I did! He said he had no plans to have a child and it wasn't fair that that girl showed up now, flaunting the boy like he was supposed to mean something to him. Then he said a couple words I can't repeat, followed with the sorry detail that it had been a one-night stand, and not even one that he could remember much about.

"I told him," she continued, "that children are often not planned for, they just happen. And since it was pretty obvious that he knew how they were made, any time that a person has sex they have to realize the liability of the act. I also told him that I didn't think anyone was trying to force him to marry the girl, just to acknowledge that the boy was biologically his."

"Did Dad ever say anything?" I asked.

"No sirree," she said. "He sat there like a bump on a log. But Charlie finally asked something that made some sense. He asked, 'So what happens if I do acknowledge that he is mine? Then what?'

"I told your boy, 'I don't think there is a clear-cut answer, but it's my understanding that Bambi has said she doesn't expect anything from him, but I have a feeling that there will be a child support demand from the state of Kansas. This isn't the first time something like this has happened, and I'm sure there is a precedence that mandates that the father will have to pay some support since that notification letter came from the state. There are laws protecting children from deadbeat dads, and I'm afraid that he'll have to face that music.'"

A little shocked at how bold my mother could be at times, I interjected, "I told him pretty much the same thing, but he blew up at me and stormed off. How'd he take it from you?"

"I think he was offended that I was calling him a deadbeat, but I reassured him I knew he was a good young man." Mom continued, "Then he asked how much money he'd have to pay in support. I told him I wasn't sure, but it would probably be a couple hundred a month or so. And maybe even some owed for previous years. He declared that that wasn't fair since he hadn't even known about him before, so how could they make him pay for the past. I calmly told him that life is often not fair, especially when you are dealing with the law. Laws are created to protect the innocent, and unfortunately that means that the finger is pointed at the other party, thereby creating a guilty party, even if the other party isn't really guilty of anything."

"How'd he take that?"

"He got pretty quiet again and said that he remembered when he was growing up that you always paid your child support without complaining about it. We were all quiet then for a bit; I could tell he was thinking.

"Then he said something that really surprised me. He told me that Flynn used to cash her child support checks and stick the cash in the cookie jar. She called it her mad money. He said that by the time he was fifteen he was sneaking money out of the jar and paying the bills before she could waste it away. He claimed that he paid the utility bills, the phone bill, and the cable bill every month with cash. He said he would get the mail every day and when he saw the bills come in, he would sneak out to the kitchen after she was asleep, take enough money to cover the bills, and the next day after school he would take the bus to the post office, buy money orders, and mail the payment. She never asked in three years how they ever got paid. When he moved out he told Hannah about it and she took over doing it. He thought that Heather probably had been doing it too, but now that the child support stopped, who knows. They probably won't ever get paid."

"Well, it doesn't surprise me that Flynn didn't pay the bills. She was always really good at spending money and wasting it on things we didn't need, but she never did write out a check to pay a bill. I had to do all of that. The mortgage was set up to be paid automatically from the bank account, so she must have put her paychecks in there to keep it paid up. Charlie has always been a pretty responsible kid. I guess that's why his reaction to Simon has come as such a surprise to me."

"Well, Jedidiah," she said, "I think he may finally be coming around. I asked him what his plans were for the Father's Day picnic. His initial reaction was a blank stare, not understanding my transition to that since we had been talking about child support and other things. I then said that I thought that his father was going to be disappointed if both of his sons weren't there to celebrate and to pitch in to help. He told me that he intended to be there to do what he usually did, to set up the tables and chairs, and get the barbeques ready.

"I asked him if he thought about the fact that since he also had a son, what his reaction would be if the boy was there. Again I got that blank stare for a little bit and then he said that he thought that maybe he'd been a jerk about the whole situation and that maybe the Father's Day picnic might be a very appropriate time for him to meet Simon and to finally accept his position as a father."

"Wow, Mom! Now I think I'm the one with nothing to say," I said hesitantly.

"He said something else, though, that told me that your troubles might not be over. He said that Caleb would pitch a hissy fit. I guess his big brother has been very instrumental in his decisions so far to reject Simon. So I guess my question is, Jedidiah, do you want me to call Caleb up here to have a talk with him, or do you want to take that one on?"

"Mom, I truly appreciate what you have done, but I think I should talk to Caleb myself. I think it is time that I figured out just what has caused his negative attitude."

"Okay then, but I don't think you have a lot of time to think it over. Charlie said he was planning to announce his intention Tuesday night to invite Simon and Bambi to the picnic. He said that you were having a family meeting to go over the picnic plans, so you might want to talk to Caleb before your meeting."

JEDIDIAH

I couldn't locate Caleb until Monday morning, when I found him on the job site. He had come home really late Sunday night and dashed out of the house before I came down for breakfast. He was helping out in the pool house where they were laying the four-by-four aqua tiles. I approached him and asked if he would come outside with me. He looked at Pedro, the tiler that he was helping, and Pedro said he could get by for a while without him. All of the materials were laid out, it was just doing the tedious job of mudding and setting, and he could take it from there alone.

Caleb and I walked toward a shady spot under one of the big willow trees where there was a picnic table set up for taking breaks and lunches. I had snagged my thermos and a couple of cups as I walked past my truck, so I poured us both a cup of coffee and sat down, nodding to Caleb to take a seat facing me.

"What's up, Dad?" he asked.

"Caleb, we need to talk about your brother."

"What about him. He's been working hard and staying sober. What else do you want?"

"Oh Caleb," I said. "It's not all about working and not drinking. Life can be so complicated at times, and I think that sometimes we get set going in a direction that we just can't find a way out, so we just keep going down that road until we crash."

"Dad, you're not making any sense. What the hell are you trying to say?" Caleb sounded defensive and ready to run.

"Caleb, I guess what I'm trying to say is that Charlie may be changing his approach to Simon. My concern is that you aren't going to like it. I think he is planning to invite Simon and Bambi to the picnic."

"Like hell he is!" Caleb declared. His face had suddenly become bright red and his posture had stiffened; he had a massive scowl on his face and his fists were firmly planted on the table.

"Calm down, Caleb! I want to know why you have such a negative attitude about this child. What is going on? I don't get it. Tell me what the problem is."

"The problem is that our family does not need to get mixed up with that Bellingham family. Gosh dang it to heck! They are trash, and I'll not stand by and see them ruin us."

"That's enough, Caleb," I said firmly. "Calm down. I don't want to hear name-calling and cussing. We are still at the job site, so please, let's try to keep this a quiet conversation.

"I know all about Bambi Bellingham's stepbrother, but that calamity does not necessarily reflect on her. She is several years younger than Reuben, and it is my understanding that she didn't really even live in the same house that he did for very long. The fact that he is in jail for rape shouldn't really factor into our acceptance of Bambi and Simon. Her stepbrother had moved out shortly after her mother married Bob Bellingham. I don't think she has any contact with Reuben now. And nevertheless, none of that is Simon's fault. I think we need to focus on the fact that your brother is the child's biological father. That doesn't change just because the Bellingham family doesn't meet your standard of expectations."

With clenched teeth, Caleb quietly said, "My expectations are that if we let her into our family, Bambi Bellingham will only cause trouble. I don't like her; I don't trust her. I've seen her around a lot, Dad, and trust me, she is not good news."

"Caleb, if there is something else that I don't know about, I think it is time that you told me. You seem to have something else that you aren't telling me. Out with it! What is it?" I asked.

I could see that he was struggling, shaking his head and taking repeated deep breaths. "I didn't want to tell you, Dad, but you made me. She's a lesbian. I saw her with my ex-girlfriend, Maggie. They didn't know that I saw them; I won't go into details, but they weren't exactly watching who came in the door. I dropped by to see Maggie, and that's when I saw them; I know it was her. I saw enough of her to know her and besides, I heard Maggie say her name. So there you have it. I guess you could say I had some sort of jealous rage going on about her for years now because she stole my girlfriend. But bottom line, she's not fit to raise my nephew, so I don't want anything to do with her."

"Okay, Caleb. If what you say is true, and I'm not doubting you, I'm just saying I need to process it a little. It's not a crime to be a lesbian, and even though I don't understand that lifestyle or that choice, if it is a choice, I don't think we can condemn Bambi for it. As far as her stealing Maggie from you, did you ask Maggie about it? What happened? Did you just walk away?"

"Yeah, Dad. I walked away. I turned around, slammed the door, and left. I never called her again, and I didn't take her phone calls. Well, crud! I was hurt. I didn't know what else to do. I left and got drunk and smoked some pot. I think I was high for about a week following that, and then I finally decided she wasn't worth it."

"You could have talked to me about it. I'm sorry you felt like you had to keep it in and deal with it alone. Son, I may not always have seemed approachable, but I am here for you now. I hope that if you ever have anything else that traumatic happen to you that you will come to me and talk it over with me. Believe it or not, I have had some pretty awful things that have happened to me too, and I may be able to help you out," I said. Then I looked at him, reached across, lifted his chin so that he had to look me in the eye, and I asked, "Okay?"

He was calmer now, almost with a defeated, sullen look, but he grinned and said, "Okay."

"So how do we go on with Bambi now? Do you want to ask her about the Maggie thing? Or find out if she has any remorse for her part in the breakup? I think it might bring a little closure to the situation, but I don't want to force you into anything. It has potential to be kind of messy, but considering the state of affairs, I think that there has to be some sort of resolution between you and her."

"Can't we just drop it, Dad?"

"I don't think so. I don't want you to blow up every time that Bambi is mentioned, and I think that until you two talk about what happened, it will be a big mess for a long time. And not only that, but your brother may be going down a path that leads to further involvement with her, maybe not on a romantic road, but at least some sort of co-parenting arrangement, so I think it may be important for your health and comfort level to solve this issue with her."

"Okay, how do I do it?"

"If you want, I could arrange a time for you two to meet and I'd be happy to be there as a mediator if you want. I know it could be kind of uncomfortable, but I'm willing to do what I need to do to put an end to this strife."

JEDIDIAH

On Tuesday morning, Caleb and I arrived at Bambi's house at ten o'clock. When I'd called to find out when she was available for a visit, she had suggested that time and day since she was off on Tuesday, and that would give her a chance for a little nap after her Monday night shift ended. I brought coffee, milk, and doughnuts to meet with her. She seemed a little surprised to see Caleb but said little besides hello to him.

She led us to the patio table, carrying a large bowl of strawberries. Simon was swinging on the tire swing hanging from a huge maple tree but came running when he saw me. Very excitedly, he called out, "Grandpa, Grandpa, I didn't know you were coming!" He ran into my arms for a big hug.

"I brought you some milk and a doughnut. Are you hungry?"

"I'm thirsty, and mom said I could have some strawberries, so I don't think I want a doughnut," he said, sounding like an adult with his sentence structure. I was so pleased with this little boy; what a smarty!

He sat next to me and ate a few strawberries and finished a whole carton of milk. I asked if he wanted to swing some more, so I followed him to his swing, leaving Caleb and Bambi alone at the table. I couldn't hear what they said to each other, but

Caleb had assured me that he would be polite. He had said he just wanted to get her side of the story, and he promised he would try to listen objectively.

I pushed Simon on his swing for a good ten minutes before we were joined by his mother and my oldest son. They were both smiling, so I guessed it had gone well. Caleb approached the little boy and said, "I don't think I've been very nice to you. But can we change that? I'm your Uncle Caleb and I'm happy to meet you, Simon." He reached forward and tousled the boy's hair. Simon just smiled and said, "I don't think I've ever had an uncle before, have I, Mama?"

Bambi had walked around behind Simon and was lifting him out of the swing and answered him, "No son, I think that Caleb is your first. The sun is getting pretty hot out here, so I think it is time that we go inside."

"Can I watch Barney?"

The mother and son were walking hand in hand toward the house. She turned to us and said, "You are welcome to watch Barney with us if you want."

We both declined, saying it was time to get to work. When we got in my pickup truck, I looked at my son and kidded him, "If you want to watch the purple dinosaur show, go ahead, I'll wait."

He just gave me a big grin and said, "No, Dad, I've done my good deed for the day. I don't think I have it in me to watch Barney!"

We returned to the work site, arriving just as they were breaking for lunch. We'd stopped at a drive-thru burger joint before leaving Manhattan and ate the food on the way home. Caleb and I went down the road to our office to check in with Hannah. She was eating a salad at her desk, and had the Goldstone schedule book open in front of her. "Hey there, you two! I was just looking this over, and it seems we are ahead of schedule." She handed me the book, and Caleb and I took it into my office to review; Hannah followed us into the office.

Caleb said, "I think that the pool house should be ready by the end of the month and the summerhouse probably about the same time. I think we should reassign those teams to build the gazebos and pergolas in the backyard after they finish; what do you think?"

I agreed that it sounded like a good idea. I asked Caleb to verify that the materials had all arrived for the gazebos; he located the file with the materials list. "The foundations are concrete of course and already poured, but all of the iron-worked balustrades are here, and Lucy approved the color and design of them. The rock supply is holding out, and I think we'll have enough to do the benches in front of each of the gazebos. The wood to build the rafters is here, and of course we have several pallets of the metal shingles. I helped put them on the summerhouse, and they were amazingly easy to apply. I hope that putting them on the round gazebo roofs will be as easy."

I commented, "I noticed that they really do look just like the red clay tiles. Lucy told me that she is pleased with them."

We continued discussing the backyard projects for the rest of the hour and returned to the job site at one o'clock to get to work. The day was a hot one, so no doubt the crew would be a little lethargic. Before we left the office I asked Hannah to run to town and get a couple cases of canned lemonade and bottled water and ice it down so that by their three o'clock break we could give them all some good cold refreshments.

During the hottest part of the summer I usually tried to run the construction crews from 5:00 a.m. to 2:00 p.m. because the mornings were just a lot cooler. So far we'd been having pretty mild weather, but I told Caleb that at the break today I'd be announcing that it was time to go on the heat schedule. Most of the guys usually didn't mind coming in early to be able to break away before the day got terribly hot in the late afternoon.

Later that afternoon, after enjoying an ice-cold lemonade together, Caleb and I were alone, working side by side in the large caterer's kitchen of the summerhouse installing cabinets.

I asked him, "Son, you didn't say, but it seemed like your conversation with Bambi must have gone very well."

He hesitated, and then Caleb answered, "Dad, I have to admit, I was wrong. She is a nice girl, and she told me that the night I witnessed her with Maggie was instigated by Maggie and she'd never done anything else ever like it. It was some kind of experiment, and she said that it had confirmed in her mind that she never wanted to do anything like it ever again. She also told me that Maggie had been coming onto her for several weeks before she finally gave in. She told me a couple of other things about Maggie that I have since discovered as well. Maggie really wasn't the girl for me, but I guess I wanted to blame the relationship failure on Bambi."

I asked, "So, all's well between you and Simon's mother?"

"Dad, I've been thinking…Simon really is a sweet little boy, and none of this is his fault. As long as nobody is insisting on Charlie marrying the girl, yeah, I'm good. Bambi's not so bad, and it'll be fun having a little nephew to spoil."

"Hallelujah," I declared. "I'm so happy that both you and Charlie have realized that having another little Jordan in the family isn't a bad thing, even if he doesn't have the Jordan name."

Just then, we were interrupted when another crewmember came in, asking a question about the hardware installation on the pool house doors. I left to help him out, walking with a bounce in my step, pleased with my life again.

Charlie, Caleb, and Bambi had finally come to an understanding. Truth be told, the discovery of a grandson had been so thrilling to me. I just didn't know how to handle my sons if they had continued down the road of rejecting the boy. The idea of deadbeat dads was so foreign to me; how could any man not want to be involved with his own child? With the Father's Day picnic looming right around the corner I was really looking forward to a celebration.

And most importantly, God had granted me the wonderful pleasure of having Lucy back near me. Our love for each other seemed to be growing daily, and even though we really hadn't yet discussed a future together, I truly believed that God had great things in store for us.

JEDIDIAH

Cling
Thud
Thud

"Well, you got one ringer, Josiah! That's not enough to win!"

My brothers and Dad were already playing horseshoes. They were just finishing up the first game when Caleb rang the old brass dinner bell, signifying that the burgers and brats were ready to eat.

The children were the first in line, and the little ones were accompanied by their mothers. There was a large spread of food— potato salad made by my mother, and my sisters-in-law kicked in with coleslaw, homemade pickles, baked beans, and veggies with dip. My brothers had all chosen very good cooks for wives, and Gretchen, Jett, and Luellen were all amazingly patient with my rowdy, pig-headed brothers. Lael, the wife of my ranch foreman, J.J. Jones, had contributed several cakes. All the rest of the guests had also brought a dish; I had spied a large bowl of Caesar salad, a couple meringue pies, an apple pie, and a big roasting pan full of fried chicken, provided by Kermie's wife, Kitty. She made the best fried chicken in the county, and I was keeping an eye on the pan, making sure I'd get a piece.

Lucy and I had been organizing the drinks and placement of the food as people arrived. Caleb and Charlie were at the barbecue grills, cooking up fifty pounds of burgers and forty pounds of bratwursts. My daughters were in charge of the ambiance, making sure that everyone found a comfortable spot and had refills as needed.

It was a perfect day for a picnic. The elm and oak trees in my front yard provided just enough shade to make the eighty-five-degree sunny day very comfortable. The morning had started off cool and dry, and there was just a slight breeze, not enough to blow around the paper plates or plastic cups.

Bambi and Simon were some of the last guests to arrive. I saw her drive in and park by the barn. I don't think that either Charlie and Caleb had noticed her arrival, occupied at the grill and flirting with a few local girls who were nearby. I excused myself from the conversation I was having with Jeff and Les Braun, brothers who worked on the pool house crew.

I walked toward Bambi and her son and was pleased to see that both of my daughters had spied their arrival too, and they joined me as I welcomed them to the picnic. Simon was holding hands with both of his new aunts as we approached the lawn where the picnic tables had been set up in the shade of the trees. I introduced Bambi and Simon to my brothers and their wives as we walked by them. My father and mother were curiously absent just then, so I explained to Bambi that I'd introduce them to her later.

I noticed that Lucy was tugging on a large cooler of iced-down sodas, trying to get it in front of the drink table, so I quickly returned to my post at the drink station, telling Bambi to have a good time as I left her and Simon with Gretchen and her two daughters, Georgie and Ginger.

Shortly after returning to Lucy's side, I saw my parents coming out of the back door, each carrying a large watermelon. They had set up a watermelon-cutting table near the water hydrant. From our stance by the drink table, Lucy and I watched as my parents worked at cutting up the watermelons and lining up the large slices of the bright red, juicy fruit. No forks were allowed; watermelon was strictly finger food at the Father's Day Picnic.

When they had it all cut up, Grandpa whistled and declared, "Watermelon time; come and get it!"

Several of the children had been anxiously waiting, watching my mother cut it up. They knew the routine, though; nobody could have any until the whistle sounded.

Laid out about six feet from the table was a large blue tarp that had horizontal lines of red tape. The taped lines were six inches apart, and with white paint, the lines were identified as "So-so, Keep Trying, Good Job, Great Spit, Nearly Amazing, Fabulous, and The Best." This was the watermelon-spitting tarp, and some version of the game had been played at the Father's Day Picnic ever since I could remember.

The game drew a small cheering section, parents and older siblings encouraging the young children to spit the seeds higher and farther. The game was limited to ages ten and younger, but everyone looked forward to it. And at the end, Grandma and Grandpa always had great prizes for the winners. They never revealed the prizes until after the game, though, so the anticipation of the prize was almost as fun as the contest itself. Then I noticed that my son and his son were bonding; Charlie was teaching Simon how to spit watermelon seeds, and Caleb was standing next to Bambi. All of them were smiling and enjoying the experience.

I was watching the event with Lucy, standing with a casual arm draped across her shoulders. I suddenly realized that my life was just about perfect. For the first time in a long time, I was genuinely quite happy. My parents were healthy and enjoying their grandchildren. My brothers and their wives and children were all attending the picnic, and also having a great time. I was very proud of my children. The girls were wonderful hostesses—

beautiful, charming, and beaming with joy and grace. And my sons were finally showing maturity and responsibility, attributes that every father dreams for their sons. And I had an amazing grandson to dote upon.

But most important, Lucy was back in my life in a grand way. She had such a radiance of peace and affection for life. Lucy was the perfect addition to our family, but more than that, she was the completion of me.

We had been spending a great deal of time together the last couple of months, and when we couldn't find time to see each other, we talked on the phone at length. Actually, reflecting upon our phone conversations, it was a refreshing way to get to know one another again. When we were within arm's reach, I had a hard time keeping my hands off her. I had been trying very hard to be respectful, mature, and honorable. So far, I had been able to refrain from making love to her, but now, looking at her with the sun shining on her beautiful face, I could feel that resolve passing away.

She looked up at me, and innocently, she said, "Tell me about your thoughts."

I felt myself blushing and could not stop myself. Quietly, I said close to her ear, "I'm thinking about making love to you. Lucy, I've never been happier than right now at this moment in my life, and I want to celebrate tonight!"

With a slight pause, she responded, up on her tiptoes, she whispered in my ear, "My place, nine thirty tonight; bubble bath, candles, and romance." We looked deeply into each other's eyes and kissed passionately.

Loud applause and whoops interrupted our moment, and my brothers were all three standing directly in front of us, carrying on.

Playfully, I said, "Show's over, boys. What's up?"

Elijah looked conspiratorially at Darwin and Josiah, and they rushed me, hauling me upon their shoulders, and Darwin said, "Looks like you're up!" And they marched me around the crowd of the onlooking friends and family, repeating a mantra, "Diddy's in love, Diddy's in love, Diddy's in love!"

They stopped their march at the rear of the property near the cattle barn, and I swiftly realized that their intent was to dunk me in the stock tank. I struggled, trying to free myself from their hold on me, threshing about and saying, "No, no, don't you dare."

Josiah, in a booming voice, said, "Big brother, are you daring us?"

But before I could protest again, my beautiful blonde savior stood between my three brothers and the stock tank, slimy with green water. Lucy posed, hands on her tiny hips, standing as tall and serious as her five feet and a few inches could muster. My boisterous brothers were sniggering and protesting that I needed to cool off. Her brilliant lavender eyes were shining and twinkling with amusement. Flirtatiously, Lucy looked up at me nearly ten feet high and winked. With mock seriousness, she voiced, "Boys, now you don't really want to do that, do you?"

Lucy was joined by my children—Charlie and Caleb on one side, and Hannah and Heather on the other. All five linked arms in front of my brothers, and unless they were prepared to break through the barrier, they were going to have to give up their quest of dunking me in the green, slimy water.

Darwin spoke first, "Now, this won't hurt him at all, and I think you all could agree that big brother Diddy needs to be dunked!"

And then, slipping between the giant and rowdy overexcited Jordan men, little Simon toddled toward Lucy. He turned, and defiantly, in a bold little boy voice, declared, "Put my Grandpa down. Don't hurt him." The little guy had tears forming, and my solid wolfen brothers swiftly turned to Jell-o. They quickly lowered me to the ground and assuredly proclaimed to Simon that they weren't going to hurt me. Simon stood his ground, not letting the tears loose, but when I picked him up, he flung his little arms around my neck and gave me a big sloppy kiss on my cheek.

"I saved you, Grandpa. I love you. I didn't want those men to hurt you!"

Gently, but with conviction, I said to Simon, "It's okay, Simon. They weren't really going to hurt me, but I'm so glad you saved me!"

The group gathered around, and my brothers took their turns warmly tweaking a cheek, ruffling his hair, and plucking at the little guy's nose. We had a group hug, joined by my kids. But not able to spy my girl, I broke loose from the throng to find her sitting up on the corral fence next to the tank. I handed Simon over to Charlie and walked toward her, reaching out to pluck her down from the fence.

Flirtatiously, I said, "Ready for that bubble bath?" Suggestively, I maneuvered her in my arms above the slimy tank, bouncing her a couple of times for effect.

Giggling, she said, "Oh, Jedidiah, you wouldn't!"

I pulled her closer to me and said into her floral-scented hair, "No, I wouldn't ever do anything to harm you, Lucy. I love you!" Greedily, I sought out her mouth and kissed her with passion.

I heard one of my brothers moan and say, "Look, they are at it again. I think Diddy has finally fallen hard!"

JEDIDIAH

Precisely at nine fifteen that evening I ducked into the kitchen and searched the refrigerator for refreshments to share with Lucy. Into a plastic grocery bag I slipped a bottle of Riesling wine, a bowl of strawberries that had been forgotten at lunchtime, a block of sharp cheddar, and a loaf of pumpernickel. Hoping to sneak out without my family missing me, I made it to my truck, which, miraculously, wasn't blocked in by other vehicles. Most of the guests had departed, but my children had built a bonfire, and Josiah, Elijah, and several of the kids' friends were enjoying the peaceful setting around the fire.

As I drove away I saw my brothers standing and watching me, and they gave each other a high-five. Shrugging them off, I turned my heart and mind toward my luscious Lucy, who awaited me just down the road.

She greeted me at the door, wearing a long, white T-shirt, barefoot, her dark blonde hair flowing seductively around her face. I wasn't sure if she wore anything else, but I hoped it wouldn't be long before I solved that mystery.

"Hi, Lucy. You look wonderful," I said. Then, uncomfortably, I followed by presenting the bag to her. "I gathered up a bottle of wine and a few things to eat. Hope that's okay."

With a soft laugh she said, "That's perfect. I've been so nervous since I got home that I totally forgot about food or drinks."

There was music playing, and candles were lit in every room. She took my hand, handed the bag back to me, and said, "Will you carry this? I'll get some glasses, a corkscrew, a cheese slicer, and we can go try out that huge bathtub." Not letting loose of her hand, I followed her through her kitchen as she gathered some things into a wicker basket, and then she led me toward the bedroom and onward to the attached large bathroom.

I'd been in the room before, of course. Lucy's ex-husband, Tony, had hired our construction company to do a total remodel of the cottage. He had passed away abruptly on the day it was finished. I hadn't known at the time that Lucy was Tony's ex-wife; he had always referred to her as Lula. He'd had aspirations of winning her back into his life, and with his newfound wealth, he'd been setting a deliberate lure, if not a trap, hoping to entice her to remarry him.

However, I wasn't thinking about Tony at that moment; I had my gorgeous Lucy seducing me in her opulently tiled bathroom. I had been the one who had done a great deal of the tiling and the installation of the fixtures. But it was not the same. Now the black marble and copper faucets gleamed in the flicker of candlelight and Lucy had painted the walls a soothing, shimmering tone of a light orange-ish brown color. "I like your paint color choice," I commented.

"It's called glistening ginger," Lucy answered in a seductive tone.

Crazy, but I thought I could smell the ginger. Taking a deep breath, I looked around and noticed a bouquet of flowers, some baskets filled with towels, and bottles of shampoos. On a curio shelf hanging on the wall was a collection of miniature owls. I stood looking at the owls and heard her behind me, arranging the food and drink on a cabinet top between several candles. From a few feet away, I heard her say, "The owls were my grandmother's.

She liked birds of all kinds, especially owls. When she passed away I got her collection and have added a few of my own in the last couple of years."

Then I felt her hands on my shoulders, rubbing my neck, and slowly I turned toward her and gently kissed her. We kissed for a few minutes before she broke away. Turning, she asked me to open the wine while she started the bath water.

By the time I had the wine open, she had the tub nearly half full of water and some cheese cubes, strawberries, and bread slices on a pewter tray. She carried it to the tiled tub edge, and I added the wine and glasses next to the tray before turning back to the beautiful woman I had declared my love to only a few hours before.

Shyly, she started to undress me, cooing that I was way overdressed compared to her white T-shirt. Before long, we were both lounging in the hot bubbly water, moaning with contentedness. We fed one another berries, cheese, and sips of wine, and the night progressed from there—seductive, stupendous, and sheer heavenly.

Before the food tray was emptied, and long before the water had started to cool, we were making passionate love in Lucy's four-poster bed. She was amazing, gorgeous in every way. When we had been teenagers in love, we had enjoyed many nights of sexual encounters, but almost always in the front seat of my parent's big Buick. We didn't even take the time to crawl around to the backseat—our passion seemed to have no end during our teen years.

Now, my expression of my love for Lucy was with a fervor and intensity that I had never dreamed about. I couldn't get enough of her; I stayed with her that night, not sleeping for long before we again roused the force of affection toward one another, locking in a coupling together, experiencing a zeal that I had never before known. The moonlight shone through the lacy curtains, illuminating the face of my angelic Lucy. She smiled in her sleep, echoing my happiness. I smiled and nestled her closely to my body, relishing the comfort of her body warmth on the cool June night.

LUCY

My relationship with Jedidiah was wonderful. My faith in God also increased exponentially, accordingly. I had thought I had a good life when I was living in Maine in my little house, going to work each day and coming home to my fluffy but petulant cat. The sedative of time had softened the pain of two failed marriages and the geographic separation of my children from me. I had been involved at my local church, and the friends I had made at church became my second family.

My new life in Whitney, Kansas, was a 180-degree change. I no longer got up each day and went to a job that I had no excitement for. My little stone cottage was less of a haven and more of a home of joy and life. My townhouse in Maine had been my hideaway from the cruel world.

I hadn't become involved with church life here yet, other than to accompany Jedidiah to Catholic Mass most weekends. And while to a typical Christian, this may seem to be the expected involvement with church, I knew that having a true relationship with God and fellow Christians was truly what God expected. And having had that in the not-so-distant past, I did miss that.

And, of course, there was Jedidiah here in Whitney. I had accepted my life as a single person when I was living in Maine, and even after I initially moved to Kansas I didn't have any aspirations of ever marrying again. One evening while I was talking to Jedidiah on the phone, I mentioned this to him. I told him that I didn't realize how lonesome I had been before. I was amazed when he told me that I was an answer to his prayer.

He explained that after his divorce he had been lonely and had tried dating a few women. But none of them had felt right. Before moving to Kansas, he had said a prayer to God, asking God to help him to find the perfect mate for him. He'd had a heart-to-heart talk with God, telling him that he had given up on dating and would wait for God to lead him to the right woman. Since moving to Kansas he had not dated at all until he had found me again. It was indeed an impressive miracle of God's, at least an amazing answer to his prayer. Our Lord had arranged the whole situation with his amazing, holy magic.

It explained why Tony's heart had been softened to want to include me again in his life and why he had set up his will to give me the property in Whitney; God had a plan. And Jedidiah, Tony, and I had been molded by God. He does indeed work in amazing ways!

And even though I had allowed my weakness for Jedidiah's flesh to overtake me on the night of the Father's Day picnic, I knew that it was not right. Jedidiah and I both agreed that we needed to abstain. God had been so good to us; we couldn't deliberately continue to flaunt our disobedience. Our love was growing deeper daily, but a life together forever was our ultimate goal, and we made a promise to one another to make great efforts to keep our hands off of each other in the foreseeable future.

LUCY

The progress on the inn and the other buildings was astounding. Jedidiah, his family, and the crew worked relentlessly through the summer heat. They started early in the morning, trying to escape the worst of the intense Kansas heat. The pool and the building that housed it were nearly finished.

I was planning a family celebration on the Fourth of July. I wanted the entire crew and their families to come enjoy the water, a barbeque picnic, and after dark we would have fireworks.

Several of the workmen had small children, and since the rest of the buildings were still far from completion, I was worried that the little children and their parents would be exhausted early and there would not be a suitable place for them to nap. I didn't want the crowd to clear out before the fireworks. The air-conditioned room that would eventually be the gym would be filled with tables and chairs; with a forecast of temperatures over one hundred degrees for the Fourth, I didn't think that everyone would want to be outdoors all day.

My solution had been to rent six large motor homes for the weekend. When the plumber and electrician had finished the pool house, I had asked them to install twelve full hookups for RVs in a shady spot east of the summerhouse. In anticipation of future large wedding parties, I thought that we would be sure to have plenty of room to entertain the entirety of family and friends, even if they filled the twelve rooms in the inn.

The RV parking would not be visible from the front of the inn, thus preserving the Tuscan façade of the inn. There were several willow, birch, and oak trees on the east side of the property that would shade the trailers, and the view of the river would hopefully be inviting to campers to join us at Goldstone, even when they weren't part of a wedding celebration.

I was envisioning that the inn would stand as a noble garrison atop the cliff, overlooking the river below. The double, half-rounded, massive front staircase with iron railings would bracket the ornate stone fountain and lead to an amazing, carved, double-door entrance. I hoped that I wasn't biting off more than I could chew, being an innkeeper, owner of a wedding business, and now managing a small RV park too, but I truly wanted Goldstone to put Whitney on the map as a destination. The mayor and the rest of the town council applauded my ingenuity, and all of the permits for my projects had been handed over to me with acclaim.

The Fourth of July was a mere two weeks after Jedidiah's fabulous Father's Day Picnic, and I wasn't looking to compete with the immense spread that his family had presented. I wanted my celebration to be somewhat different, but I knew that there would be some similarities. You couldn't have a picnic without potato salad and baked beans, but instead of burgers and brats, I planned to serve steak skewers and chicken breasts.

The local Future Farmers of America club, the FFA, had large grills that they cooked on, and often did so as a moneymaking venture. I hired them to grill our meats, and I would personally make the large Crock-Pots full of baked beans and two huge bowls full of potato salad. My new friend and neighbor, Lael Jones, volunteered to create several beautiful flag cakes using strawberries, blueberries, and white frosting as the stars and stripes on the cakes.

Lael and J.J. were also planning to clean several dozen ears of sweet corn and arrange for huge pots of boiling water on portable stoves to cook the corn. My new friend Kitty Weed would bake two hundred cornbread muffins. I told her that we weren't expecting as large a crowd as at the Father's Day Picnic and that two hundred seemed overkill, but she assured me that the leftovers would freeze nicely.

My twins, Jude and Jade, both promised to come for the weekend, but I knew from experience that neither of them would arrive early enough to help with the preparation. I loved them very much, and I thought I had taught them the value of family and pitching in to help out; but as young adults, they seemed to have very independent lifestyles, and they were not always considerate of my needs.

Nevertheless, I was happy to have them come home, and one of the motor homes was reserved exclusively for them. My small house did have a spare bedroom, but at the present time, I had a lot of things stored in the room that would ultimately go into the inn. I had rented a small storage unit in town, and my garage and shed were also filled with furnishings for the inn, but there were a few of the nicest pieces that I did not want to relinquish to a non-climate-controlled environment.

All of my family was coming to my Fourth of July celebration, including my parents, my brothers, and my sister. And, of course, the Jordans were all joining us too, so it would be the first opportunity for our families to meet each other. I had arranged for my parents to sleep in my motor home. I'd kind of forgotten that I had one, but when I had the electrician and plumber installing the hookups behind the summerhouse, I remembered the one that Tony had left me in the shed.

I had offered them my bed, but they declined, saying they didn't want to put me out. They were coming on Friday to spend the whole weekend, but the rest of the family would be arriving Saturday and staying for the Fourth celebration on Monday; some would be spending Monday night too. I had stocked each of the motor homes with some basic food supplies—bread, butter, eggs, cereal, milk, peanut butter, and fresh fruit—so they could snack and not be underfoot the whole weekend.

LUCY

As it turned out, Independence Day weekend was wonderful. The weather had not been as hot as had been predicted, and rather than feeling exhausted when they all left on Tuesday morning, I was disappointed that the weekend had ended so soon. Jade and Jude had even come early and stayed until Tuesday morning. I had a bit of special time alone with each of my children, but the time went by too quickly. My family and Jedidiah's family had got along together famously; no arguments, no jealousies, and no bitter remarks were heard. I shouldn't have worried; they had all been so wonderful.

My mother had helped with the food preparation, and Daddy had helped Jedidiah line up the tables and chairs, and together they had erected a huge, white canvas tent. The grounds had been transformed into a wonderful party zone.

Hannah and Heather decorated with red and blue streamers and foil stars. Caleb and Charlie were in charge of the fireworks, and the show late at night had been monumental.

I love my family, but I hadn't really wanted to cater to them for the whole weekend. They were welcome to use the pool as much as they wanted, and I was hoping that I would get some volunteers to help with the picnic. I knew my brothers would kick in, and I was counting on my sister Bryn and Frank, her fiancé, to lifeguard at the pool.

But I needn't have worried; I had a lot of help with the celebration. Jedidiah and his children were wonderful, and so was my family. Perry, Tommy, and Wes—my brothers—and their wives and children, had all been cheerful and helpful, and Bryn and Frank had seemed to enjoy their pool duties. I think nearly everyone was in the pool at least once, and some of the children had hardly ever left the pool. I know that nearly every time I looked for Jude or Jade that weekend they were either in the pool, or in wet bathing suits, just leaving the pool.

After the food had been served on the Fourth and leftovers tucked away in coolers and refrigerators, I sat down at one of the large tables in the air-conditioned room to enjoy a tall glass of iced tea. Kitty Weed was sitting nearby with a woman I hadn't been introduced to yet, but she quickly caught my attention, calling to me, "Lucy dear, I have someone I'd like you to meet."

I didn't rise, but twisted in my seat so that I could see Kitty and the other woman easily. I smiled at them and said I was happy to see them. Kitty introduced the woman as her sister, Bea Butler, saying, "Bea just lost her husband about a year ago, and she's been talking about moving to Whitney after she gets her house sold."

I moved my chair closer to Kitty and Bea. I gave her my condolences regarding the death of her husband and told her it'd be nice to have another new citizen in town. Kitty then asked me an interesting question. "Have you considered hiring a housekeeper for your new inn? It sounds like it is going to be quite the happening place, and pretty big. You surely will need some help keeping it clean and organized."

I took a moment to think about that, and then I said, "I suppose it is time to start considering hiring some help. So far I've only got a couple fellas lined up to clean the pool, but I will need a staff to run the inn, and you know, it is going to be more than just an inn. I'm hoping to make Goldstone into an all-inclusive wedding retreat. We'll have a fabulous backyard where we can hold garden weddings, and also a ballroom indoors so that we can have weddings year round. And I'll have a greenhouse, a caterer's kitchen, and hopefully I can hire a wedding planner."

Suddenly, I seemed to have caught the ear of every woman at my party. They all started firing out ideas.

Kitty said, "Bea kept a beautiful house and raised five wonderful daughters. I'm sure she would make an extraordinary housekeeper for you."

Lael Jones said, "I love weddings, and I'd love to try my hand at being a wedding planner."

Shelby, my sister's oldest daughter, said, "I've been studying portrait photography at college, and I plan to be a professional photographer when I graduate at the end of summer. Maybe I could be your wedding photographer."

Frank, Bryn's fiancé, asked, "Have you hired a landscaping firm yet? Even though we are a couple hours away, I'd love to give you some design ideas and then establish your landscaping for you. We'd help you find someone locally to do the routine maintenance."

Holly, a beautiful, petite girl with long black hair, a new girlfriend of Caleb's, said, "I've been working as a florist in Manhattan. But the commute is awful, and I'd love to do just wedding flowers, and to work here at a wedding retreat would be fabulous! I have a degree in floriculture from K-State, so it would indeed be my dream job to work as your wedding floral designer."

Bea chimed in and said, "One of my daughters, Gianna, has been working in the bakery at the large supermarket in Manhattan. She's their cake decorator, but Gianna and her husband are building a new house just a few blocks away from here. Her husband is a doctor, so they don't really need the money, but she loves to be creative, and since they haven't been able to have children, she likes to keep busy. If you're interested, I could give you her number and you could maybe talk."

My sister-in-law, Perry's wife, Jill, said, "I'd be happy to help with the decorating. You have really good taste, so you may already have most of it planned, but I'd love to give you some ideas." Jill was a consultant for a home-party sales group that sold interior design reproductions.

My head was spinning, but I was overjoyed to have so many suggestions. "I am so thankful for all of your ideas. And yes, I want to talk to every one of you; I love your ideas. First, Bea, I am looking forward to getting to know you better, and I'm betting that yes, you could be a wonderful housekeeper for my inn and retreat."

I turned my eyes toward Shelby. "I have considered creating a photography studio in one of the lower-level rooms. But where would you live?"

Then my sweet Jedidiah spoke up, "Lucy, I think that perhaps we need to consider adding a few staff cottages to the property. Maybe we should build two, three, or maybe four little houses— one for your housekeeper, one for the photographer, and maybe one for the florist too." My wheels were spinning in my brain as Jedidiah talked about the cottages, and I must have had a concerned look on my face.

"Lucy, maybe I could even invest in the business, or I could pay for my own cottage," Bea said.

With gratitude, I answered, "I think these ideas are all wonderful. I hadn't really thought it through, I guess, but indeed I will need a wedding planner." I made eye contact with Lael, smiling. "I will need a housekeeper with years of experience running a household and catering to young women." And I reached a hand toward Bea, grasping her hand in mine. I turned slightly to see Holly and Shelby. "And I can't put on any kind of a wedding without a florist and photographer. And of course they would need someplace to live close by."

I looked again at Bea. "Yes, I'd love to talk with Gianna about her wedding cake skills and possibility of hiring her. Does anybody know of a caterer? I think we might as well get one of those lined up too."

Several people were talking at the same time; Jedidiah's mother mentioned someone named Pearl, and Frank said, "A friend of one of my employees was trained in Paris as a chef, but he's living back here now, and he may be interested in a job here. I've heard he wants to get out of Metro KC and live in the country. I think his name is Unger Vassar."

"Okay then, have Pearl and Unger call me. I'll interview them both, and Bea, please let's talk later, and I'll want to interview Gianna too. And Holly, Shelby, and Lael, you too, let's talk later, and we'll come up with a plan. This is so exciting!"

I moved over to where my sister was sitting with her family and talked to them about photography and landscaping. My world was expanding! And I was loving it!

The fireworks later that night were dim compared to my excitement; I couldn't wait for the wedding retreat business to start. Even if these particular women did not work out—and I could see no reason at the time for any of them to be less than what they claimed—I had an amazing new venture ahead of me. And with enough of the right help, it would be grand.

LUCY

Without going into a great deal of detail about the interviewing process, which truthfully had intimidated me, it was amazing how quickly I was able to put together a wonderful staff of talented people.

Bea Butler was a wonderful multitalented woman, and I knew that she would be a perfect mother hen to the rest of my staff. It was decided that, as the housekeeper, she would have quarters in the basement of the inn. The lower level of the turret that was nearest to the kitchen would be her living room and kitchenette, and adjoining that would be her bedroom, bathroom, and also a garage. She would have access to a small private patio area via French doors.

I hired my new friend and neighbor, Lael Jones, to be the wedding coordinator. She didn't have any experience exactly in that field, but she had helped put together many family weddings, and she'd worked as a housecleaner, bookkeeper, and waitress, so that coupled with her enthusiasm and delightful personality, I felt confident that she would be a very good wedding coordinator.

Actually, none of the staff that I hired had any true experience working at a wedding retreat, and one of them, my niece Shelby, had never worked at any job ever. But Shelby had always had a special place in my heart, and after seeing her portfolio, I knew she would be a very competent and creative wedding photographer.

Gianna and Holly would be the pastry chef and florist, respectively. Gianna, Bea's middle daughter, had a lot of experience working as a wedding cake baker, and after seeing photos of her creations, I had to call her an artist. She had put together some truly amazing cakes. Holly, the girl who had been Caleb's girlfriend, was also an artist, but with flowers. She too had shown me photos of some of her wedding floral work that had amazed me. Holly, on the other hand, was less than thrilled with Caleb, so even before our interview, that relationship was over. But she assured me that they had broken up amicably, and if she ran into him at Goldstone, it would be okay. She said that she would never dream of making a scene, especially about some boy.

My sister's fiancé, Frank, came through for me when he recommended Nester Washington to be my grounds maintenance man and Unger Vassar as the chef. Nester had worked for Frank for a few years in his landscaping business. He had also moonlighted at the Harley Davidson factory as a security guard and had skills as a computer programmer, so I was confident that Nester would be an asset to Goldstone Inn. However, I was a bit concerned about one thing with Nester. I didn't want to appear to be a bigot in any way, so I had a bit of a struggle asking him about what worried me, but he quickly put me at ease.

"Nester," I said with a tremble in my voice during his interview, "have you had a look around the town of Whitney?"

"Why, yes ma'am, I have. Unger and I came up early this mornin' and walked up and down Main Street, pokin' our heads inside all of the businesses that were open, and givin' a howdy to everyone. I was pleasantly surprised at the genuine acceptance from all the folks that we met." Nester was beaming, speaking with a bit of a southern drawl. "I grew up in Miz'ssippi, and I have to say for a bunch of white folks, these people in Whitney seem almost as friendly and hospitable as they do back in my hometown of Biloxi."

"Well, that is a relief," I said. "I was afraid that you might feel uncomfortable or that the citizens may not be very cordial to you because, well, without sounding like a bigot or something, your skin is obviously a lot darker than your average Joe here in town. I really hope you don't mind me saying this, and I'm not really a very professional interviewer, so maybe it is a big faux pas to even bring up your race."

"Miss Lucy, I have no problem talking about race. I'm actu'ly admiring of you that you had the nerve to speak up and say what you were thinkin'. I know that in all-white communities, a person like me is going to stand out like a sore thumb." He paused, scratched his head of short black hair, and continued with a huge grin on his face, "But in a way it's kinda' cool. I've never really craved fame, but I'll kinda' be an instant celebrity in town. Everybody will know me and remember my face!"

He had me grinning too, and I felt very comfortable with this tall, muscular African American man. What he said next was a bit disconcerting, though. "Wait till you get a load of my friend, Unger Vassar. He's a very tall, lean white Russian with fastidious manners. I know you're interviewin' him next to be your chef. Since we are talkin' frankly here, I think you should know up front that Unger is more than just my friend. He is my life partner; you see, we are gay."

I'm not very good at hiding my feelings most of the time, and even though I was trying hard to remain professional, I perhaps seemed stunned and paused a bit too long before I said, "Nester, you and Unger will definitely be unique to Whitney. I appreciate your candor, but your relationship with Unger will not factor into my decision at all. I do have a question, though. And this may be a bit presumptuous since I haven't even met Unger yet, but should I consider that you are a...how shall I say this"—I paused—"a package deal? I either hire both of you or neither one?"

Before he had a chance to answer, my doorbell rang, indicating that my next potential employee was there for his interview: Unger Vassar.

I looked inquisitively at Nester quickly, and he simply said with confidence, "Miss Lucy, I think that you are goin' to love both of us, so I don't think you need to worry about that yet."

The bell rang again, and we both stood. I went to answer the door, and Nester followed me. At the door was a very tall man, broad-shouldered, with a square head and a crew cut. He was wearing all white—white jeans, a white chef-style shirt, and white sneakers. As he entered and stood next to Nester, I realized for the first time that Nester had been dressed entirely in black. "Welcome, I'm guessing you must be Unger Vassar. I'm Lucy Golden. Please come on out to my sunroom; that's where I've been conducting all of my interviews."

"I'm pleased to meet you, Ms. Golden. I've brought you a small snack so that you could sample my cooking." For the first time I noticed that he was holding a small cooler. But before I responded to his comment, Nester said, "I think I should leave you two alone so that you can do your interview. It has been very nice to meet you, Miss Lucy. I can tell you are a very nice lady, and I hope that I'll be seein' a lot more of you."

"Unger, would you please go ahead and make yourself comfortable? I want to see Nester out the door." I had a couple more things I wanted to say to him, but I wanted to say them without influencing what Unger might tell me about himself.

Outside, after the door was closed, I said, "Nester, I think you will be a fabulous employee. I want to offer you the job." I had explained to him about the wedding retreat and the plans for the large landscaping. He had really impressed me, and despite his bodybuilder appearance and his other obvious differences, I knew that he would fit nicely on my team.

"So you don't want to wait until you've interviewed Unger?"

"Nester, I haven't had a lot of time to think, or in fact much experience with hiring a staff, but I've got a really good feeling about you, and I wanted you to know that my decision is based solely on your qualifications and personality. I had already checked out your references from what Frank sent me, and after my interview with Unger, then I guess we'll know more."

Nester had thanked me profusely and said he was going to go wander around the building site some, checking out the landscaping.

For the next hour I talked with Unger, and snacked on the hors d'oeuvres that he had brought to tempt me. The food was delicious, and Unger was even more engaging than Nester, but he had a very professional demeanor. To make a long story short, I hired both of them. Before they left, I called Jedidiah on his cell phone and asked him if he would have some time to talk to the three of us together at the site.

While we showed them around the building site, I engaged them in a lively conversation about the staff cottages that had been Jedidiah's suggestion. With the assistance of Nester and Unger, we came up with a plan for placement of three cottages between my cottage and the inn, creating a third driveway that would be restricted as "staff only." There would be two smaller cottages for Holly, the florist, and Shelby, the photographer. Each would be two stories, with a studio and showroom on the main level, with the living quarters on the second story. The cottage for Nester and Unger would be somewhat larger and would have garages on the main level to house part of the fleet of vehicles that we planned to purchase, as well as landscape maintenance equipment.

That day ended with a solo bubble bath and then a dinner date with Jedidiah. We went out for pizza and later went for a long walk strolling around town. I told him about the staff that I'd hired, and he praised me for acting upon my dreams. "Lucy, I'm very impressed that you have developed such an elaborate business plan for your wedding retreat, and how fast you are finding quality people to staff your inn."

Nervous that I was attacking my plan too fast, I said, "Jedidiah, maybe I should slow down, and take more time interviewing several candidates for each position."

"No, Lucy. I think from what you've told me that each of these people all came highly recommended by friends or relatives, with the exception of Holly, and you checked her references. Don't let the fact that she and Caleb broke up already give you any cause for doubt; he's not exactly notorious for making the best choices with relationships."

With a silly, pensive grin on his face, he continued, "Actually, maybe he got a little of that skill, or lack of it, from me. I certainly made poor choices in my younger days when I let you go without a fight. I should have looked you up after I got settled out in Seattle and insisted that you come out to give it a try."

"Oh, Jedidiah, I can't honestly say that I would have been very receptive to that plan. I was still very much a small-town girl and extremely tied to my family. I don't know that even if you had offered, that I would have followed you to Washington. I think that maybe it was God's plan all along to allow us to have other relationships before we met up again. We both learned a lot from our previous marriages, and we are better people today because of it. I know that I learned that patience, compromise, and making allowances for your partner's imperfections are very important. Of course, as we age, some of those qualities become a bit easier. Young people aren't especially known for their patience or willingness to give and take."

"Yes, I agree," Jedidiah said. "I know when I was young I thought that I knew it all, but now I realize that I was sorely misinformed. Experience is in fact a very good teacher. Another thing I have learned is that nothing is certain but change."

"You're right. Even though it is a trite adage, I have to agree. Change is indeed certain."

LUCY

I engaged the services of a tax accountant and a business lawyer so that they could advise me how to create a partnership with these talented professionals that I'd hired to run Goldstone Celebration Inn. I would want to pay them all a salary or a percentage of the event income. Additionally, a few of my new employees expressed interest in investing in the business, so I needed assistance from my accountant with that too, knowing that those who invested would need to have a return on their investments as well, that is if we made money.

I also spent a great deal of time in prayer that week that I was busy hiring staff, asking God for assistance and confirmation that I was entering into a venture that I would be able to handle. I read my Bible and found many references to brides and bridegrooms. And I knew in my heart that providing a joyous place and services for weddings would be a special way to use my God-given talents. I enjoyed helping people find happiness, and what happier moments in life are weddings and the birth of babies? Between the two, I was much more comfortable with weddings than births, though.

After I had a preliminary business plan from my accountant and attorney, I called together a meeting of all of my new team on the first Saturday in August. I wanted them to get to know one another, and to hear their ideas and have a brainstorming session. I had given each of them the task of putting together a four-tier package so that we could start developing multi-level options. We would customize and personalize but keep each wedding within the parameters of a certain price frame. Allen Anderson, my accountant, was still working to come up with the pricing structure, but I hoped our first business meeting would give us a good start.

Since the pool house was still the only large structure that was almost completed, we again met in the gym. I hadn't yet purchased any gym equipment since it was the one room available to hold meetings. The summerhouse was completed, but it was still being used for storage.

It was a hot, windy Kansas day, so meeting outside in the grand pavilion wasn't really a great option either. The gazebos, pergola, and pavilions were all nearly completed, though, and the landscaping had begun, so the backyard was beginning to take shape nicely. With the extreme heat, the construction teams had continued on their early morning schedules, and Jedidiah had given everyone the weekend off. They had been working Saturdays most of July and would also be working Saturdays until Labor Day, so they deserved a weekend off.

Therefore, the construction site was eerily quiet prior to the arrival of the team. Jedidiah had joined me for an early morning swim, and then he had helped me to set up for the meeting. He would, of course, attend the meeting because he was a very important part of the team. Even though his part as the builder would eventually be finished, it was clear that he would continue on in the capacity as my one and only special love. We found that we were becoming inseparable, and neither one of us wanted to be apart from the other for very long.

I had dressed carefully in an ivory linen embroidered pant-set and matching high-heel sandals. I wanted to appear professional but to also keep cool in the heat as well.

I wasn't providing any refreshments for the meeting, but I had asked Bea Butler, her daughter Gianna, and Unger, the Paris trained chef, to all bring some snacks and beverages as a way to showcase their talents.

Mrs. Butler and Gianna were the first to arrive. With Jedidiah's help, they brought in a large cooler. Inside were Tupperware boxes that held miniature, decorated cakes. Gianna explained, "I made seven different flavors of cakes: German chocolate, pound cake, devil's food chocolate, red velvet, white cake with raspberry filling, lemon, and carrot cake. And I have iced and decorated them in a multitude of different frostings."

"Oh yes, aren't they amazing?" her mother cooed. "And I don't think I'm just prejudiced because she is my daughter. I think she made some wonderful treats."

"Yes," I agreed. "They look delicious, and they're beautiful too!" And turning to her mother, I said, "Mrs. Butler, what did you bring for us?"

"Now, Lucy, please, you must call me Bea. And I brought several pitchers of ice-cold fruit juices and flavored teas, all with chunks of fresh fruit swimming in them. There is another box in our car. Would you please bring that in, Jedidiah?"

While we waited for him to retrieve the box, I helped the two women arrange the refreshments on a table. When he returned with the box, Jedidiah said jovially, "What's in here? Rocks? It's pretty heavy."

Bea chuckled and said, "I found these beautiful, heavy, green glass tumblers and matching snack plates; they were on clearance. They really weren't much more than if I would have bought disposable ones, and I always find that cold drinks taste so much better when you drink them from a real glass and not something made of plastic. There are some coasters in there too, so they won't sweat onto the table. The humidity is pretty high today, so we don't want to leave water circles all over the table."

Just as we got the glassware unpacked, Unger arrived with his partner, Nester, who would be our maintenance and security agent. They carried in several stoneware casseroles and some stainless chafing dishes. Unger explained as he was unpacking them, "I wanted to bring some nourishing hot foods. I had talked with Gianna and knew she was bringing sweets, so I thought we should have something to balance that out. I made three flavors of miniature quiches and tiny sausage burritos. They are best if they are kept a little warm, thus, the chafing dishes were the obvious choice. I did buy these, Lucy; I hope that's agreeable to you. I'm quite certain that we will be using them in the future."

"Yes, Unger, that is perfectly fine, and those quiches and burritos smell delicious. Can I try one?"

"Certainly." Unger beamed with pleasure. He started describing the fillings in the quiches, but before he got past the ricotta and spinach, we heard the unmistakable noise of a loud Harley Davidson motorcycle arriving. The door burst open to admit a tall, beautiful blonde woman, with her hair in braids, wearing a white tank top, an open-zippered, hot pink sweatshirt, and skin-tight blue jeans. "Hello all," she greeted with a flourish, and with a Scandinavian accent said, "Ingrid has arrived!"

LUCY

I laughed and went to welcome Ingrid, our new salon manager.

Ingrid had been a surprise to me in many ways. To begin with, I hadn't even considered having a spa at the inn, but on the Friday of the week when I'd been doing all of my hiring, I had an unannounced visit from Mayor Harvey Coldwater. He told me the story of Ingrid and Bjorn Johansson and strongly recommended that I consider finding room at the inn for a spa and Ingrid. "Several years ago the Johanssons were high-school teachers in West Virginia. But they'd been lucky enough to win a huge lottery jackpot and decided to live out some of their dreams. Bjorn and Ingrid bought a big RV, two Harleys, and set out on the road. They traveled around for a couple years, exploring about half of the states and a bit of Canada, but when they found Whitney, they fell in love with our little town and decided to call it home. They bought a house, and both of them went to tech school to learn a new trade. But even more important than that, they have become Whitney's greatest cheerleaders! They are on the city council, they've started several programs for kids, and they've planted a lot of trees to help beautify the town. Bjorn is working at one of the trailer factories now, but Ingrid is still kind of at loose ends. She's a trained masseuse and hair stylist, but as she's explained to me, she doesn't want to just open up a little shop on Main Street. She wants to be part of a bigger enterprise, something over the top. Ever since she found out about your enterprise out here, she's been itching to finish her schooling so she could approach you and hope that you would fit her in out here."

"Harvey, she sounds like she'd be an asset to our wedding retreat, but I hadn't thought about putting in a spa," I told him.

"Well, your plans are on file at the city office, and she's been looking at them, and has a proposal she wants to share with you. She's confident that there is space in the pool house for a small spa, and she could do her massages in the sunroom that is on the west.end of the pool house."

"I'd love to talk to her. When do you suppose she could come for an interview?"

"Lucy, she's waiting outside," Harvey said sheepishly. "I wanted to kind of pave the way, because she can be a bit overwhelming if you aren't prepared for her. And I wanted to be sure that you understand that she and her husband have become very valued citizens of Whitney in the short time they've lived here. And considering that the city has given you the tax concessions and helped all of your permits fly through quickly, I think you owe us the little favor of at least giving her a try."

Coming from someone else, this may have seemed a little threatening or even like an ultimatum, but Harvey Coldwater was very unassuming and genuine, so I trusted him. "Send her in," was all I had to say, and he popped up out of his chair and scuttled to the door to wave her in.

She didn't have to duck to come through the doorway, but she was one of the tallest women I had ever seen. She had long blond hair, large blue eyes and a bright pink lipsticked mouth. She was wearing a pink tank top with black leather pants and boots. I couldn't see any tattoos, but it wouldn't have surprised me if she had several in hidden places. She strolled into my sunroom very confidently, and the room seemed to fill with her presence. "Hello! I am so very pleased that you agreed to speak with me. I am, of course, Ingrid Johansson, but I'm sure that Harvey already told you that."

She gripped my hand in a two-handed handshake, and I could see that her upper arms were very muscular. I noticed her arms because of her height. I stood face-to-arm with Ingrid as we shook hands. I looked up, greeted her, and asked her to have a seat. Harvey sat down again too, so even though I would have preferred a one-to-one interview with Ingrid, it was not to be.

But in the end, it had been a very enlightening hour and a half, and suffice it to say, Ingrid had it all figured out where her spa would be, the client services she would provide, how much extra we could charge the bridal party for the spa services and massages, and even offered to use her own money to install all of the fixtures necessary to run a hair salon. I felt a bit railroaded, but she was indeed a very wonderful lady, and I knew she would be an asset to Goldstone Inn. Nevertheless, I felt that she was perhaps going to have a hard time fitting in with the rest of the female staff at the inn, who, in comparison, seemed prim and proper. But because of her eagerness and Harvey's glowing accolades, I agreed to go with her plan to add the spa to the Goldstone Wedding Retreat and Inn.

I also had a sneaking suspicion that perhaps the Johannsons had been the anonymous donors who had contributed the half-million dollars to enlarge the pool. During the interview with her, she had twice spoken of the pool, once saying, "Having this pool is going to be such a blessing to the community," and later she said, "Having the spa in the pool house will give me the opportunity to do some swimming too; it's my favorite way to exercise."

She would be doing the bridal party hairdos, manicures, and massages. Her husband, Bjorn, would also be helping her with the massages, and she would need to hire some part-time help to assist with the shampoos and manicures.

As she strolled into the pool house for the staff meeting, Ingrid said, "Lucy, you look marvelous! I'm afraid I may be underdressed in my redneck twin set, but I'm not much for dressing up. I hope that's not a deal breaker."

I assured her that she looked fine for our meeting.

Following close behind Ingrid were Holly Ford and Shelby Stewart, the florist and photographer. Lael, the wedding planner arrived next, carrying a box full of employee manuals that she and I had worked on together.

I announced in my loudest voice, "It looks like we are all here. If you'd like to get something to eat and drink, then please gather at the large table and we'll get started." The team got in an orderly queue after putting their belongings at the table to free their hands.

While they filled their plates, Bea placed a linen napkin and a coaster at each place at the large table. There were ten of us altogether, and I was pleased to see that they were a lively and pleasant group of people.

Once everyone was seated I said, "I'd like to go around the table and everyone give us a little background information about you. We will be working closely as a team, and I think it is important that we all become well acquainted."

I nodded toward Bea to begin. Bea was wearing a cotton, casual pant-set, made of a large, bold, floral print. It resembled a scrub set that nurses and dental hygienists usually wear.

Standing, Bea started, "My name is Bea Butler. I've been living in Wichita, but was widowed about a year ago. I've raised five beautiful daughters and taken care of my husband and a large house, but I have never worked outside the house before, so I'm so very fortunate to have been given this opportunity to show my prowess as the new housekeeper for Goldstone Inn.

"I have a sister who lives here in Whitney—Kitty Weed— and one of my wonderful daughters is here today. She will also be on our team." She paused, and, smiling, she poised her left hand toward her daughter. "This is Gianna, my middle daughter."

Gianna took the floor next. "I'm Gianna Graydon, and yes, I'm very much looking forward to working here as the pastry chef. My specialty, of course, will be wedding cakes, but as needed I will be baking cookies, muffins, or any sweet that suits the occasion." Gianna was dressed simply but looked elegant in a baby blue, sleeveless shift, and her blonde hair was pulled back into a French twist. She was beautiful and exuded confidence and poise.

She continued, "My husband, Don, and I are building a new home here in Whitney, but we have been living in Manhattan. Our new home will be completed soon, so it looks like we'll be moving in sometime this month. I've been working at the Hessing Supermarket in Manhattan baking and decorating cakes in their bakery department. I just love being creative with food, so I can't wait to start working here!" She sat down and looked to her left.

My niece, Shelby, was next. She introduced herself and revealed in a soft, but quick-paced recitation, "My mother and Lucy are sisters, but more than that, I've been studying portrait photography in college and just graduated, in fact, a couple weeks ago. I did an internship with a very talented and busy studio in Lawrence, and I received a lot of praise for my ideas and beautiful moods created with my photos. This will be my first true job, and like Mrs. Butler, I appreciate the opportunity that Aunt Lucy has given me. I promise I won't let you down." Shelby looked sincerely at me with her large blue eyes and smiled nervously.

"I know you won't, dear. And after seeing your portfolio, I would have hired you even if you weren't my niece. You are very talented," I said. Shelby had sat down already, and I looked to her left. "Okay, Holly, your turn."

"I'm Hollis Ford, but everyone calls me Holly. I'll be the in-house floral designer. I've been working at Manhattan Posy Designs for a couple of years and have primarily been working on their wedding flowers, so I've got quite a bit of experience. Since my parents moved out of Manhattan last year, I've been living here in Whitney with my grandmother. I didn't really like driving to Manhattan every day, but I wasn't able to afford a place of my own in Manhattan either. I'm excited to be the new floral designer here at Goldstone, and it'll be great to live here too."

I interjected a comment, "We plan to build three cottages to house part of the staff, and I'll explain that in a little while. And Holly, we are excited to have you on board too! Now Unger, you are next."

Unger, sporting a fresh square crew-cut, wearing a white cotton chef's tunic, pushed back his chair and stood proud and tall. "My name is Unger Vassar, and I will be the head chef here at Goldstone Inn. I've been working in Kansas City for about a year, and before that I was the Head Chef at the Metro restaurant in downtown Seattle for ten years. I began my love of culinary arts from my talented and beloved mother, who passed away recently. I perfected my culinary skills in Paris, France, several years ago. I grew up in Kansas, and even though I've lived in several places around the world, I love it best right here.

"The crowds and crime in the cities are not to my liking, and even though you can easily blend into a crowd, I have found that I prefer to be where people know me and where I know them. I enjoy working with talented people, and even though my lifestyle is not always one that other people can understand, I have found that it is a lonely life living in a city, so my partner, Nester, and I are very glad to be a part of this team. And just so that everyone is aware, yes we are gay, but neither of us likes any PDA, or public displays of affection, so you needn't worry that we are going to make things uncomfortable for anyone."

There were some pleasant words of acceptance from the team: "No problem with me," "Glad to have you on board," "I agree, cities are too impersonal."

As Unger sat down, Nester stood up. Nester, who was a large man with light brown skin and dark brown eyes, was wearing a tight black T-shirt and tight black jeans. He said, "I am Nester Washington." And, smiling, he continued, "I am black and gay, so

I probably will stand out as an unusual person in this small town in Kansas, but I can already tell I'm going to love it here. I will be doing all of the maintenance on the property and keeping you all safe and secure too. I have experience doing both; I worked at Boeing for twelve years, first as a maintenance millwright and the last few years as a security guard. I was with Unger for a couple of years when he said he wanted to move to Kansas City. I was at first a little reluctant to give up such a good job, but I had to agree with him that we should get away from that terrible traffic and crime, so I moved with him. Since living in Kansas City I've been working at two jobs, the Harley Davidson factory, doing plant maintenance and security, and on weekends I've been working with a landscaping crew. In fact, the boss on that crew is how we became acquainted with Miss Lucy.

"Lucy's sister, who is Shelby's mother, is engaged to Frank Krug. Frank owns the landscaping business that I've been working with on the weekends, and he was the one who recommended that I give Lucy a call about working for her. I've learned a lot from Frank about plant care, and he has assured me that he will be available if I get in over my head with landscape maintenance. But I'm pretty confident I can handle it, and I know I'm the right man for the job with the building maintenance and security."

"I agree, Nester. I'm sure you're the right man for the job," I said.

As soon as Nester sat down, Ingrid stood tall and straight. "I'm Ingrid Johansson. My husband, Bjorn, and I moved here a few years ago from back east. I grew up in Sweden and learned to be a masseuse in Sweden. I met Bjorn when he came to visit my country. He had cousins who live in the same small town where I lived. We fell in love twenty-five years ago, and I followed him back to the States. We got married and had two children right away.

"Bjorn was born near Trego, Nova Scotia, but his family moved to Lubec, Maine, when he was very young. His mother was originally from there and he has dual citizenship with the US and Canada. I'm also a citizen of both Sweden and the US, but I don't have any family left over there, so I have no plans to ever return to Sweden. Both of our boys have grown up and have lives of their own, so we decided to set out and travel for a while. We sold our home in West Virginia, bought a motor home and a couple of Harleys, and started driving west. Oh, and I forgot to tell you, we won a lottery jackpot too, so that's how we could afford to do all of this. We got as far as Whitney and fell in love with the little town and its people.

"We decided to stay here, bought a house, and have had the opportunity to fulfill some of our dreams. Bjorn is a welder and loves it; he works for one of the local trailer manufacturers. I've been going to beauty school, and now I'm a licensed beautician as well as a masseuse. We'd been talking about opening up a salon, and when I heard about this place, I thought I'd check it out. I'm really happy to be working here, and, in fact, I've already got the salon open. I had to put off a couple of ladies who wanted their hair done this morning, but I've got them coming in later this afternoon. Lucy let me invest in the salon, so I've agreed to keep the wedding and other celebration customers as first on the list always, but we'll squeeze in some other locals for appointments in between."

"Thank you, Ingrid. I'll be explaining that a little later too, how a few of you are actually investors too. We've got a couple more to hear from first though. Lael, your turn."

Sitting next to Jedidiah, Lael stood. She was wearing a long, flowing, multi-colored broomstick skirt and a pear-green, georgette-embroidered tunic. With her dark hair and olive complexion she looked very exotic. "My name is Lael Jones. I live just down the road; in fact, my husband and I live in a mobile home on Jedidiah's ranch." She made eye contact and smiled at Jedidiah. "My husband, J.J., is his ranch foreman. Like some of the rest of you, I don't have a lot of experience doing the job I've been hired to do here at Goldstone, but I'm quite sure that I can do a good job. I will be the wedding planner or coordinator. I'll be the one that ties all of the different departments together, assuring that our customers have a truly wonderful experience here at the inn.

"I come from a large family, and most of my sisters are married. I've been very involved with the planning of all their weddings, and I also have been a bridesmaid in over a dozen weddings, so I'm very familiar with all that is involved. I've also worked at several jobs over the years—administrative assistant, waitress, seamstress, florist, and tour guide—so I've had some experience doing a lot of the tasks involved with weddings. I know how important it is to keep the event running smoothly, and I love to organize and keep track of details. I guess that's enough about me for now. Jedidiah, I think you are next."

My sweetheart stood, purposefully situating his chair at a safe distance behind him, he stood casually but smartly, wearing a gold-colored, button-down, short-sleeved, cotton shirt, and khaki shorts that were so long that his knobby knees were covered. He grinned, and his eyes twinkled as he started with his self-introduction. "I'm Jedidiah Jordan. I'm the general contractor and builder of Goldstone Inn. I'm also very fond of your boss, Lucy. She and I go way back to our teenage years. We were sweethearts in high school, but because of my own stupidity, I lost her for nearly thirty years. Either by coincidence or God's hand, we ended up as neighbors and have renewed our relationship. My family and I live at the end of the road to the east of here. I've got two sons and two daughters; they all work with me in our construction business that we call The Rocking J.

"We also raise registered Hereford bulls on our ranch, so that's where J.J. Jones comes in." He looked at Lael and said, "Lael has been very helpful with many aspects of our ranch, and I'm sure she'll be great here as the wedding and event coordinator.

"As far as the inn goes, we completed the insulation last week and got a good start on the drywall. But there are a lot of rooms in there, so it will take us two or three weeks probably to get the drywall completed. We are right on schedule, actually a couple days ahead. The front double staircases and stone fountain were finished a few days ago, but the stonemason wants us to leave the fountain dry for a few more days. I gave the crew the whole weekend off because we'll be hitting it hard until the drywall is done. The backyard construction projects are nearly all completed. We are just waiting on some concrete balustrades to finish off the portico over the banquet area.

"After we get the build completed I'm sure you'll see me around a lot because I'm not going anywhere. I'm planning to be a big part of Lucy's life for a long time to come, so I'll be available to help out wherever I'm needed. I don't need a title of any kind, as long as she'll keep me around!" He leaned down and kissed me sweetly on the lips. "I hope you don't mind, but I do like to have a little PDA once in a while!" Everyone laughed and Ingrid and Nester clapped a little.

I stood then and said, "Yes, I plan to keep Jedidiah around for a long time, even if he does want to kiss me in front of my team once in a while!"

Next, I passed out the employee manuals that Lael and I had created.

"On the front cover, I have a scripture there that I believe is very appropriate. Ingrid, would you please read it aloud?"

"Gladly," she replied, and she began reading in a clear voice, with a slight Swedish accent:

> Therefore, as God's chosen people, holy and dearly loved, clothe yourselves with compassion, kindness, humility, gentleness and patience. Bear with each other and forgive whatever grievances you may have against one another. Forgive as the Lord forgave you. And over all these virtues put on love, which binds them all together in perfect unity.
>
> Colossians 3:12-14 (NIV)

"I love those verses, and I think it is a great foundation for our team as we begin on our journey working together," I said.

There were remarks of agreement around the table, and I continued by reading aloud the company mission statement: "Goldstone Celebration Inn team of professionals will present a venue for celebratory events: weddings, vacations, reunions, and other social gatherings. We will strive to create dream festivities so that the fantasy of the customer is met with an abundance of personalized details, and orchestrate the entire event from start to finish. The Celebration Team will present an all-inclusive event and do so in a manner as to make the event a treasured memory for all who attend, and to be profitable as well. Affordable luxury will be our goal."

I paused for effect and then asked if there were any questions or remarks, to which I received applause and positive comments from the team.

"One little sidebar on this before I move on: I had considered Blushing Brides as a possible name for the wedding retreat, because when I was playing around trying to come up with an idea I noticed that if you take the first letter of all of the team members and sort them just right, you get the word blushing!"

Bea remarked, "That is quite clever. There may have been a higher power bringing this team together. That is special."

"I agree, Bea. I have felt throughout the entire planning of this project that God has been with us. And that brings to mind something else." I paused, and then continued somewhat hesitantly.

"When I interviewed each of you, it wasn't an appropriate time to bring it up, and even now, I don't want anyone to feel any religious pressure, but I am a Christian, and it is my plan to operate the business on biblical principles of a fair and true, ethical and right basis. I don't want to knowingly cheat any customer, and even though we will have our prices marked at a relatively high mark, I don't want anybody to get the idea we are only in this venture only to make a fortune. I believe that God has led me to use my talents in this way, to bring people who are in love together in a God-blessed union."

Ingrid spoke up, "I'm a Christian too, and I agree with you Lucy. Thank you for saying so, and I too love the idea of using my talents to bring together blessed couples, and to be able to help create a memorable start to their marriages."

Next Unger and Nester simultaneously said, "I'm a Christian too." They smiled at one another and Nester continued, "Being a black man, I have experienced my share of discrimination, but I'm not afraid to declare that I love Jesus and I hope I don't offend anyone, but when I work I tend to sing hymns."

Unger laughed heartily and said, "He sings loudly too, but he has a wonderful, melodic voice, so it is a very pleasant sound!"

I said, "I'm looking forward to hearing Nester singing! This is such a fabulous team. And I'm happy to hear that so many of you are Christians too. Are there any comments?" I could see that the five as-to-yet silent women—Bea, Lael, Shelby, Gianna, and Holly—were making eye contact, and together as one they rose from their chairs. "Ladies," said Bea, "can we make this unanimous?"

"Yes," the other four answered.

Bea said, "I noticed that these young ladies all bowed their heads and said a silent prayer earlier before we began eating. Besides that, I can just tell that we have a fine bunch of people here, and now that I know we are all Christians, I hope you will all understand that any time I serve you a meal, be it a snack or a breakfast, or whatever, I'll expect you to pray before eating. It is only right for us to thank our Lord for all of our blessings, and today, I feel so very blessed to be a part of this team."

Unger stood and said, "I think before we go any further that we should join hands and say a prayer together. Would that be agreeable to everybody?"

The team all stood, joined hands around the table, and together we said the Lord's Prayer. I felt that God had definitely directed my life to a very blessed group of people, and he was watching over us.

"Thank you, Unger, and everyone else too."

I gave Jedidiah's hand a little extra squeeze and saw he was grinning at me. "I had asked you all to do a little homework, and bring me an outline of four different plans in your specialty. If you will all leave your plan ideas on the table, I will quickly review each of them while you take a short break. Let's take fifteen minutes, get a little fresh air, refill your glasses. The restrooms are out the door and to the right."

LUCY

After the group returned, and quieted down, I continued the staff meeting, "We already have four weddings tentatively booked: New Year's Eve, New Year's Day, January fourteenth, and Valentine's Day. The brides want to meet with the team the first week in October to come up with a plan. Jedidiah has assured me that we will be ready to open by Thanksgiving, so weddings more than a month later should be no problem. The one on the thirty-first of December is rather large, but the other three are relatively small, so unless we can get another booked before then, that means our first wedding will be an elaborate affair, but it will be an opportunity for us to showcase our talents. And as long as we keep it highly structured, we should be able to pull it off. We might pull in some out-of-town hunters to book rooms in November and December. We'll also do a little advertising and hope to host a few Christmas parties. They probably won't bring in a lot of money, but it would help to get our feet wet with something small first.

"Lael and I will review your plans more thoroughly this week, but it looked to me that you all have done a wonderful job, and I'm very pleased with your creativity and organizational skills. With these plans, we will create color brochures. The brochures will serve a couple purposes. Marketing, of course, will be one advantage, but we can also use the brochure to help compose each wedding. We want to make each wedding as individual as possible, but also keep in mind some standardization will make all of our jobs a little easier, and consequently, the perception will be that we are more professional. Of course, each bride will probably have at least one thing that she will focus on. For example, one bride may want the most elaborate wedding florals that money can buy but be satisfied with just cake and punch, but no meal at her reception. Or the family of the couple may want to look at the event as an opportunity to take a lot of family photos, so the wedding itself could possibly be a rather simple affair, but the photography package would be the primary moneymaker.

"The names of the four plans will be Basic, Traditional, Premium, and Elite. So hopefully your plans that you worked up will all fit into those headings and we can move forward with the brochures quickly. We may need to call each of you if we need more details or if there is something that just doesn't seem to fit. I think that the brochures should include our photos too, so before we leave today, Shelby will be taking some photos, both of the entire group and individual ones too. For the photos, I have matching shirts for everyone with our logo."

There was a bit of discussion about the photos, and then I continued my explanation. "What I'm thinking is that as we have prospective brides come to us, we'll want to first meet with the bride, and perhaps her mother and fiancé. Initially, I think it should just be Lael, and perhaps myself too, meeting with the customers. If they show interest, then we can book a second meeting with the prospective customer, and at that time we could have personal visits with each team member. If we have a brochure outlining our options, they can pick and choose from the different packages."

Ingrid interrupted, saying, "I hope it's okay, but I'm thinking that perhaps we want to overwhelm them initially by speaking to everyone on the team. If they walk away with only a basic brochure, and not seeing the entire impact of our team, or without a thorough tour and understanding of what we can do, I'm afraid that we might lose them. I'm thinking it's best to get that *wow* factor solidly in place before they leave."

There followed some lively discussion, and after putting it to a vote, it was decided that Ingrid's ideas were favored by the majority of the team; new prospective customers would be wowed by the entire team on the initial visit.

I continued, giving another example of how the options could be potentially mixed and matched. "Perhaps we'll have a bride who wants to choose the Level Four or Elite Photographic package, but wants to have just a simple Level One Basic wedding feast. We want to be very flexible, and even though I've never been a salesman, I know that it is good business practice to always be ready to upsell, so even though we get a bride who wants to go with the Basic wedding feast, perhaps we can convince her to go with Elite Spa and Floral packages and maybe add on the chocolate fountain to the Basic meal."

Pausing, I looked at Unger and said, "I was impressed with that idea in your plan. I foresee that we'll have a lot of brides who want the chocolate fountain. Good job."

Then looking around the table, I went on, "I noticed in my quick review that most of you mentioned an item to be optional that can be added to any package. I really like that idea, and it will help increase sales.

"As each of the brides meets with you and you are finalizing the plans, you will simply mark up one of the brochures, circling the plan, and make additional notes in the margins. Then each department will submit their brochure to Lael and she'll put together a formal agreement that addresses all facets based upon what is signed off on in each of the departmental brochures. Then we can present this to the couple as the contract for services and ask for a deposit.

I think we should ask for a twenty-five percent deposit at the time of booking; then another thirty-five percent two months before the event. The final forty percent would be due one month before the event. We'll need this monetary commitment from our customers so that we can purchase supplies in advance. Also, since we will be blocking out time on the calendar for the event, we can't afford a cancellation at the last minute. If they are required to pay in advance, I believe there is less opportunity to be left holding the date for a non-event.

We will of course need to leave leeway for changes and alterations, but that will be worded into the contract too so that anything that is major will hold an additional fee attached to the change. Minor changes we can do complimentary, but it will be important that as a team we communicate all changes to one another, primarily to Lael, as she will be the one holding the entire event together. For instance, if a bride calls up two weeks before the event and wants to change to all silk flowers instead of fresh, this will obviously be cause for a pricing fee addition. We don't want to be hard-nosed business executives, but we can't let the customers walk all over us either. Please make them feel special and that they have control, even though in actuality, we have taken the control away from them once they signed the contract. You will each need to develop the demeanor of Princess Diana while maintaining the business shrewdness of Donald Trump. Any questions?"

Shelby asked, "So what you're saying is that we have individual determination to make alterations to the packages prior to the signing of the contract, but after it is signed, we will need to consult with the rest of the team, and especially with Lael?"

"Yes, that's right, dear. Some brides will be sneaky and try to change something with each of you, and while you think it is minor, it may influence what the rest of us are planning. I have another example. If a bride wants Ingrid to add flowers to her hair, say daisies, and she also wants to add on several arrangements of daisies to the floral package, and later she calls up Unger and asks him to arrange platters of fruit and cheese to resemble daisies, perhaps we all need to re-think the entire ambiance of the day. Is she making it more casual? Sometimes daisies speak the language of simple and casual, but on the other hand, maybe she has just discovered that her groom's favorite flower is the daisy and she wants to be sure to include them in her day. I think in this instance that Shelby would want to know that her portraits might also need to include daisies, and Gianna might also want to have daisy decorations on the cake. Obviously all of these last-minute changes would be cause for additional work and purchases, so the bride should pay more. But if she *only* wants a few daisies in her hair, and asks for none of the other changes, then we can probably let her slide in this one little change at the last minute. Does that make sense?"

The team members all nodded in agreement.

"There are still a couple of areas that I think we are weak on. One is wedding music, and the other is wedding attire. I don't want to get in the business of wedding dresses and tuxedoes, but I'd like to see us have a good working relationship with a seamstress and perhaps a dress shop and tuxedo rental store. If anybody has any ideas, I'd be glad to hear about them."

Holly said, "I played the harp for four years during high school. I was pretty good, and I'd love to play for some weddings. I don't have a harp of my own, though."

Ingrid volunteered, "I've played the piano for many years and played keyboards in a small all-girl band for a couple of years in Sweden. I was also the alternate pianist in my church back in West Virginia. I have a little electric keyboard that I play around with, but I'm thinking we should probably invest in a nicer electric piano. And harp music is so beautiful at a wedding. I think harps are pretty expensive, but maybe we should look into getting one. I'm thinking that would be quite a draw to have a harpist. What do you all think?"

There were several nods and agreements around the table regarding both a harp and piano.

Nester said, "I can hook up anything electronic you come up with. We'll probably want to have a pretty nice sound system so that we can have both indoor and outdoor microphones and speakers. And if we had some permanent speakers out in the garden it'd be pretty easy to set up for music and microphones out there. Shelby, doesn't your brother play classical guitar? Maybe we could get him once in a while to perform at the weddings too."

"Yeah, he's pretty good. I could ask him, but sometimes Beau kind of has an attitude and isn't necessarily the kind of person you can count on."

"Shelby, I understand, but if you'd like to ask Beau if he'd be interested, maybe we could get a commitment out of him to do a few weddings if we have an interested bride and groom. I have a CD of his, and I think I heard where he has cut a second one too, so we could perhaps share his sound with our customers, and if we can work out a deal we'd have another option." Turning my eyes toward Nester, I said, "I've always wanted to have a really good stereo system. Let's talk and come up with a plan and we can get started on that."

"I nearly forgot about the computer system. Nester is also a whiz at computers, and he is already working on setting up a network system so that each of the team members will be networked together, and he is creating a program so that all of our data regarding each beloved couple will be kept in our database," I explained.

"Oh dear," said Bea. "I don't have any experience with computers. Will I need to use one too?"

"I can teach you everything you need to know," said Nester. "We will have the schedule and the supplies list on the program, so you will need to be aware of how to get in and see the calendar. You'll be able to see things like what you will need to purchase as far as breakfasts, linens that'll be needed, and even cleaning supplies or extra housekeeping needs. It won't be a problem; I'm sure you will pick it up easy enough."

I asked, "Any other computer questions or concerns?"

Holly said, "I can foresee that it'll be a great tool to have photos of bouquets available online, so then the brides will be able to sort to a particular style, color, or flower, and see the different options. It's much cheaper and easier than printing photos of them and having her sort through hard copies. I'll also need to use the Internet, of course, to order flowers and supplies. Sounds great to me! And I can help Bea learn too."

Gianna said, "I might need a little help with it too. I'm pretty good at playing computer games and shopping on the Internet, but as far as keeping records on the computer, I've never really done that."

"No problem," said Nester and Holly simultaneously.

I looked around the table and had one more question. "The table and chairs that we have been sitting at today are the style and size that I have in mind to purchase to use in the gazebos and for the garden weddings. Do you like it? Have the chairs been comfortable?"

I heard positive comments and put it to a vote, asking if there were any objections. It was agreed to purchase duplicates and to investigate to see if we could find some that were a little nicer to use indoors in the ballroom.

"Does anyone else have any comments or questions?"

Ingrid asked, "What about a preacher? I don't think we can put on weddings without a preacher or at least a judge."

"I have to confess, I really hadn't given much thought to that," I said. "Does anyone have any suggestions?"

Holly volunteered, "My Granny and I go to the Methodist Church here in Whitney. The preacher there is kind of dull and old-fashioned, but we could maybe get him to do a few of the weddings."

Lael said, "There is a retired judge who lives in town. I've run into him several times at the library. He seems to be a very likable person, but I don't know the legalities of it; can a retired judge still marry people?"

Nobody seemed to know the answer to that.

"We have been going to a church in Manhattan that has a pretty dynamic preacher, Dennis Wilkens, but he just announced last week that he is going to be moving on soon," commented Gianna. "Actually, he is going to be going back to school to get his doctorate and won't be moving exactly, but he won't be having as much time to devote to the church, so they are trying to find a youth pastor to step in and take on some of his duties. Anyway, I'm afraid that Pastor Wilkens won't be able to help us out."

Jedidiah spoke up. "The only one I know of is the priest in Express. I think he serves three or four small towns in the area, so I would think he's probably not going to be available to do weddings here either."

"I guess we'll all have to pray about it and keep our eyes and ears open. Maybe God will supply us with a preacher too. He has been very good to us so far, and I'm sure if we all just ask him, he will surely step in and help with this too." I looked around the table as I said this and everyone was nodding and agreeing.

"All right, Nester, I see you brought a box with you. I'd asked you to get cell phones for everyone. Is that what you have in your box?"

"Yes, ma'am, it is." Nester started handing the phones out. "I've programmed all of the phones and added everyone's numbers on the contact list. We are on a shared plan of minutes; I believe there is a sheet in the employee manual that gives you more information about the phones. If you have any questions, feel free to ask me."

"Now, one last bit of business. I know that you all took time out of your personal schedules to come today and devoted several hours to your presentations, so I have a five hundred-dollar check for each of you. I hope that will cover your travel and time for attending. If you will give me your receipts for anything you purchased for today's meetings, I'll write you a check before you leave today. I'd like to have our second team meeting in six weeks on September sixteenth. We should have our brochures printed by then, and the inn will be a lot closer to completion so we can discuss move in and set up.

"You have probably all noticed that there is a big swimming pool out there." I told them the story of the anonymous donor and the request to have it open to the public. "We have started selling memberships to the local citizens so that they can use the pool too. The initial membership fee is twenty-five dollars per month, and all members are informed that they have to follow a few rules. These are all covered in your handbook under the tab marked *pool.*

"The first is that nobody under the age of eighteen is allowed in the pool. This is an insurance issue because we don't have a lifeguard. Also, it has been my experience that adults are usually more likely to be respectful of other's space. Adults tend to want to swim laps and exercise, while the younger set is more into horseplay and fooling around. Which is rule number two—no horseplay allowed. The third rule says that only paying members or guests of the inn are allowed in the pool. We have security cameras monitoring the pool area, so we will be able to see if any members abuse this rule. Should we discover that a member is bringing in a non-paying guest or allowing someone else to use their keycard, we'll suspend their membership for thirty days.

"Since we aren't going to have the pool guarded or watched closely, our members have been told these are all rules to protect themselves, as well as to keep the pool enjoyable to all who pay to use it. I'm also tasking all of you team members to keep a look out when you are at the pool. You may need to be disciplinary at times and keep the members in line. The fourth rule is that no food or beverages other than bottled water are allowed inside the poolroom itself.

"There are of course exceptions to the rules. Should there be a paying guest at the inn who is younger than eighteen, he or she must be accompanied at all times by a parent when in the pool or gym. Also, we will be open to renting the building to groups of young people, but we must provide a lifeguard in this event. I have the name of a few local Red Cross certified lifeguards who have agreed to hire on for these events.

"We will also be offering the pool as a possible venue for our beloved couples to have pre-wedding parties, perhaps engagement parties or showers, or bachelorette parties. Whenever the pool house is booked for a private pool event, our local members will be notified by e-mail that the pool is closed for the day and their accounts will be credited a dollar per day.

As members of the Celebration Team, you have unlimited access to the pool and gym. You can use the facilities any time that you want, and you may bring one guest, as long as your guest is over eighteen. Your work schedules will be set at your own discretion, as long as you perform your job, so if you want to take a two-hour break to swim and relax in the sauna, that's up to you. You will, of course, all be required to attend all meetings and events and perform your talents to your best abilities."

I looked around at my team members and saw smiling but tired faces. "I asked you to bring your bathing suits, so if you would like to, feel free to go for a swim after Shelby finishes up with the photo sessions. Unless somebody else has a comment or question, please get changed into the matching gold shirts and meet out front on the staircase in front of the inn. Hopefully in September we will have the gym equipment here too, and we will be meeting in either the ballroom or summerhouse. Thanks for coming today."

JEDIDIAH

Life doesn't have to be complicated. It comes down to love. Who you love, what you love to do with your time, where you love to be, and who the higher power is that you love and respect.

And when one is fortunate enough to have all of the sectors of your loves line up perfectly with another person, then it becomes quite obvious that the greatest treasure of your life has been discovered. That is the way I felt about Lucy. She is my treasure, and once I opened up my eyes and admitted that I couldn't live without her, I set out to find a way to convince her to marry me.

Knowing that she had two failed marriages, I knew that she would be very reluctant to marry a third time. Early on in our renewed acquaintance, she had said as much on the phone one evening. She told me that even though she eventually felt much stronger after her divorces, that getting to that point was so painful and disturbing that she didn't think her psyche could tolerate another failure of that proportion.

We had both discussed our previous marriages, and in retrospect, we agreed that the volumes of learning that the experiences had given to us were immeasurable. I had stayed in an unhappy marriage for twenty years because I was the type of person who does not allow myself to renege on a commitment. I saw friends and relatives giving up on their marriages, saying that they just knew that God would not want them to be unhappy. To me, that was stupid. God never guarantees happiness; the Bible is full of disappointments and failures and unhappiness. I was determined to try to make the best of a bad situation.

However, Flynn had seen it differently, and she finally ended the marriage. She did not appreciate my organizational skills, my determination to set the course for our children to be honorable and disciplined, or my dislike of confrontational battles. She thought life was all about fun, and I wasn't fun enough for her. So she kicked me out, and I experienced that sense of failure that Lucy had talked about with me. I too didn't think that I could ever live through another disappointment of that grandeur. Divorce taught me that even though I worked hard to follow my beliefs and morals, I could still get kicked to the curb.

But all of those negative thoughts and memories faded when I was with Lucy. Together with her, my life had renewed vigor; I felt transformed into a lovable man, not someone who could be rejected, but a man worthy of the love of a good woman.

I wouldn't say that our lives were complicated because of the Goldstone Inn project, but we were busy. It seemed that our every thought and most of our energy was focused on the build, Lucy's more so on the decorating and the business venture she was embarking on. But nevertheless, it was hard to find time to just talk about us, to focus on what our lives would be like once the inn was open.

I thought what we needed was a long weekend alone together and away from Whitney. One Saturday in August, after Lucy had spent a long day painting on the beach mural behind the Grand Pavilion, we had a particularly eye-opening evening together. I knew without a doubt that if we could spend two or three days centering only on our relationship that we could cross over to the next phase. I wanted to ask her to marry me, but it had to be at a time when we wouldn't immediately have to go back to work. I decided that Labor Day weekend would be the ideal long weekend to propose to her.

Perhaps too hastily—and admittedly spontaneity is not my strong suit—I booked a flight and made hotel reservations in Victoria, British Columbia, all without first asking her opinion. I had been there once and I remembered it as a beautiful city with romantic possibilities. I felt that Lucy would enjoy the architecture of Victoria and I knew that she loved gardens, so we would spend one whole day exploring Butchart Gardens.

On the Tuesday evening of Lucy's reveal of her mural, I took her out for dinner. There are not many choices of restaurants nearby, and she chose the Pizza Hut. After we ordered our hamburger and onion pizza and had our pitcher of beer delivered to our table, I turned to her and said, "I have a confession to make."

Whenever we eat out we always sit side-by-side at restaurants, never across the table from each other. It is easier to have a cozy conversation when we are closer, and I never tire of holding her hand. She looked up at me with her gorgeous lavender eyes, and flirtingly she said, "Jedidiah, is this about the beach mural? Did you sneak a peek before the reveal?"

"No, I can honestly say I did not look at the mural before you were ready. But in a way it is about the mural. The mural, the inn, the wedding business, the landscaping, the whole nine yards. I think it is time we get away from it. What do you say, will you go away with me for Labor Day weekend?"

"Um, Jedidiah, do you really think we can spare the time?"

"Yes, it will all be here when we get back. And after the inn is open it may be a long time before we have any more free time."

"So where do you want to go?" my lovely Lucy asked.

"Victoria," I answered.

"In Canada," she asked. "Why there?" While not truly suspicious-sounding, her voice quavered with quandary.

"It is a grand city, and there are some amazing gardens there that I know you will love to see. It is cooler there, and besides, I already bought the tickets and made the reservations. I hope it's all right."

She seemed to hesitate a bit before answering, but with only a little delay she said, "Jedidiah, I would love to go to Victoria with you. And you are right, it may be our last chance for a vacation for quite some time."

The flight was uneventful, other than a short layover in Seattle. We both started to relax and I knew that I would never forget the look on her face when we landed in Victoria.

We were both lighthearted and giggling like children while we explored Victoria. There was an antique wooden sailboat show in the inner harbor with over 150 boats on display, as well as several merchants who were trying to sell their marine-related products in booths scattered around the harbor. On Friday afternoon, after we had checked into the hotel, we casually walked around near the water, boarding some of the boats and taking lots of photographs. There were some magnificent sailboats, all sizes and colors, some that glistened with many coats of marine varnish, and others that were in the beginning stages of restoration, showing age and weather-related rough spots.

In a way, I could see the similarities between the antique boats and my relationship with Lucy. We both came into the relationship needing some restoration, with the varnish worn thin in places, the upholstery torn a bit, but with love and attention we were building a lovely craft.

There were vendors and street acts everywhere in the harbor district. Holding hands, we wandered around watching some of the acts. In a sunny spot, we watched while a young fellow was completely wrapped in cellophane, round and round and round, leaving only his head and feet free. Within a few minutes, he comically was able to work his way out of the plastic trap. The sun's rays were shining brightly and the young man's bare legs and arms were slick with sweat in all that plastic wrap, aiding in his ability to slip out of the hot plastic. There were jugglers, musicians, and a lot of costumed people walking around—some singing or acting out short skits. Everyone seemed to be enjoying the sunshine on that fine September day.

We paid a couple of bucks to see the Harbor Aquarium, which was a large boat that had aquariums lined up around the lower level. In the aquariums were a variety of marine animals, and in one extremely large aquarium was a diver who was pointing out all of the life in the glass cage. They had a huge octopus in that aquarium and some other unique creatures that one doesn't see in an average day on the prairie in Kansas.

There were horse-drawn carriages giving rides around the grand building that they called Government House. We didn't take the carriage ride, but instead we sat in the shade of a large maple tree and relaxed a bit, watching the people and gazing at the amazing architecture of the building. The exterior of the three-story building was faced with granite in shades of gray, blue, and pink. We asked a couple of the locals who wandered by where they recommended we go for dinner, and following their directions, we ended up in a pub-like establishment. The food was good, but the atmosphere wasn't exactly romantic. It was fun, though, with a lot of colorful and expressive patrons having a good time around us.

On Saturday we slept late, and after a scrumptious brunch at a little mom-and-pop restaurant, we drove a few miles to the Butchart Gardens. The fourteen-mile trek to the gardens in the rental car was slow; it seemed that we were not alone in the plan to spend the day there. But once we finally arrived, it was well worth the time spent waiting in traffic. The story of the woman who had reclaimed the land from an old limestone quarry and created the beauty of the acres and acres of gardens was inspiring. There were many separate-themed gardens on the property, and all of them were beautiful and immaculately tended. I think Lucy was most fascinated with the wide variety of trees—everything from monstrous redwoods to banyan trees, to monkey-puzzle trees.

We sat on some benches and watched a musical show for a while—some very talented Scottish lass was singing and dancing to tunes unfamiliar to me, but quite fun. Most of the songs were ballads, telling stories of love and adventure. We ate a quick meal of German sausages on crusty buns at the Blue Poppy Café near the entrance of the garden and then prepared for the fireworks.

I had planned ahead for this event, hoping it would be as amazing as the hype. We carried a couple of blankets and some bottled water to a good vantage point on a grassy hill. Alcohol wasn't allowed on the grounds, so even though champagne would have been more appropriate, I settled for water. There must have been several thousand people there for the fireworks show. I wanted to create a romantic setting, because this was where I hoped to pop the question to my very special Lucy.

I had a diamond ring in my pocket. I had been a little intimidated about purchasing it without her input, but I'd bought it from a mutual friend, Kirk, who was a jeweler in Manhattan. One morning while she was in the shower and I was alone in her bedroom, I had gone through her jewelry box and tried on her rings, trying to figure out what size to get for her. I had discovered that that method wasn't going to work, so I slipped one of the rings that seemed to be the same size as several others into my pocket. That day I had gone to Manhattan and using that ring to get the size right, Kirk and I had found the perfect ring. He helped me to pick out a magnificent ring; there was a teardrop diamond in the center, surrounded by twenty smaller diamond chips. I'd later returned her ring to her jewelry case, hoping she hadn't missed it.

We had a great view of the fireworks show, and we were comfortable sitting on the blanket on the soft lawn, wrapped together in the other blanket to ward off the chill in the air. The show had been going on for about ten minutes, and the brochure had promised us that the show would be about a half hour, so I knew that it was nearing the halfway point. I was trying to find a way to lead into my proposal. The next song that was played over the speakers, with the fireworks orchestrated to match the tune, was *Still the One*, by Orleans. My darling Lucy was quietly singing along. This had been our song in the seventies, and I took it as a sign that it was the time to declare my intentions, to ask her to marry me.

I turned slightly so that I could watch her sing, and she turned to look at me; it was a special moment, and it seemed as though we were all alone with her singing her promise of love to me. I shuffled slightly so that I could retrieve the little red velvet box from my pocket. She looked at me kind of curiously but continued to sing along until she saw what it was that I had in my hand.

I opened the box and displayed the ring to her, saying, "Lucy, my love, I will always love you. You are still the one for me, baby; you always have been. Will you marry me?"

"Jedidiah, you are still the one that makes me glad. With you I am stronger and better than I ever thought I could be. You are still the one I dream about. I love you with all my heart. Yes, I want to marry you."

We kissed passionately, and the rest is a bit fuzzy. I just remember being extremely happy. The fireworks in the sky echoed the explosion of joy in my heart, and my life was only getting better!

JEDIDIAH

On the drive back to the hotel we passed by a small church near the water, and Lucy asked me to circle the block so she could read the sign in front of the church that advertised the service times. We decided that we would go to services at the little church the next morning to praise God for our good fortune to have found each other again.

The church was small and very quaint. The morning was clear and the air was fresh; they left the doors wide open during the small gathering, which seemed more like an adult Sunday school gathering than a regular church service. The parishioners had gathered in a small side room, not the actual church sanctuary, sitting in a circle around the perimeter of the room, on old-fashioned wooden folding chairs that creaked with every movement. The people were all very friendly and greeted us with genuine hospitable hearts; we felt welcomed. I told them that we were there for the weekend only and had just become engaged the night before. Our future marriage was included in their prayer time, and we felt truly blessed.

During the teaching it was so special and memorable that through the open doors we could hear the seagulls squawking and the ships' horns blaring. It felt very exotic, definitely far away from Kansas.

After church we wandered around downtown for a while, always holding hands. We found a lovely little butterfly sanctuary. It was in an old brick building, with high ceilings and many skylights. The sanctuary was lush with vegetation, jungle-like, very warm and humid, and there were thousands of butterflies fluttering around inside. I loved seeing my fiancée in such a striking setting—another extreme contrast to our homes in Kansas. Lucy took many snapshots, but I just enjoyed watching her childlike interest and fascination with the multicolored butterflies.

In the lobby of the butterfly sanctuary we found a brochure advertising a castle in Victoria that really caught the interest of Lucy—Craigdarroch Castle. We followed the tiny map and found the huge stone castle standing on a hill overlooking the city. It was open as a museum—four floors and thirty-nine rooms of grandeur built in the last decade of the 1800s. We enjoyed touring the castle, which was surprisingly very sparsely attended that September day. After we climbed the eighty-seven stairs to the tower on our self-guided tour, we sat and looked out over the city, undisturbed for nearly an hour.

"Jedidiah, thank you so much for bringing me to this lovely city. This has been a very special weekend. I will always remember this," Lucy said.

"I wanted to share some time with you somewhere out of the ordinary, so I'm glad that you like Victoria."

"We probably should talk about a few practical issues," she said. "Will we live in my cottage after we are married?"

"If that is what you want, yes, I think that would be the best. My kids can stay on at the big old house on my place, and the commute to work will be very minimal," I continued humorously.

"I like that plan," she said. "But that brings to mind another thing. You are undoubtedly aware that I hold the contract for purchase on your acreage and house. Once we are married, that will be yours, of course, free and clear. Well, let me rephrase that, it will be ours. All of what I have will be ours. I don't want any division of our finances."

"Are you sure about that, Lucy? I'm not marrying you for your money; I'm marrying you because I love you and can't go on without you as my wife. I'm a little uncomfortable that your wealth will be ours to share."

"Jedidiah, I'm not usually a pushy woman, but I'm not backing down on this topic. I had a prenuptial agreement with Tony, and because of that he always seemed to have the attitude toward me that I was free to go at any time, but I'd be leaving with nothing. I felt trapped until I finally was strong enough to understand that his threats could not keep me under his control and unhappy.

"And the more I think about it, it wasn't so much that I was unhappy, but that the marriage was unequally yoked. I heard a radio sermon on that topic a while back, and it finally dawned on me what that really meant. Tony and I were unequally yoked in many ways—financially, on our Christian beliefs, our child-rearing methods, disciplinary viewpoint, and our ideas of family values. But you and I are one hundred percent different from that.

"We have the same Christian belief, we both believe that all children are gifts from God, and I don't want finances to be in any way a knife that cuts our relationship in two. I won't marry you, Jedidiah, unless you agree that what I have is yours and what you have is mine. We are going to be joining as one, period. I hope that's not a deal-breaker, but I have a very adamant belief that if we can't share our finances, there is no way that our marriage will work. I want you as my equal partner for the rest of my life; I'm not entering into this by holding back anything."

"Yes, ma'am," I answered. "I understand. And no, it's not a deal-breaker. I agree and I thank you for being so clear. I want us to be able to talk about anything, and it makes me very proud of you to know that you aren't afraid to stand up for what you believe in. I love you with all of my heart, Lucy. I'm planning to be with you for the rest of my life too."

"You know all about how I got that money. I didn't really earn it. I was just awarded it as part of Tony's misguided plot to win me back. I would have never come back to him, especially not for the money. But as it worked out, his twenty-five million dollars has allowed me to fulfill some of my dreams, especially my dream about finding you again!

"I think of it as just money, a tool to use to achieve my goals. I don't think of it as Tony's because, actually, it was Turner money, and he only had it for a little while. So if there are any projects that you've been holding off on because of finances, you will have the freedom to go ahead. If you want to remodel the house or buy more bulls or buy a new car for your daughters, whatever you want to do, you won't have to hold back."

"Lucy, I would never just go ahead and do anything of that magnitude without discussing it with you first. Since it is our financial package, then it is something we need to decide upon together. And as far as new cars for the girls, I don't think so. Neither one of them has proved to me yet that they can take care of their used cars, so they have to keep driving the old ones, even if my net value increases exponentially the day I marry you.

"We'll need to decide when to tell our families about our engagement and when we want to get married. I'm assuming you'll want to get married at Goldstone, right?"

"Yes, you're right, the wedding will certainly have to be at Goldstone. And what do you think about telling the families on Thanksgiving? They should all be together then, and we can announce it at dinner."

"I'm not sure if I can keep it a secret until then," I replied.

"Well, if you really want to share it sooner, I suppose we could, but I kind of like having a secret with you that no one else knows about, at least for a while. Maybe we could let Lael in on the secret so that she can help us to plan the wedding."

"So, my future wife, do you have a date in mind for the wedding?"

She looked up at me with her sexy eyes and said, "What would you think about the Saturday after Christmas? Christmas is on a Monday, so our wedding date would be December thirtieth. I would've liked New Year's Eve or New Year's Day, but we already have those dates saved for other brides."

"That gives you a little less than four months to plan it. Do you think that's enough time?"

"What do you mean *you*?" Lucy looked playfully at me. "This is a joint venture, buster. You have to help too, you know. Even though I'm in the wedding business, I'm not going to do this without your input."

"I'm sorry, I guess I kind of slipped up there. Of course I want to be involved in the wedding plans," I admitted. "I didn't mean to say that it would only be you doing the planning. I think that December thirtieth would be a wonderful day to get married. Do you suppose that by announcing our date only a month before on Thanksgiving Day that is enough notice for our families to hold the date?"

"Thanksgiving is on the twenty-third of November this year, so it is actually five weeks. That is a week short of the traditional, expected notification date, but we'll just have to take who we can get, I guess. If people already have other plans, they'll just have to choose to either break those plans or not come to our wedding. As long as you and I are there, the rest of them can come or not. It is going to be our special day, and I'm not going to worry about anyone else's schedule."

"I like the way you think, my darling girl. So, what else have you been thinking about for this special day?"

"I was thinking, of course, depending upon what you think, but perhaps we should have our kids stand up with us. Since we have three girls and three boys, our attendants would be an equal number."

I answered, "I love that idea. Including them in the wedding will be good for them too. They will not only be onlookers, but participants. I think that is an important way to begin our new life together. I want all of our kids to feel like they are part of a new, larger joined family."

"The only other thing that has crossed my mind is that since it will be a winter wedding, perhaps we can have the girls wear white furs and red dresses, and maybe the guys would be more comfortable wearing leather jackets instead of tuxedos."

"I like it," I said honestly. "I think the boys would appreciate not having to wear a suit, and our girls would look lovely in white fur, and maybe more of a cranberry or burgundy than Christmas red. What do you think?"

"Oh, yes, I think you are right," Lucy agreed, and continued, "I think we should have lots of Christmas decorations in the inn, maybe a huge tree, all decorated in cranberry, white, and gold. I think it will be amazing."

At that moment we heard approaching footsteps and suddenly remembered we were in a public museum, so we relinquished our private tower to the next couple who came through the arched doorway, descending the stairs to continue viewing the fine craftsmanship and amazing lavish furnishings in the 20,000 square foot Craigdarroch Castle.

JEDIDIAH

On Monday, Labor Day, we were traveling most of the day, and by the time we finally arrived home it was nearly dark. We had stopped in Topeka and had dinner at the Cracker Barrel. Lucy had spent a little time shopping in the gift shop, finding some wrought-iron table lamps that she wanted to put in each of the guest rooms. She purchased all that they had and arranged for them to be shipped so we didn't have to try to load them all into the car. The shades for the lamps were packaged separately, and not to Lucy's liking, so she did not get the shades. She was a very determined shopper, and I enjoyed watching her in action.

The crew had all taken a three-day weekend, but they would be back to work early on Tuesday. We would be doing finish work—the trim and installation of the cabinets. Hopefully by the next scheduled Celebration Team meeting on the sixteenth we would have that phase completed and be starting with the priming and painting.

Nester and Unger had moved to Whitney already and were living in Ingrid and Bjorn's motor home. It was one of those huge luxury models, so they weren't roughing it, but living quite opulently. Lucy had, in the end, decided that the landscaping project was too large for her to take on now that she was also planning a wedding business, so she had worked with Frank Krug and come up with a plan that incorporated a lot of her ideas. Nester had supervised the installation of the plant materials, working side by side with the crew, and the result was a magnificent garden.

The backyard was lush with trees, bushes, and lots of perennial flowers. There were vines growing on the columns and large planters strategically placed to both beautify and define the space. There were several of the original trees still gracing the front of the inn, but the landscapers had added a beautiful lawn, more trees, and a lot of flowers in raised stone beds. It looked superb. Nester assured me that most of the plants were very hardy and would stand up nicely to the harsh Kansas summers and winters and would need minimal maintenance to sustain the brilliance. They had, of course, installed an irrigation system to keep the gardens watered.

Unger had been very instrumental with the setup of the three kitchens. The summerhouse was complete, and Unger had started cooking meals for the crew. He was cooking and selling meals for about five dollars apiece, and since most of the crew had been at the job for several months already, they welcomed a chance to have a meal that they didn't have to eat out of a bag or lunchbox. The summerhouse had become a very grand break room for the help, and I'd been proud of my crew, fascinated really, how the men all seemed to get along, laughing, joking, and telling off-color jokes together. It didn't seem to matter at all to the small-town fellows that Unger and Nester were gay, black, or were from far-off places like Russia or Mississippi. And by the end of the first week of eating in the summerhouse cafe, I saw all of them sharing a good-hearted chuckle, mimicking Unger's Russian accent and Unger poking fun right back at J.J.'s southern drawl. They were all very accepting and made me proud to live in Whitney, where people were very welcoming and tolerant, not discriminatory or rude at all. It affirmed to me that this small town was exactly where I wanted to be for the rest of my days.

The fleet of Goldstone vehicles had been delivered at the end of August. The housekeeper's double garage was finished, and two of the new vans were parked in there. We had built a carport next to the summerhouse and the two vans for the caterer and pastry chef were parked in that space. Both of the chefs had been using their vans already—Unger for food shopping, and Gianna, who had baked two wedding cakes, used it to deliver them to the wedding reception sites. Nester was using his new pickup truck daily and parked it under a tree by the motor home at the end of the day. Lucy was gone for the day, driving her new PT Cruiser, and her VW was in her double garage at her cottage. The other two vans were parked in Lucy's large shed until the garages were completed at the new cottages.

I was running this all through my mind the Wednesday afternoon following our return from Victoria because the weather was turning ugly. There was a thunderstorm warning and grapefruit-sized hail was predicted. I didn't think there was much we could do to protect the newly planted landscape, but at least the vehicles should be safe, other than maybe Nester's pickup truck. I said a quick prayer that the roof and windows of the inn would be protected; it was such a beautiful building, and even though it was massive and grand, a storm of large hail could do a lot of damage.

I went looking for Nester and found him consulting with some of the men in the back garden. I asked him, "What do you think? Is there something we can do to protect the plants?"

"We've been troubleshootin' here, and short of coverin' everythin' with those new canvas shades that connect to the gazebos. We can't think of any way to keep the hailstones off of the new landscaping," Nester answered, rather frantically.

"Yeah, but I don't think Lucy would like it if they got torn to shreds."

Lucy was shopping for lampshades and wasn't expected home for a few hours. I suddenly had a thought, "What about chicken wire? Would that work to cover everything?"

"Well, that would probably help, but it'd take a lot of chicken wire." Nester looked a little hopeful. "Where are we goin' to get that much chicken wire in just a short time? That storm's only about an hour away."

"We've got several rolls of it in our barn. I was going to build a large chicken coop last year and never got around to it. I'll run home really quick and load it up. I'll take a couple of the guys with me, but maybe you ought to see about moving Ingrid's motor home under a tree and park the new truck under one too. It's probably the best we can do to protect them for now."

So the Braun brothers and I ran to my pickup, which was parked in front, racing against a storm. Within fifteen minutes we had driven to my place, loaded the wire rolls, and returned to Goldstone, parking in the back by the summerhouse gate to the backyard. Nester had moved the motor home and all of the guys had moved their cars and trucks, parking them under willow trees. Nester had rounded up all of the hands to help save the landscaping from the hail.

All of the men were wearing leather gloves and had pliers or wire-cutting tools, and we started by unloading the wire netting rolls and placing them strategically around the garden. The wind had picked up, and we all had to yell to be heard over the roar. There were five teams of four each unwinding the wire, fastening it to the gazebo iron railings on one end, unrolling it the length of the garden, and fastening it to poles or other railings—whatever they could find that was sturdy and in the path. We worked at it nonstop for forty minutes, effectively making a canopy of one-inch chicken wire over about three-quarters of the back garden.

The sky had turned nearly black, and the wind was roaring. There was lightning in the north sky—brilliant, wicked streaks. I knew that Lucy was far south in Topeka and all the weather reports I had heard claimed that the storm was moving in from the north, so I was relatively certain that she was safe. That didn't keep me from worrying about her, though. I said a prayer, asking

God to keep her safe and to bring her home as soon as the storm passed.

With minutes to spare, Nester took several of the guys and one last roll of wire out to the front, and even though there were fewer structures to fasten the wire to, they hoped to secure a couple lengths over the raised flowerbeds and the young trees. As long as the predicted hail was at least an inch in diameter, most of the plants should survive. We'd done all we could do, and suddenly the rain came.

It just let loose in buckets! It came down fast and hard, and the few of us that were in the backyard sought cover in the summerhouse. I hadn't seen Nester and his bunch, but I supposed they were inside the inn. The wind got even stronger and the lightning was closer. Unger, who'd been inside the summerhouse kitchen watching us from a window, looked rather green. I went to him to see if I could comfort him a bit and discovered that not only was he deathly afraid of storms, he was frantic because Nester was not with us. I tried to assure him that we would be fine and that surely Nester was in the inn, so he was safe too.

Suddenly the front door of the summerhouse burst open and Nester came running in, followed by four carpenters, frenzied and yelling, "The tornado siren is going off. We need to get to the basement." Unger rushed forward, hugging his dear friend, who was soaked clean through with rainwater. They were the first to head down the stairs to the basement storage room.

There were over twenty of us crowded into the basement, which was almost filled to capacity with stored furniture, anxiously awaiting the storm to pass. Nobody was saying much, and it was remarkably quiet down there. We couldn't hear the wind or the siren; we couldn't even hear whether or not it was hailing. Finally, after twenty minutes, Nester became restless and boldly proclaimed that he had to go check it out. He wouldn't allow anybody to follow him up the stairs, though.

He'd been gone only a few minutes when he returned, grinning widely. "It's over," he declared. In his hand he held a huge hailstone, every bit as big as a grapefruit. "Look at the size of this thing! It doesn't look like we've suffered much damage, but there is bound to be some cleanup."

Miraculously, he was right. Even though there were thousands of the huge hailstones atop the chicken wire canopy, none had broken through the canopy. The plants were all safe. But even more amazing than that, the inn and summerhouse hadn't sustained any damage. There were no broken windows and the metal-tile shingles didn't show any sign of dents, scratches, or pits.

The wind had retreated and the rain had lessened to a mere sprinkle. I walked around surveying the entire property and was in awe; God had indeed protected us. He had saved us completely from the wrath of the storm. Or so I thought anyway. Nester found me at the pool house, staring up at the glass roof of the sunroom. There weren't even any broken skylights! The ground around the pool was littered with the monstrous hailstones, but none of them had broken through the glass.

"Hey, boss," he said kindly. "You'd better come see this." He had a worried look on his face, and his concern translated that there was a problem. I hurried to follow him, cutting through the backyard and through the gate by the summerhouse.

I had left my pickup parked there, totally out in the open. My wonderful, red, four-wheel drive, double cab pickup was destroyed. Every window was broken out; shards of glass were everywhere. The red paint was devastated to the point that you could hardly see any color. There were so many huge dents in the truck that it looked as if one more punch would make it collapse. I couldn't speak. I didn't know what to feel. Should I feel thankful that it was only a truck that was injured? I felt that surely I would have been dead if I were inside the truck. But it was ruined; I'd never seen hail destroy a vehicle to such a magnitude! I found myself wondering if the hail had caught any motorists unaware on the roads.

Abruptly, my thoughts turned to Lucy. Where was she? Was she in the path of this awful storm? I fumbled in my pocket for my cell phone, called her, but the call went to voice mail. Unger was at my side and slowly led me into the summerhouse. He knew the look on my face; it was the same that had been on his own a short while ago when he didn't know Nester's fate in the storm. He tried to comfort me; he brought me a cup of coffee. He called out to Nester and told him to go find Lucy. I tried to protest, saying that I wanted to go find her, but Unger wouldn't let me leave. He joked with me then, saying, "Your bucket of bolts wouldn't get you out of the driveway."

JEDIDIAH

Nester was gone for hours. I kept trying to call Lucy every ten minutes, but it always went to voice mail. I called Lael and told her my concern, and she thought she knew of some of the stores that Lucy hoped to shop at, so she made some phone calls, trying to discover if they had seen Lucy yet.

Unger kept trying to assure me that she was safe; after all, she'd been in Topeka, and the storm had turned toward Wichita after going through Whitney. It had finally petered out about thirty minutes after it dropped its wrath on us. I told the crew to leave the chicken wire netting in place and to go home. They undoubtedly were concerned about their families too. Nester called Unger every half hour to report his progress, but he hadn't found Lucy. Unfortunately, there were several roads she could be on; there was more than one way to get to Topeka, and even once he got to Topeka, he didn't know how to find her. Eventually, Unger told him to come home but to drive a different route just in case she was stranded along a different road. Nester reported that the storm had headed west at a point about ten miles south of town, so it was clear to him that Lucy had to be safe, but until she was home, I couldn't rest.

At the point where Unger told Nester to turn around and head home, he tried to convince me that it was time to go home and wait. Nonetheless, I didn't want to go to my house; I let him take me to Lucy's house, though. Unger had only been inside Lucy's cottage once before, and he tried to put my mind to rest by making pleasant comments about the charm and quaintness of her home. He cooked some pasta and tried to get me to eat, but I had worked myself up into such a quandary that I felt physically ill. All I could do was pace from window to window, looking for Lucy to drive in. I couldn't eat, and Unger was at a loss as to how to ease my stress any other way than with food.

He lit some candles and put on some soft music. He tried to be funny, and said, "I'm not trying to seduce you, Jedidiah. I just can't stand to see you so fraught with unrest, and you are making me stressed out. So the candles and music are to make me feel better."

I said nothing, just dialed Lucy's cell phone again. Unger found Lucy's huge white family Bible on her coffee table and opened it up to the middle. He started reading aloud from Psalms. He had only been reading about five minutes when we saw headlights shining through the front windows.

I jumped out of the chair that I had only been sitting in for a few minutes and raced toward the door. I threw it open and ran out to the car that was driving in. I could tell by its shape that it was a PT Cruiser; I kept running toward the car until I could see Lucy's face through the windshield.

She stopped the car, curious, I'm sure, as to why I was greeting her in such an unusual fashion. She rolled down her window, but I quickly got the door open and reached in to hug and kiss my bride-to-be.

"Jedidiah, I'm happy to see you too, but you're scaring me. What has happened?"

"Oh, Lucy, I've just been so worried about you. I'm so very glad that you are home safely. You are okay, aren't you?"

"Yes, Jedidiah, I'm fine. What's going on, and where is your truck? Why did you drive a Celebration van over here?"

Unger came out of the cottage then and waved wildly at us.

"Jedidiah, why is Unger here? Did something happen to Nester?"

"No, I'll tell you all about it as soon as you come inside," I said. "But why weren't you answering your cell phone?"

"Oh my," she said nonchalantly. "I turned the ringer off when I went into the lamp showroom, and I guess I forgot to turn it back on. And I was so involved in the audiobook that I was listening to on the way home that I forgot to turn it back on."

"I'm just so relieved that you are home. We had a bad storm here this afternoon, but other than my pickup, we are fine. Well, at least I'm fine now that you're home."

JEDIDIAH

The next day, things got back to normal, but I was suddenly rather gun-shy; I couldn't stand to let Lucy out of my sight. I convinced her to come to the building site and work with me on Thursday and Friday, and on the weekend we were virtually inseparable as well. Finally, Monday morning rolled around and she said, "Jedidiah, I need to go to the printers today and pick up the brochures. Would you like to go with me and we can see about getting you a new truck?"

I'd only had liability coverage on my ten-year-old truck, so I wasn't entitled to an insurance settlement. "Lucy, I'm not sure if I can afford one right now. I can just drive the Winnebago van for now."

"Oh, come on, let me buy it for you. Don't be silly. You know I can afford it, and remember, we agreed that what's mine is yours, and yours is mine."

"That's only after we are married," I argued.

"Jedidiah, you know that is only a formality at this point. I feel as married to you as if we already had the license. And speaking of the license, we could get that while we're in town too. What do you say?"

"Don't you think it is a little early to get the license?"

Lucy's face became distorted as if she were fighting off tears. She said, "You aren't backing out on me are you?"

"Never, my darling! I just don't want anybody to think I'm taking advantage of your wealth. And I only meant, are you sure that a license is good for several months? We aren't getting married for nearly four months."

"It is three and a half months, and I checked; the marriage license is valid for six months," she countered.

"But, Lucy, do you really think you want to buy me a truck?"

"Jedidiah, let me put it this way: I love you, I trust you, I will marry you in less than four months and never let you go. If you don't let me buy you a truck, I'll have to wonder if you are serious about truly accepting my condition that we will totally be combining our finances."

I looked deep into the pools of her lavender eyes, swimming with unshed tears, and I could see that she was serious. I thought about it and realized there was really no valid reason why I shouldn't let her do this if that was what she wanted. I answered, "There is one condition."

"Yes?" my bride replied.

"I'm going to pay the fee for the marriage license, all right?"

Smiling, she agreed, and we set out to go shopping.

We stopped first at the printers, and picked up the brochures for the Goldstone Celebration Inn Weddings. They were very professionally done, colorful, and the information was concise but very descriptive. They were letter-sized and printed on shiny paper. Lucy exclaimed, "They are beautiful, aren't they, Jedidiah?"

I answered, "Not as beautiful as you, my love, but yes they are quite nice."

I loaded the boxes of brochures into the rear of the PT Cruiser, Lucy's fleet vehicle that had the logo advertising Goldstone Celebration Inn. Holding her hand, I gazed down into her eyes and said, "Are you ready to get a license to marry me?"

"Most definitely," she answered and offered her lips for a kiss, which I gladly participated in.

"It seems a shame to leave that diamond ring in a box; are you sure you don't want to announce our engagement sooner?" I asked.

"Unless someone finds out about the marriage license, I still want to wait till Thanksgiving Day, if that's okay," she replied.

I relented easily, saying, "As you wish, my love."

The courthouse was across the street, so we walked to our next destination, actually nearly skipping with joy.

We filled out the necessary form, presented our identifications, and after paying the fifty-dollar fee, we left with a little piece of paper that carried much value.

We had been talking about the pickup truck on the way to Manhattan. I told her that I wanted a Dodge Diesel four-wheel drive. She had asked, "What color?"

"The color isn't really important to me," I had said. She gave me a quizzical look, not understanding that to me it was more about the power and size than the color, but I finally conceded that if I had a choice it would not be red again. I joked, saying, "The last red truck I had kind of ended in a miserable way, so I don't think I want to test my luck with another red one."

At the dealership, we were allowed to wander around about ten minutes before a salesman confronted us. When I told him what I was looking for, his first question was, "What color?"

I felt a bit exasperated; was I the only one who didn't pay much attention to color? I asked him, "Could you please just show us all of your four-wheel drive diesel trucks, and I'll decide if a color appeals to me?"

He led us to four trucks parked off to one side; there were two red ones, a white one, and one that was the same champagne gold as the Goldstone fleet. The last was the one that immediately caught my eye, but it was a three-quarter-ton dually. The red, hailed-out one had been a half-ton, and I didn't want Lucy to think I was expecting her to go to that expense.

The salesman keenly picked up on my interest and he started reeling off the features of the gold truck. "This is a Dodge Ram

3500 Mega Cab Dually with a 5.9 liter Cummins diesel engine, a six-speed standard transmission, and it's a four-by-four. The color is a custom one; the guy who ordered it backed out of the deal after it arrived, so you're in luck; we can give it to you for stock color price today. This is the Laramie Edition, with leather interior and sound system upgrades. There is a Bose six-disc CD sound system and a Sirius satellite radio. It has a lot of luxury in there for you and the little lady. Of course, there is air-conditioning and heated front seats, and the pedals are even adjustable so the little lady could reach to drive this big boy. It's one strong, smooth-riding workhorse. It is last year's model, and since the new ones will be out soon, we need to clear out the old stock, so I'm sure we can make you a heck of a deal."

I could tell that my little lady really liked the gold one too, and since the red ones were the only half-ton ones at the dealer, Lucy asked, "What do you say, Jedidiah? Could you live with the bigger one? You said you didn't want red, and I like this one."

Not comfortable discussing it in front of the salesman, I asked, "Can we test drive it and have a few minutes alone to discuss it?" The salesman agreed and returned with a magnetic license plate.

In the truck, driving down Fort Riley Boulevard, I said, "Lucy, this truck is probably about ten thousand dollars higher than the half-ton ones. I don't really need a three-quarter ton truck; it'd be nice to have it, but maybe we should look somewhere else."

"Oh, come on, my darlin'," she replied. "I can tell that you really want this one. Why go somewhere else? Let's see what kind of a deal he'll make for us once he finds out we're going to pay cash."

"Are you sure? I bet this guy makes some kind of snide comment about the *little lady* writing the check."

"I can take it if you can, big boy!" she said playfully. "I love this truck, and I might even want to drive it since the pedals are adjustable!"

She was being lighthearted and mischievous, even more confirmation that she was the woman for me to love the rest of my life. "Okay, sweetheart, let's go back and talk to the man about buying a truck."

JEDIDIAH

On the following Saturday I led the Celebration Team through the property on an extensive tour. The cabinet and trim installation was complete, and some of the walls were primed. We'd been having beautiful weather, so all of the crew had temporarily been reassigned to working on the cottages, hoping to get them all framed in and weather tight before the fall rainstorms started. Once they were closed in, then the painting could be done in the inn, but we had to take advantage of the weather while we could.

The members of the team who had not yet been in the inn were awestruck. I don't think they had any idea of the sumptuousness that their employer had in mind for her inn. The carved heavy front doors had been salvaged from the livery stable, and Kermie had meticulously worked his marvel on the doors, bringing their glory back to life. They glistened with multiple coats of varnish, and the beauty of the mahogany attested to over a century of strength and endurance. No wear and tear was visible; Kermie had indeed worked a miracle.

The chandeliers and other light fixtures were hung but were bulb-less, draped in plastic to keep them paint free. Lucy and Scarlett had designed a magnificent entry to the grand ballroom, and my crew had done an amazing job realizing the plan into actuality. The windows showed layers of sheetrock dust and would need a good cleaning. But even with the limited light and sun shining through the dirty windows, it was obvious that the inn was glorious. It was affirming to hear all of the compliments of the craftsmanship. I knew that my crewmembers were talented, but to hear comments from people who had never seen the inn before assured me that it was indeed a place of splendor. I had never doubted that Lucy's dream, and my sister's design would be anything but fabulous, but still, I loved hearing comments such as those coming from Bea, Shelby, Holly, and Gianna.

Bea was chattering like a teenager. "It is awesome! I never dreamed that I'd get to live in and work in such a gorgeous place. Those cabinets are amazing, and the moldings and trim work truly make it into a one-of-a-kind beauty. And an elevator! Oh my, that will really be nice too!"

Shelby's comments echoed Bea's, and she added, "I'll be able to take amazing photographs in the ballroom. The light will be perfect, and those turrets are so romantic and charming."

Holly added, "I can't wait to put a huge flower arrangement in that grand entrance under that opulent chandelier! And all of those columns give it such a Mediterranean essence. The wide overhanging eaves outside will keep the interior cooler and also provide protection on the verandas. We can maybe even have some potted palms near the entry vestibule. Oh, and I love the arched doorways; the whole ambiance makes it seem like this inn has been here for centuries."

I added, "It is the first structure of such magnificence that my family has built, so I was learning along with my crew how to build those arched doorways, but yes, I think they turned out really well. I love the deep overhangs too. I always love a porch, and even though this house technically doesn't have porches, but verandas and loggias instead, they really extend the living space so that the exterior feels more comfortable on hot days. What do you think of all of the wrought iron embellishments?"

Gianna answered my query. "I wish we would have had you build our house. I love wrought iron, stone, and stucco. It feels so European, and even though I love my new house, I'm very thankful that I now get to work at such a magnificent property. I've been in the summerhouse, of course, but this is my first time stepping inside the inn. I'm awestruck; it is amazing."

Lucy had paint and fabric swatches that she was showing the team, explaining the color schemes of the rooms. Nester and Unger disappeared for a few minutes and suddenly reappeared as the elevator doors opened. Nester commented, "That's a great feature. I'd been a little afraid that I'd hafta tote suitcases up and down stairs for the old folks, so that gets me out of that task! And the bedrooms are all pretty good sized upstairs."

The group ascended the stairs, except for Bea, who joined Nester and Unger in the elevator. We continued the tour on the upper floor, starting at the west end and finishing in the bridal suite. Lucy explained her plan. "This room is huge because the bride and her attendants will undoubtedly need a place to dress and hang out until the wedding starts. There will also be a dozen different colors of drapes for backdrops hung high on the bare south wall; Shelby will be able to choose the different drapes as backgrounds for bridal portraits, and also other special shots of the bridesmaids, and perhaps a tender photograph of the bride with her father.

"The night before the wedding, we plan to have the rehearsal and dinner in the ballroom or sunroom. Then the gentlemen will have the lower level available for a bachelor party, and the women will have free reign of the second floor and the pool house too. Ingrid will be on hand for massages and manicures and pedicures. Are you all ready to see the lower level?"

On the basement level, Lucy notified everyone that they were to call it the lower level, never the basement. "We don't want anyone to feel like they are second-class citizens and are being abandoned to the cellar."

I continued showing the group around, starting with the groom's quarters. Shelby and Holly climbed the circular staircase to the room that Lucy was calling the Dance Circle, giggling upon returning at some private joke. It was good to see that the two were becoming friends; we had a good team, and it was going to be a pleasure to be part of it with my dear Lucy.

They all liked the theater and didn't seem to have any problem with imagining the big screen and comfortable chairs that would eventually be in the large empty room, that, to me, seemed rather cave-like since there weren't any windows.

Unger said, "This room would probably serve as a tornado shelter too. The basement in the summerhouse was a bit too cozy and since we will be storing the garden tables and chairs there, it may not be the right atmosphere for our guests in the event of an emergency."

Lucy joined Unger on the topic. "Actually, you are correct. We are planning to outfit the room with emergency, battery-powered lighting, and the door is an extra heavy-duty steel door with a heavy iron deadbolt to secure it. The bolt can be opened from either side of the door so it won't trap anyone inside, but it should keep the door closed due to air pressure changes during a tornado event. In the corner closet we will keep a battery-powered radio, a case of those emergency space blankets and bottled water, and also candles, matches, and extra batteries for the emergency lights."

Unger shook my hand and thanked Lucy and me for being so thorough. We continued the tour, and when we reached the housekeeper's suite, Bea was conspicuously hushed. I showed the group the walk-in closet, the bathroom—complete with a Jacuzzi tub and separate shower with an upgraded rain-style showerhead. In the lower level of the east turret was the lovely little kitchenette and living room. I heard pleasant *oohs* and *ahs* from the team. I led them to the entry of the attached double garage where the two of the fleet vehicles were parked. They all walked around the

PT Cruiser and the cargo van, admiring the Goldstone logos that were painted on the vehicles. Bea wandered slowly around the room, gently touching the tiles in the bathroom, gazing out the triple-paned windows and nodding as I described to her the heat pump that would allow her to have the rooms as warm or cool as she desired.

Gianna asked about the large rectangle marked off with blue painters tape on the floor near the kitchenette. Lucy explained, "Your mother has a couple of big, old, marble-topped lab cabinets that she wanted to bring here. She'll keep one here in her suite, but the other will be used in the entry of the inn as the guest reservation desk and will double as a bar during parties. This taped-off section shows where that will go when we get it moved in."

Gianna said, "Oh yes, I'm happy that those aren't being sold with the house. I remember when I was a child that my father brought those home from the college when they remodeled the chemistry lab. They were scarred and chipped, but Daddy spent hours and hours in his workshop stripping, bleaching, and sanding the wood and then putting on the lovely new finish. It will be nice to have those pieces of home here at the inn." She gave her mom a little hug; her mom still not said a word.

Finally, I couldn't take the silence any longer and asked her point blank, "Are you upset with the suite?"

With tears in her eyes, she answered, "No, not upset, but overwhelmed with the beauty. I would have been satisfied with a tiny room and a simple bathroom. I can tell, though, that there was great care and thought put into the design of my rooms. And, Jedidiah, it looks finished; the painted walls are perfect. I'm surprised; you said that the painters had been reassigned, so I wasn't expecting the suite to be done."

"Yes, I admit I was a little devious," I replied. "I wanted to surprise you with the completed room, so I did mislead you a bit. But Lucy assured me that these colors were what you had requested. Did we get it right?"

"Absolutely perfect; I'd asked for a smoky sage green in the bedroom and a cheery sunny peach color in the rest of the suite. The paint colors are gorgeous, and the window shades and drapes are so much more than I expected. In fact, I never expected so much space." She turned around and returned to the bedroom and loudly declared, "The ceiling in here is my utter favorite. I've never seen anything like this before. It's like looking through a huge glass ceiling."

Lucy spoke up, explaining, "I got the idea when I went to the doctor a couple of months ago for a check-up. I asked how they made the ceiling look like a beautiful sky, and the nurse hooked me up with the catalog where I could order the panels. They are called sky ceiling light diffuser panels. We actually have them for the other three bedrooms on the lower level too, and a couple of the bathrooms upstairs that don't have windows in them. So you like this one? I thought that this one with the pink flowering tree hanging over added a bit of a feminine touch."

"Oh yes," Bea responded. "Every morning I will get to wake up to a lovely spring day. You know, with all of this special attention, I'm kind of feeling like a house mother, and I can tell you all that I am looking forward to mothering all of you."

Gianna stepped forward and hugged her mother. She took a step back and said, "Mother, you are worth all of this and more. And this team of people will be very fortunate to have you mothering them; you are the best! I'm looking forward to being able to spend more time with you. For years now I've dreamed of being closer to you, and now we finally have that opportunity. God is good, and I count myself very lucky to have been handed this chance to work with this awesome team."

Lucy edged her way so that she stood front and center and said, "I agree with Gianna, God is good, but it's more than good luck. God has blessed us, and I would like to ask for God's blessing today as we move forward and begin this venture. Would you all join me in prayer?"

Circling around the perimeter of the turret, we joined hands, bowed our heads, and Lucy prayed, "Father, great and almighty, thank you for all of our blessings. You are the most holy and deserve our honor. We are gathered here today, relishing in our good fortune to have been chosen by you to be your blessed children. Help us to do good work and to always focus on love— your love, the love of our beloved couples whom we will be helping to begin their married lives together and the love for one another. You have commanded us to love each other. Help us to always focus on you, God, and remember that our dreams are yours too. In Jesus' name I pray, Amen."

I interrupted before the group moved out and said, "Bea, your suite is one hundred percent complete, so you can move in anytime. Lucy told me that your house sold this week, so whenever you are ready, just let me know, and we'll be there to move you, okay?"

With tears brimming from her gray eyes, Bea Butler said, "It's going to be bittersweet moving; I'm leaving my home behind that I shared with Efram for almost three decades. We had so many memories made in that house and raised our five daughters there, but I'm going to love living here. Jedidiah, I will take you up on your offer to help me. Thank you all!"

Later, after completing the tour of the rest of the property, and a subsequent short break, the team gathered in the summerhouse. Lucy opened the meeting of the team by saying, "I've been thinking a lot about dreams lately. I wanted to share with you the dream that I initially had regarding these gold stones."

She opened up a photo album and unsnapped the three rings holding the pages together, removing the front page. She gazed at it lovingly and passed it to her right, asking Lael to pass the photo page around the room. "I found this old barn in Whitney—the mortar was cracked, there were broken windows, the roof had holes in it, and there were bats living in the rafters. But I started dreaming about a way to resurrect the structure and to make it livable. All I wanted initially was to make it into a home with an art studio on the top floor. I found myself doing research about rebuilding stone barns, and I said prayers to God asking for direction.

"I did not dream about beginning such a magnanimous venture as this wedding-planning business, or even an inn, until many months later when I received notice of my inheritance. I guess what I'm trying to say is, dream, just dream! Everybody should have dreams and ask God to help you fulfill your dreams. Only with his help can you achieve momentous, fabulous, even stupendous dreams. God wants to give you all anything that you can dream about. I guess you could say this is my *I Have a Dream* speech, but because I am your leader, I want you all to be happy here at Goldstone. If there is ever anything that you would like to change or do differently, please come to me or someone else on the team and we can discuss it.

"My way of thinking is that Goldstone is only a building, well, actually several buildings now, but rock and mortar and wood, just a place for us to become all that we can be. I'm not your conventional, stuffed-shirt businesswoman, and we probably will never have the structure that a Fortune 500 corporation could relate to, but I want to see us as successful and fulfilled business people.

"Now, I think I'll step off of my high horse and let us start by looking over the brochures."

LUCY

September flew by, and I praised God daily; the carpenters, electricians, plumbers, and roofers finished closing in the cottages by mid-October, making way for the drywallers. The painters returned to the inn after painting the apartments.

The walls on the main floor of the inn were enhanced with moldings, creating a mock-wainscot complete with a wide chair rail. The paint on both the walls and moldings was monotone—a soft golden tan. The light in the room bounced off of the walls, making it look sunny even on dreary rainy afternoons.

The walls in the guest rooms were unique in each of the rooms. I had attempted to pick out colors that would reflect light and give the impression that the rooms were larger. We'd be able to accommodate most of the wedding party with private rooms, each with their own bathrooms. In the rooms large enough to allow it, I had purchased a trundle or a sleeper sofa so that families with children could be comfortable in a room together. There were also two pairs of rooms that had adjoining doors.

Bea had moved into her suite long before the rest of the inn was completed. I had wondered if she would be spooked, being alone in the big building all alone after the workmen went home for the day, but she assured me that she was used to living alone in a large house. "Besides," she said, "I'm really looking forward to getting to know this house well, and I think it will be exciting to be able to wander around in the evenings and see what has been accomplished during the day. I'll be available to help out with the construction cleanup too. You'll need help with hanging draperies and dressing the rooms; I hope you will let me assist you."

"Certainly," I replied. "I think it will be fun to work side by side putting the finishing touches on the inn."

Holly was diligently setting up the flower shop with the assistance of Les and Jeff Braun. I think that they were both a little sweet on the cute little Asian florist. She was a pretty, petite woman with long black hair, pearly white complexion, and always a big smile on her face. Holly had drawn a crude sketch showing where she wanted the workroom to be, design table, shelves, and cubbies for supplies, and a pegboard hanging on the wall to organize her tools. The showroom included a conference table where Holly would meet with customers, and of course, a counter with a tiny cash register too. We had decided that there was no reason she couldn't have a small retail business as well, as long as she focused primarily on the wedding business. It would be nice for the local citizens to have a local florist.

She had a large cooler in the back and a smaller one in the front showroom to display bouquets for retail sale. The Brauns had created a small office tucked in close to the stairway that connected the shop to the upstairs apartment. There was also an exterior staircase so that her guests would be able visit her without going through the shop.

Holly had also been very busy in the greenhouse, planting a perennial garden, and most recently, she'd been planting roses near the windows in the sunroom. She was planning to grow some of her own flowers and to have a lot of large green plants like ferns, azaleas, and miniature roses. She was still living with her grandmother, but the time was nearing when she'd be able to move into her apartment over the flower shop.

Shelby had also moved to Goldstone, living in the Winnebago since mid-September. She'd been getting her studio set up with the assistance of Karl Schmidt. Karl was the rude waiter Jedidiah and I had encountered several months ago; his father had directed him our way shortly after that and he'd been a big asset to the construction crew. Shelby seemed to be enjoying his company too. She was also very helpful with the move-in of the furnishings in the inn once the painters had finished.

In fact, all of the team was helpful setting up the beds, moving in the dressers, sleeper sofas, and hanging the artwork. We had three wedding consults the second week of October. The conference room was complete by then, and we gave tours to the brides, the mothers-of-the-bride, and two of the grooms; the third was living in Chicago and would only be arriving the week of the wedding. These were the weddings that were scheduled for New Year's Eve, New Year's Day, and January fourteenth; the first one was for Lila Penrose, the friendly and helpful gal from Tile-O-Ramma. We also had three wedding dates blocked out for February—one for Valentine's Day and another for the Saturday before and the Saturday after.

The mayor had eagerly been watching our progress because he had scheduled a party with us to celebrate his twenty-fifth wedding anniversary. Harvey said that he and Mrs. Coldwater wanted to be our very first customers, and if we were ready to accommodate them, their party would be on November eleventh. He wanted a very elaborate shindig, a ceremony reenactment, a dinner, wedding cake, and a dance. He also had booked the honeymoon suite and six other rooms for his children and grandchildren. The other two rooms on the upper level were also booked by out-of-town guests that would be at the party. Mrs. Coldwater had worked with Holly, ordering several large floral arrangements, as well as a duplicate of her bridal bouquet that would have gardenias and yellow roses, accented with verbena. There were also low table arrangements ordered that would be created with more gardenias and yellow roses.

Shelby had taken formal portraits of them, using the lower level of the inn as a temporary studio because the cottage that housed the photography studio was not completed just yet on the date that they had arranged for the sitting. Shelby had made a hundred four-by-six-inch prints that the couple had inserted into invitations; it seemed that they had invited half of the town to their party. Unger was giddy with anticipation; the Coldwaters requested a formal dinner with elaborate food choices, starting with giant mushroom caps stuffed with chopped bacon, sun-dried tomatoes, and feta cheese. The entrée was a sophisticated version of beef stroganoff, which was Harvey's favorite food. I wasn't sure what the salad choice had finally ended up being, but on the Thursday before the party I had seen several large pumpkins in the caterer's kitchen, so I believe that they had agreed on either pumpkin pie or pumpkin soup.

Quite upsetting to me, though, I missed the party. I had come down with a bad cold about the first of November, and I just couldn't kick it. I kept pushing myself, trying to get everything just right, setting up furniture and hanging the window shades and draperies. I had a great team assembled, and they all pitched in and helped. Finally, on that Thursday before the Coldwater party, when Unger saw me in his kitchen, he joined forces with Gianna, and together, the two of them convinced me to go home, take a hot bath, and go to bed early. In fact, Unger nearly carried me to his van, plopped me in the seat, and drove me to my house.

I think he would have undressed me and helped me into the bath, but I had enough energy left to convince him I could do it on my own. When I came out of the bathroom, wearing my warmest flannel pajamas and snuggled into my heaviest robe, he was waiting for me in my bedroom with a cup of steaming chicken noodle soup, with a double shot of Drambuie. He stayed with me, making sure I finished both the soup and the whiskey, and then he tucked me into bed. "I'll check on you in the morning, and I'll tell Jedidiah that he should probably pop in this evening to make sure you're okay," he said before he left.

It wasn't long before I fell fast asleep, and if Jedidiah popped in, I was not aware of it. I slept soundly for fifteen hours, only waking the next morning when my feline roommate started his hunger march across my chest. I slowly crawled out of bed, used the bathroom, and shuffled into the kitchen to feed the cat.

But when I saw the light on in the kitchen, I was startled! Unger was in my kitchen and seemed to be cooking. My mind was fuzzy, confused, and not able to decipher the reason that Unger was cooking in my kitchen. That's when I started coughing and coughing and coughing some more. I sat down clumsily into a dining room chair, but I couldn't seem to quit hacking. It was a deep, painful cough; my throat felt raw and my chest hurt with each hack. I was also very warm but clammy feeling, so I knew I must have a fever. Unger brought me a cup of warm milk and encouraged me to drink it. The milk soothed my throat a bit, and the coughing eased momentarily, but when I tried to speak, I started coughing again.

Unger helped me back to bed, found some Nyquil in my medicine cabinet, poured some in the little plastic cup that sat atop the lid, and watched as I drank it all down.

The thick green liquid had a calming effect, and I was able to settle the cough down again, huddled under several layers of blankets. This was the routine I kept up for three days, with Gianna, Lael, and Jedidiah taking turns checking on me and bringing me hot liquids, Nyquil, or whiskey shots. Finally, Sunday evening when I woke up, I discovered that I was alone and decided a hot bath would feel wonderful.

I let the water run until it was as high as the back-fill drain, and then I slid down below the layer of bubbles to soak. A short time later, perhaps ten minutes or so because the water was still warm, I woke from my relaxed stupor and discovered my fiancé sitting on the edge of the tub. When I opened my eyes he asked, "Are you feeling better?"

"I think so," I answered softly and cautiously. "I haven't coughed once since I've been up, and I'm feeling human again."

Then, trying to be humorous, I added, "At least I feel human enough to take a bath. I'm also feeling pretty hungry."

"Do you feel up to some leftover beef stroganoff? There was a little left in the kitchen last night after the mayor's party. It was delicious, and I felt certain you would like to try it."

"Oh, no," I moaned. "I missed Harvey's party? I hope he wasn't slighted."

"No, not at all. We told him about your bronchitis, and he was very understanding. In fact, he made sure that I bring you one of the gardenia bouquets. Did you notice it on your bedside table?"

I admitted that I must have overlooked it, and then I added, "I would like a bit of that stroganoff."

So Jedidiah stayed with me for several hours, sharing the leftovers with me and describing the party that I had missed.

LUCY

As soon as I felt fully recovered, I started planning my huge Thanksgiving dinner. Only Jedidiah and I knew that it was also our engagement party. I was thrilled that both of my children were flying into Kansas City on Tuesday before the holiday, and they were both staying for a week, so we'd have a good long visit at last. Nester and Unger volunteered to go pick them up at the airport, actually going to Kansas City the night before so they could go out to dinner with some old friends while they were in the neighborhood.

Jude's plane was due to land at ten thirty, and Jade's was an hour and a half later. They had all met each other at the Fourth of July picnic; my twins had seemed to form a special bond with the couple. Jude always has seemed to seek out anyone who may be an underdog, or at least the odd man out, not that either Unger or Nester were odd, but a large black gay man and his white Russian lover were something of an oddity in Whitney, Kansas. Jade has always been easily influenced by her brother, and since Jude had befriended the couple, it followed that Jade would too.

But the anticipated reunion at the airport turned sour when Jude did not disembark from his plane. He was supposed to be on the Southwest flight number 1212; Unger and Nester watched keenly while all of the passengers got off of the plane and walked through the door at the mouth of the Jetway. Impatient to see their little friend, they kidded one another, betting that Jude would be the last off when he didn't show up right away. Alarmingly, though, he wasn't the last off; the crew was the last that came through the door—two stewardesses wearing trim, navy blue suits and a pilot in a white shirt and black pants—who were all pulling their rolling luggage. Unger got their attention and asked, "Is there still another passenger onboard? Our friend was supposed to be on your flight, and he didn't get off."

They gave the men a puzzled look and then assured them that the passengers had all gotten off of the plane. They led the worried men to the customer service desk, explained the dilemma to the agent, and waited with them while they searched the roster of customer names who'd flown with them. Jude's name was missing. And when they researched it a bit more, they discovered that he had been a no-show at the Las Vegas departure. Unger reported to us later that the Southwest personnel had all been very kind and helpful, but nevertheless, they weren't able to help locate my son.

My daughter's plane landed a few minutes before noon, and when Nester and Unger explained the situation to Jade, she started crying. She said she'd had a bad feeling that there was something wrong. Jude was supposed to call her the night before their flight, and he hadn't called. She said she'd tried to call him, but Jude's roommate at the missionary dormitory had answered the phone, telling her he hadn't seen Jude for two days. He claimed he didn't know where he was, but Jade thought he was lying.

Unger called me with his cell phone from the airport, filled me in on the problem, and asked me what to do. I told them to sit tight, maybe get some lunch at the airport, and call me back in about thirty minutes. I planned to call the YWAM base office and see if I could figure out what was going on.

It took me a little rifling through papers to locate Jude's last newsletter that was on the YWAM stationery. As I'd hoped, the base office phone number was listed, so I called the number. A young woman answered and I asked to talk to the director. She was a good gatekeeper, not putting me directly in touch with him, but after a bit of frantic explanation, she transferred me to Tom Southwick, the YWAM Las Vegas Director.

First, I identified myself as Jude King's mother, telling him, "I'm worried about my son. He was supposed to be on the flight to Kansas City this morning, and he was missing. Can you tell me where he is?"

Tom Southwick was a slick talker, one of those who tries to calm situations with a soothing voice and charm. "Now, Mrs. Golden, I'm sure the boy is fine. He probably just missed his airplane and will be on the next one. I'm sure there is no need to be alarmed."

"But he did not call his sister last night as he promised, and his roommate seems to know something he's not telling. My daughter called their room last night and she said he sounded like he was lying when he said he didn't know where Jude was. Can you talk to the roommate and get him to be straight with you?"

"Well, ma'am, I can assure you that Jimmy is a fine boy and he's not prone to lying. Like I said, I'm sure there is nothing wrong. But if it will make you feel better, I'll go speak with him and give you a call back."

"How about you put me on hold, go talk to him right now, and come right back and tell me what's going on? I don't have a good feeling about this situation," I asserted.

"Okay, it's your dime," he said sassily, losing a bit of his smooth talking. "I'll be back on the line in a few minutes."

When he put me on hold, the line was silent; none of that canned music assaulted my ears. I was calling with my cordless phone, so I was able to pace while waiting for Southwick to return. Unger must have called Jedidiah, because he suddenly bolted through my front door, moving faster than I'd ever seen him move before. "Lucy, are you all right? Have you found Jude?"

"No," I said. "I'm not all right, and no I haven't found my son yet. I'm on hold with the director of the missionary training facility, waiting for him to ask Jude's roommate for help."

Just then, Tom Southwick returned, saying, a little less calmly, "Ma'am, it appears we might have a situation here."

"What do you mean, a situation?" I countered.

"I don't want to alarm you, but Jimmy just told me that Jude went into the tunnels Sunday to give his possessions away to the homeless people that live there."

"What? I don't understand," I said abruptly.

"Jimmy says that since Jude was leaving and going home, he decided it'd be better to give away everything except one change of clothes, his Bible, and his guitar, rather than have to buy luggage to pack it in to fly home. There are flood tunnels under the city that are meant to control the heavy rainwater when it comes during the winter, but there are several hundred, maybe thousands, of homeless people who live in the tunnels during the dry season.

"Thankfully, the weather has been dry so far this fall, so the people have not had to move out yet, but Jude wanted them to have his clothes and bedding, even his bicycle so that he didn't have to deal with bringing it all home."

"So what you're saying is that my son disappeared two mornings ago to go into the dangerous tunnels with the homeless people? Has anyone tried to find him?"

"Well, no, ma'am, we just now discovered that he is missing. I'm sure we can get the police to go find him right away and everything will be just fine. No need to worry," Tom Southwick answered.

"No need to worry," I yelled into the phone. "No need to worry! My son is missing, and with drug addicts or worse, and you don't think I need to worry?"

"Ma'am, please calm down."

"I don't think calm is the correct reaction to the situation, Mister Southwick," I taunted, drawing out his name into long syllables. "I'll be getting on the next plane to Las Vegas, Mister Southwick," I said, repeating his name in the same extended version. "And when I get there, I'm going to find my son. And after I find him, I plan to meet with you and show you what I think of your rinky-dink operation there in Las Vegas. I can't believe that you don't take some security measures; you're in one of the ten worst neighborhoods in the whole country, and you seem to think there is nothing to worry about! You yank young men and women into your clutches, throw them out into the streets with the scum of the earth, and just remain calm while they get themselves into situations that they don't know how to get out of. Do you even give your trainees any defense training, Mister Southwick? Do you ever think that a lot of the people they are confronting out there on the street don't want to be taunted by a young kid preaching to them? Huh? Do you ever think about how crazy it is to send these young people out into the world of sin in Las Vegas armed only with a Bible?"

"Mrs. Golden, I hope you realize that the best armor anyone can have is a Bible," Southwick replied.

"I know how valuable the Bible is, Mr. Southwick, but I also think you are very naïve if you think it is sufficient defense against drug addicts and prostitutes and the rest of the trash that breeds in Vegas. A Bible cannot stop a bullet or a hypodermic needle, so you'd better be praying very hard and fast that my son has not come up against any real danger in those tunnels under your crazy little Sin City."

My blood pressure was reeling! Jedidiah took the phone from me, introduced himself to Southwick as my fiancé, and told him we'd be arriving just as soon as we could get a flight. He added, "You'd better be available when we get there, because we will have a lot more questions for you when we arrive. I'll call you back with our expected arrival time. Good-bye for now."

LUCY

Jedidiah and I had quickly gathered up a few things—some bottled water, the cell phone charger, a recent photo of Jude, and a coat—and after putting out some cat food for Jethro, we drove to Kansas City. I called Unger back from the car on my cell phone. Nester had a friend who owned a small passenger plane, so he was making arrangements with him to fly us to Vegas. Jedidiah was driving the PT Cruiser; it was the vehicle that had been sitting in the driveway.

I was anxious and kept looking at the speedometer. "Can't we go any faster?"

"I'm driving the speed limit, and we'll get there safely," my fiancé assured me patiently.

Two and a half hours later we parked in the garage at the airport and raced inside to find Jade and her companions. We found them just inside the door, sitting in the hallway. I gathered my weepy daughter into my arms for a big bear hug. Nester introduced us to the young man who was with them, Graham Sealove. He told me that Graham's plane was ready to go and if we were ready, we could get going. The five of us followed Graham, quickly passing through the preferred traveler section of security, only showing them our IDs. With very minimal luggage, we made it to the plane that was waiting in less than five minutes.

Once onboard, Graham explained, "This is a Lear 60, and we should be able to get to Vegas in a little over three hours. Please get comfortable and relax and help yourself to drinks and snacks in the galley." Jade took the initiative to explore the refreshments in the galley, and she put an assortment of the snacks on a tray. She offered her tray to everyone, and then unexpectedly, when Graham asked her to join him in the cockpit, she sat in the co-pilot seat. They were talking animatedly the whole flight, but I could only watch them through the open curtain; the engine sounds were too loud to overhear what they were saying. I searched through my purse and found a small New Testament that I kept in there and started reading. I wasn't comprehending the words at first, but I kept reading and flipping the tiny pages. I came to the section in the book of Matthew where Jesus calmed the stormy seas. He drove evil spirits out of men possessed by demons, and he healed a paraplegic, telling the man to *Get up and walk*. In later verses, he was with Matthew eating supper, and Jesus explained to his companion that he was about mercy, to invite outsiders into his mercy, not to coddle the insiders.

It dawned on me then that that was what my big-hearted son was doing too. He was showing mercy to the people who lived on the outside and trying to emulate Jesus's love. I continued to read the small Bible, and like often happens when I read, I fell asleep. I woke up when I felt the jolt of the wheels setting down on the runway at Vegas. Jedidiah, who was sitting next to me, reached out and took my hand. "We are here, my love. It won't be long now. I'm sure we'll find Jude."

As we taxied to the gate, Graham spoke to us over the public address system, "I have a vehicle waiting for us, and I'll join you on our quest. I've done these sorts of missions of mercy before, and I'm pleased to be able to help find Jude."

I didn't really understand the importance of what he was saying, but after we left the plane and waited for him to finish his paperwork and make arrangements for his plane, Jade explained to me what she had found out about Graham Sealove.

"Mom," she said, "Graham runs a charitable organization called Sealove, Be Love. He has this airplane, and also a helicopter, and lots of contacts around the world so that he can go wherever he is needed to help find missing people. He's helped out during floods and hurricanes to find people, flying overhead to find people who were stranded on their rooftops or on small hills that the water hadn't covered yet. And when Hurricane Katrina hit, he was on the job, helping to rescue hundreds of people.

"And Mom, he lives in Hannibal, just a few blocks away from me. He says he's not home very much, but when he is there he says he loves the little town, the peace and quiet that is the opposite of disaster scenes. He even implied that when this is over he wants to take me out on a date! How's that?"

"Wow, sweetie, it seems we have the Lone Ranger on our team. That makes me feel a little better, and even though I don't know him very well, it sounds like he'd be a very good potential date for you. Maybe you could even help him out with some of his rescue missions."

"That's exactly what I was thinking. He said it gets lonely sometimes because he is gone for long lengths of time. His only living relative, other than a couple of sisters, is a great aunt who lives in his family's large home in Hannibal with him; in fact, she's a granddaughter of the Lear guy who founded the Lear Jet company." Jade continued singing accolades about Graham. "And he's cute too, don't you think so?"

Graham was a little taller than my daughter, probably about six feet tall. He was thin, had curly brown hair, and sky blue eyes that seemed to sparkle. I agreed that he was cute, just as he joined our group, coming up behind Jade and placing a hand on the small of her back.

"Okay," he said, "looks like we are ready to go. There is a small Winnebago out in front that will be our ride and home away from home until we can locate Jude."

LUCY

Graham continued in his role as navigator, and he drove us immediately to the YWAM Center. Jedidiah had called Tom Southwick and announced our arrival at the airport; he was expecting us and had Jimmy in his office with him. We all crowded into the office together, and, perhaps feeling a bit overwhelmed, Tom suggested we move to the dining hall where we'd have more room.

I demanded, "Just tell us where my son is!"

But Jedidiah led me through the doorway, following the rest of the group.

"Now," Tom began in his infuriating calm tone once we were all seated on the cold benches of a folding metal lunchroom table. "We don't exactly know where Jude is, but we do know that Jesus is watching over him, so he is most assuredly safe."

I interrupted, "Jimmy, what can you tell us about this?"

Jimmy, looking very nervous, with beads of sweat on his brow that caused his long blond bangs to stick to his pale and pimpled forehead, stammered, "I don't know for sure where he is, but I went with him last week to a place under Caesar's Palace where you can enter the flood tunnels. Some of the local artists have been working on a mural on the wall there at the mouth of the tunnel. I'm pretty sure Jude has been helping out with that, so that would be my best guess as to where to start looking for him."

Jedidiah posed the question, "Has anyone gone there to see if they can find him?"

"Well no," Tom uttered. "Most of our team is gone this week on an outreach mission. Jimmy stayed behind because he had the flu, so there really wasn't anyone to send down there."

Nester piped up with, "You mean to say that you haven't gone there yourself and looked? Weren't you at least a little curious to see if the boy was laying there hurt or needed help right there at that place? What kind of a mentor are you for these kids if you can't step out and do at least that?" Nester's voice was rising, and at that moment, he reminded me of Mr. T from the old A-Team TV show. He was getting in the face of Tom, and without physically poking him or even touching him, I could see that Tom was a bit scared of the large black man.

Nester demanded, "Have you at least called the police?"

Tom answered meekly, "No, but I've heard that the police won't go into the tunnels. The people who live there don't hurt anyone or anything; they keep to themselves for the most part, so the cops don't want to rile them up."

Nester exploded, "Rile them up, rile them up you say..."

Graham moved forward, and, seizing control of the situation, he said, "I think what we need to do is get in the motor home and head to Caesar's Palace. Jimmy and Tom, would you like to join us, or would you feel more comfortable leading us in your own vehicle."

Tom pulled some keys out of his pocket and agreed to lead the way in his van.

Ten minutes later we were parking at the back of the huge parking lot near the ornate casino known as Caesar's Palace. Nester was holding something that looked like a weapon. I knew he'd purchased a large duffel bag at the KC airport, and he'd stuffed it with airport purchases such as T-shirts, sport socks, baggy sports shorts, travel-size toothbrushes, ball caps, and sunglasses. He had explained this when I gave him a curious look as we passed through security at the Kansas City airport. He'd said he knew we wouldn't take time to pack, and since he had time wasting at the airport, he did a little shopping so that we'd all have a few necessities if our trip turned into a several-day wait.

But when I saw him bouncing the rod off of his leg, I asked, curious if he'd been able to buy such a thing at the airport.

"No," he answered. "It's just an old length of copper pipe that I found laying in the lot at the YWAM Center. I thought it might come in handy, so I picked it up."

Graham passed out large flashlights to everyone, explaining that he had a contact in Vegas who had rented the RV for him and stocked it to his order. He asked us all to put on our jackets or coats and to tuck our pant legs inside our socks; he cautioned us to stick together. Nester handed each of us a white ball cap too; they sported the blue Kansas City Royals logo. He led the way, holding Jade's hand. She had always been timid, so I was bewildered to see her bravely walking into the dark tunnel holding this young man's hand.

At the mouth of the tunnel there was indeed a boldly painted mural. The words *Jesus Loves You* were centered, with psychedelic greens, yellows, pinks, and oranges circling the words. Flowers, musical instruments, smiling faces, and peace signs decorated the concrete wall; it was an awesome masterpiece, and it indeed looked like artwork that Jude would have a hand in creating.

Jedidiah and I followed Graham and Jade, with Tom and Jimmy behind us and Unger and Nester behind them. I wasn't sure if Tom and Jimmy would have joined us in the tunnel, but Nester seemed to intimidate them, bouncing the pipe alternately off his thigh and the wall of the tunnel.

It was utterly dark, damp, and quiet, other than the rhythmic bang of the pipe against the wall. The air was fetid, with horrible odors of human waste and rotting garbage. We walked slowly, close together, walking nearly five minutes before we saw any sign of human life. There was a makeshift room half-blocking the tunnel; it had low walls of cardboard. Looking over the walls, we peered inside, seeing a cot, a hotplate on an orange milk crate with a long orange extension cord, a sleeping bag rolled up and tied inside a clear trash-bag. There was also a suitcase that was zipped shut, but this *room* was empty of human life. We did spy a scorpion and a spider crawling on the cot, but nothing else. I shuddered, and Graham urged us forward.

As we continued deeper into the tunnel we saw three more rooms cordoned off with makeshift materials. One was outlined with wooden pallets on end, tied together with twine. Another demarked with lengths of black plastic attached to stanchions with gray duct tape. Considering that it was nearly dark outside, I was curious that none of the residents so far seemed to be home.

We'd been walking about thirty minutes when we saw the first people. There were two men lying together, both of them unmoving and lying on old couches that were pushed together to form one large bed. Graham bravely reached forward to touch them, and, feeling for a pulse, he said they were alive. He pointed out the hypodermic needles laying close to their bodies and said that most likely they were in a drugged stupor.

We could hear someone moaning or crying just a bit farther into the tunnel, so we kept going. We came upon a black woman who was in much the same condition as the other two men, passed out on a cot. But she was not alone; there was a man sitting in a metal folding chair, with a dirty length of Berber carpet pulled around his shoulders. In his lap was a young child, the source of the crying. I couldn't tell if it was a boy or girl, but the child looked to be about three or four years old. The man was lackadaisically trying to comfort the little child.

Graham spoke to the man, but the man did not acknowledge us at all. He continued to stare into space and rock the little child on his lap. One of the flashlights lit up the man's face, and I could see that his eyes had the milky, glassed-over appearance of the blind, and since he did not flinch or move at all as we approached and made noise, it was clear that he was deaf as well as blind.

At that point, I could see that Jade was wilting. She clung to Graham's arm, and there were tears streaming down her face. Graham quietly motioned us to turn around, and when we were out of range of the little disturbing family, he said, "I think we should retreat for now. We need to regroup and possibly get more help."

We all were troubled by what we had seen, and nobody talked as we returned to the mouth of the tunnel with the wall that reminded us that Jesus loves us. Outside in the fresh warm air, Graham said, "I think we've had enough of the tunnels tonight. Maybe we should go to the police station and file a formal missing persons complaint." We mutely agreed and marched toward the RV. Tom and Jimmy slipped away unnoticed, and when I saw them driving away, my first thought was, *good riddance*, but I chided myself for my thoughts. They were only human too, and it had been a horrific experience traversing that tunnel for nearly an hour. God knows I'd rather be anywhere else than searching through the maze of storm tunnels for my lost son.

At the Las Vegas Police Department, the desk sergeant was kind and helpful, and he was impressed with Graham's presence. It seemed that Sergeant O'Bryan was familiar with Sealove, Be Love, and he was awed to be included in a rescue mission led by Graham Sealove. He helped us fill out the proper forms, and when he asked for a photo of Jude, I handed him the one we'd picked up right before leaving home. O'Bryan made several copies of it on a color copier that was near his desk before returning the original to me. I held the photo lovingly, looking at the likeness of my son through puddles of tears.

With a distressed but listless expression and tone, he explained what we were up against. "The tunnels are very dangerous places. There are a lot of indigents who live in them, and they do not like to be disturbed. They create havens to escape to, and in their minds they are safe from the outside world. They don't focus on the dangers of the tunnels, black widow spiders, rats, drug addicts, and criminals, or the worst fear of all, floods.

"You see, the tunnel system is built to carry away the heavy rain water that comes most of the time in the fall and winter seasons to Las Vegas. With all of the miles and miles of concrete that there is in Vegas, there's no place for the water to soak into; it all flows down into the series of tunnels via the storm drains. There's a maze of hundreds of miles of storm tunnels under Vegas, and who knows how many people live there. Every year we have a couple hundred deaths due to drowning in this city. The vast majority of them die when the rains come and the tunnels fill with water."

It was then that I remembered seeing storm clouds in the distance across the desert when we came out of the tunnel. I think I even saw some lightning. I asked the sergeant, "Is there rain forecasted for here tonight? I saw some clouds and lightning."

"Thankfully, we have that in our favor," he answered. "Those clouds are way off in the desert, and the prediction is that they are moving away from the city. We aren't expecting any rain here till the weekend." He stood up and said, "If you'll excuse me, we have a shift change going on, so I'll go back behind where they are having their duty assignment meeting and announce to them our concerns for your boy. It's my guess that they will at least do some extra patrolling at the mouths of the tunnels and talk to some of their snitches to see if we can get some more information."

Unger, who'd been largely silent for most of this affair, waited for O'Bryan to leave, and then he said, "I think a group hug and then some prayers are in order." Looking around the group, he spread his large arms and gathered us all together. We joined together, putting our arms around one another's shoulders or waists, and there in the police station in our football huddle, Unger started praying. He asked God to keep Jude safe wherever he was, to help him to keep the faith, and to send him the message that we were going to find him. Unger continued his lament, asking God to keep all of us who are present safe, to ward off the spiders, rats, and other vermin that we might encounter while in Las Vegas, and to help us return to our homes as a complete family unit. He ended by saying, "God, you are the most high heavenly father. We love you, we respect you, and we ask for your favor and mercy. Help us to learn from this situation and to remember that we are on this planet to love and help our fellow man. Amen."

It was Graham who continued the prayer, leading us all in the Lord's Prayer. And upon finishing the final amen, we dried our tears and saw that Sergeant O'Bryan had returned. He assured us that the police would be doing everything they could possibly do to find Jude. He asked us what our plans were for the night, and when Graham explained that we had a motor home that we had at our disposal, the Sergeant wisely said, "That might be kind of tight quarters for all six of you. Why don't you get a room and let us do our job tonight. Come back in the morning, and we'll fill you in on what we have discovered. Hopefully we can find him tonight and get you all home by Thanksgiving."

I had forgotten that the holiday was only a little more than a day away by now. But we agreed to find rooms for the night. Graham drove us to the Alexis Suites and assured us that he'd stayed there before and it was quiet and comfortable. We booked two suites at the end of the hallway, each with two bedrooms. After Nester sorted through his large rolling duffel, he supplied us all with the basic necessities that he had purchased for us hours before at the KC airport.

Jedidiah, Jade, and I were in one suite, and Graham, Unger, and Nester were in the other one across the hall. Jade asked if it'd be okay if she had a room to herself. She said, "It's pretty obvious that you two want to be together, and I need to be alone tonight; I have a lot of thinking to do."

So Jedidiah and I showered and changed into clean T-shirts, socks, and baggy blue shorts. Just as I realized my stomach was growling and I hadn't eaten for hours, we heard commotion in the hallway. Jedidiah checked it out and found that there was a pizza delivery guy who had delivered us four large pizzas. Apparently, Graham's rescue experience had saved the day again; he had ordered for us all and he had kindly left the anchovies off the pizzas.

Everyone had had the same idea to shower immediately, to wash away the stench and memory of the journey in the tunnel. It was almost comical to see the group gathered together in our living room of the suite to eat pizza, everyone in matching blue Royals shorts, white tube socks, and black T shirts that sported pictures of Harley Davidsons. It seemed that there was a bit of an air of relief. Maybe it had been Sergeant O'Bryan's assuring tone that had put us at ease, but I believe it was the praying. There did seem to be some true hope that we would find Jude tomorrow.

LUCY

After a mostly sleepless night, the morning of the day before Thanksgiving arrived with rays of Vegas sunshine streaming in through the windows of the suite. Gathered once again in the living room of our suite, we prayed over the leftover pizza and ate our cold breakfast. Jedidiah made a pot of coffee with the small Mr. Coffee that was in the kitchenette. Everyone was wearing the matching Harley Davidson black shirts, blue shorts, white ball caps, and disconcerted expressions on our faces.

Graham, who was ever on his toes and very professional in his organizational skills, laid out the plan for the day. "I think we should start by getting some supplies. We'll need more drinking water, flashlight batteries, and maybe some rolls of colored tape. We can leave a trail showing where we've been so that, number one, we don't get lost, but number two, we don't need to waste time by going in circles. This is all assuming we are all going back down in the maze of tunnels, right?"

He looked us all pointedly in the eye and waited for each of the team members to agree that they were indeed planning to return to the tunnels.

"Okay, I think we should all have a backpack and be prepared with water, snacks, first-aid kits, and maybe some noisemakers.

Can you think of any particular noise, or perhaps a song that Jude would relate to, and if he would hear it he would know his family was there to rescue him?"

Jade and I looked intently at one another, trying to meld our minds together to answer Graham's question. Jade answered tentatively, "What about the Beatles song, *Hey Jude*? We used to sing it together all of the time, and you know how he loves the Beatles."

"I think you might be right, Jade," I agreed. "He loved that song, and also *Yellow Submarine*. What do you think, should we sing it repeatedly, or maybe play it on a Walkman or something?"

Graham explained, "I noticed that sound seemed to echo down in the tunnel, and I like the idea of us singing it better than playing it on a Walkman. It would make more of a personal connection with him if he heard your voices. I have a laptop in the other room. I can look up the words to both songs and get them printed off down at the front desk."

Jedidiah asked, "Don't you suppose we should go to the police station right away and see if they have any developments?"

"Yes, of course," was Graham's answer. "I think we want to get supplies first, though; I'd hate to be tempted to go down into those tunnels again without being prepared.

"One more question before we leave. What do you think; should we book these rooms another night? Because of the holiday we might have difficulty getting a room again if we let these slip through our fingers."

"Don't you think we'll find him today," I asked painfully.

Graham answered, "It's not so much that I don't think we'll find him, but even when we do, we'll want a place to come back to and get cleaned up and regroup. So unless there's any objection, I'll go down to the front desk to book the rooms for another night, and let's plan on leaving in about fifteen minutes. Everyone should probably be wearing those heavy tube socks too; we'll get some sweatpants when we stop for supplies. I noticed that there were black widow spiders everywhere. You don't want one of them crawling up inside your pant legs." With that word of warning, he left the room.

After fulfilling Graham's shopping list at Wal-Mart, we went to the police department. Sergeant O'Bryan wasn't at the front desk; instead we were met by Lieutenant Shoemaker, a tall, buxom, redheaded female officer wearing a very tight blue uniform shirt. But she was just as friendly and every bit as helpful as O'Bryan had been the night before.

She offered coffee and doughnuts to all of us and led us into a larger room with a table and about a dozen chairs. It reminded me of an interrogation room that I'd seen on *Law and Order*, but none of the walls was either windowed or mirrored, just all concrete blocks painted with high-gloss gray paint.

The lieutenant insisted we all sit down before she began her review of the case. She introduced herself as Salli Shoemaker. Since we were all eager to hear what she had to say, it didn't take long for the chairs to be pulled out and quickly sat upon.

She started, "As you may have already deduced, we have not yet found Jude." Turning toward me, she said, "I'm assuming you are his mother, right?" And then looking at Jade, who was again close to Graham, she queried, "And you must be his sister, Jade."

"Yes," I answered quickly, hoping she would get on with the report.

"I know this must be very difficult to have to experience the mystery of not knowing where your son, or brother, might be and if he is in any danger. So I'm just going to start reading through the report on the case, okay?"

She cleared her throat and began reading aloud. "Ten o'clock p.m. November 21, Officer Grady approached a male person leaving the tunnel near the Hard Rock Café. This male person, whom we will identify only as MP1, is a known informant for the PD and is known to live in the tunnel system beneath Las Vegas. MP1 was questioned regarding the disappearance of Jude King.

MP1 categorically denied any knowledge of the young man in question. However, when asked about the missing bicycle, he was more helpful. Jude King's bicycle had been described to the PD as one that was perhaps ten years old, with black and orange tiger-striped paint. The bicycle had a cartoon-personalized tag of sorts on the rear under the black banana seat; the tag had the likeness of the Kellogg's Tony the Tiger, and the word *Great!*

"After hearing the description of the bicycle, he responded affirmatively that he had seen the bicycle. MP1 told Officer Grady the name of the man who had the bike in the tunnel and gave the officer directions to find this man.

"Grady waited for backup." Looking up from the report, the lieutenant said, "It is our policy to never enter the tunnels alone."

Continuing with the report, she went on. "When Officer Christian arrived, they walked into the tunnel and, following MP1's instructions, located the bicycle and the man whom MP1 had called Running Bear.

"Running Bear was described as a young American Indian man, small bone structure, and five-foot-seven, weighing approximately one hundred and twenty pounds. His dark eyes were penetrating, clear, not glassed over, and alert; the man did not appear to be a drug user. When asked about the bicycle, he became vocally resistant but did not attempt to flee. With repeated questioning from the police officers, he admitted he had found the bicycle leaning against the wall under the 'Jesus Loves You' mural entrance of the tunnel near Caesar's Palace on Monday afternoon.

"He became tearful, with evident fear that he was in trouble. The officers conferred and decided it would be best if they insisted Running Bear come to the station for more questioning. He complied without resistance and only asked to take the bike with him. It was pushed out of the tunnel by Running Bear, and the officers put it in the trunk of the squad car. Running Bear was questioned again by another officer when he was brought in. He was treated with humane care, offered a hot shower, a hot meal, and clean clothes, all of which he initially refused.

"When another officer offered the same to him, this one a female officer, he agreed shyly, saying it had been several months since he'd had a real shower and a full meal had been even longer ago than that. The boy is still here, in fact, but he is sleeping in a small conference room. When his true identity was discovered, we found that he was a runaway sixteen-year-old from southern Missouri near Carthage.

"His real name is Matthias Greensborough, but he was our only lead to date on the efforts to locate your missing son, Mrs. Golden." Officer Shoemaker rose and walked to where I was sitting. Placing her hand gently on my shoulder, she said, "I'm so sorry that I don't have more to tell you. I do know that the officers on duty have again been filled in on every detail regarding Jude's disappearance. I feel very confident that he'll be sitting down to Thanksgiving dinner with you tomorrow." She paused, looked thoughtfully at us, and then continued. "So, will you be returning to the Alexis to wait for word?"

"No," I answered weakly. "We aren't going to sit and wait; we are going down into those tunnels ourselves, and we are going to find Jude."

"I can't advise you to do that," the redheaded officer said with alarm in her voice, her green eyes kindly trying to persuade me. "The tunnels can be dangerous, and if you are hurt in there, medical attention is very hard to provide in the tunnels. The EMTs don't like going into the tunnel system, and there is always the possibility of getting lost."

Jedidiah spoke. "We are aware of the danger, but we have to give it another try. We can't just let Jude remain lost in those tunnels without trying to find him."

Graham came forward and introduced himself to Officer Shoemaker. There were signs of recognition when he told her that Sealove, Be Love would be represented in the search, but she still was not convinced it was a good idea.

Graham asked, "If I could, I'd like to talk with the Greensborough boy. I've helped to return a lot of runaways to their families; I'd like to have the opportunity to help this boy too." Salli led Graham back to where the boy was resting, and he went into the room to talk to the boy alone.

While he was gone the team said little. Unger had a terrified look on his face; Nester just looked mad. Jade had her eyes closed, her head bowed, and her lips were moving in silent prayer. Jedidiah was holding my hand, and I was telling him a story about Jude when he was in elementary school. I'd helped him to construct a crude wooden cabinet for a school project when they were reading *The Indian in the Cupboard*. We had resorted to using a little duct tape to keep things in place. A few days later, Jude was evidently working on another project of his own, when he came to me, asking to borrow the goose tape. I had tried not to laugh at him at the time, because he was very serious, thinking that the tape was called goose tape. It helped to ease the ache in my heart a little to remember how sweet my little boy had always been, and throughout his life, he had always been the epitome of unguarded enthusiasm. Plus, foremost, he had God watching over him.

When Graham came back to where we were waiting, he only said he had a few phone calls to make.

Salli said, "Frankly, I know that you have a lot of experience, Mr. Sealove, with rescue missions, but I hesitate to think that you have ever experienced the likes of those flood tunnels before."

She sat silently for a few seconds, chewing on her bottom lip, and then said, "Oh heck, I can see that you are determined to do this, so if you can wait just fifteen minutes, my shift is ending and I'll go with you. I've been down there lots of times, so I know the layout of the cross-sections and the most dangerous spots."

I said with sincerity, "Officer Shoemaker, that would be greatly appreciated. I can't thank you enough for your offer to help."

"Think nothing of it, but you're all going to have to start calling me Salli. We've got a long day ahead of us, so we may as well be on a first-name basis. Why don't you all go out front and wait for me? I'll be out as soon as I can finish up here."

LUCY

It was indeed a blessing to have Salli Shoemaker with us on our second day in the flood tunnels. When we got to the tunnel entrance where we had entered the evening before, we explained to her that we had gone straight in, not turning at all from the straight path from the "Jesus Loves You" entrance. Salli explained that we could save some underground steps and go in another entrance near the Bellagio that was probably very near where we had ended our trek yesterday. We all piled back into the RV, and Graham drove us to the Bellagio lower parking lot. Upon arrival we all donned our rescue gear—the backpack filled with water bottles, snacks, first-aid kit, and extra flashlight batteries. We had also purchased identical bright yellow, hooded windbreakers that had white reflective stripes on them and light gray sweatpants. For once, I was a little glad that Wal-Mart had something for every occasion. We'd been able to get everything we needed for our mission with just the one stop earlier in the day.

Everyone was wearing the jackets, soft cowhide leather gloves, and our pant legs were tucked into the white tube socks. I'm sure we looked like we were wearing some sort of Halloween getup, but at least the spiders would have less body surface to attach themselves to. We also had odor-control facemasks that were made of activated charcoal cloth to help us tolerate the intense odors of the tunnels. We had purchased enough gear so that Tom and Jimmy could go with us, but they were nowhere to be found. We'd stopped by YWAM on our way to the police station, but the place was locked up tight; nobody answered the phone either. Nevertheless, Salli was wearing the gear meant for Tom, so the seven of us in our yellow windbreakers and backpacks marched from the RV toward the tunnel entrance about a hundred feet from the edge of the parking lot.

Before entering the tunnel, Graham produced two more items for each of us. He said, "I got this idea from Nester yesterday when he was bouncing that length of steel pipe off of the wall; I realized that it would make a pretty effective weapon. So I purchased several two-foot lengths of plastic pipe from the plumbing department in Wal-Mart. Please don't hurt anyone unnecessarily, but if you need to defend yourself, a whack with this should give you a little advantage." He gave Salli a sideways glance. "Is that okay with you, Salli?"

She agreed. "It can't hurt to have a little extra protection. I am wearing my service revolver too, but I've got it under my jacket so it's not too obvious."

"Okay, then the last item for everyone is the headlamp. These were Jedidiah's idea, and a darn good idea at that. Hold your pipe in one hand, and tuck your flashlight into the jacket front pocket so it's easy to get at should you need extra light."

The air inside the tunnel was about thirty degrees cooler than the outside temperature, so the jackets were welcome in that aspect, as well as keeping the spiders off of us. Salli had liked Graham's idea of marking our path with colored tape. She started out ripping off two lengths and putting a large fluorescent orange X near the entrance where we entered the tunnel. She periodically stopped on our trek and marked the wall with another X. We'd gone about the length of a football field when we came to an intersection. She suggested we break up temporarily into two groups and walk ten minutes each way, then reverse direction and meet back up at the intersection. We'd be able to check out twice as much area that way.

Salli handed Graham the blue tape and she said, "I'll take Nester and Unger, if you want to lead the two women and Jedidiah. Mark a blue X every three minutes or so; it will help you be sure to find your way back and keep you very aware of the time."

We turned left and Salli's team turned right. We'd only gone about three minutes when we encountered a dwelling. We saw posters attached to the concrete wall, a mismatched table and two chairs, and two rollaway beds that were folded up and raised up on a makeshift platform of several old wooden pallets stacked together. There was a metal four-drawer file cabinet and one of those Rubbermaid cupboards meant to go onto a deck to store your outdoor furniture cushions, hoses, or garden tools.

Another four minutes into our journey the path was restricted with a small garden shed that someone had evidently hauled in piece by piece and erected in the tunnel. It was raised up on a concrete block platform and had a deadbolt lock on the door. There was an orange extension cord poked through a small neat hole near the door; the hole had been covered in duct tape to prevent the entry of even the tiniest of bugs or spiders. This was evidently the home of someone who had wanted privacy in the tunnel. Jade, exhibiting some bravery, pounded loudly on the door and shouted Jude's name. Her shouts echoed in the silent tunnel, but there was no response from within the shed.

About twenty feet from the little shed, we found a man sitting atop a large wooden table. It appeared to be a sturdy table made with a whole sheet of plywood as the top. The man had a pillow and a blanket, but also stacks of colorful plastic storage boxes piled on either side of him, creating a two-sided barrier. He was smoking marijuana and gave a little wave at us as we neared him. Graham stopped in front of his table but did not approach the man. He told the man we were looking for a young man who was lost. Edging closer, he showed the man a photo of Jude and asked if he had seen him recently.

"I ain't seen nobody for days," he said with slurred speech. "I've been sick an' not able to go out fo' three or fo' days, and there's not 'xactly a lot of tourists down here usually. Ya' wouldn't happen to have anything to drink in that pack o' yours, would ja?"

Graham unzipped his bag and gave the man a bottle of water, an orange, and a small bag of almonds. He thanked the man and said, "We'll be passing by here again in a couple minutes, so if you think of anything, just call out to us when we come back."

We continued on our way, only going about twenty-five feet before turning around. Graham marked our turn-around spot with a large blue X, and as we passed by the man on the table, we saw that he had turned around and was facing the wall. Smoke was still hovering around his head, so he was obviously still smoking his joint.

We returned to the intersection and found the rest of our group already gathered there. Graham gave a quick recap of what we saw, explaining why we were a few minutes late. Nester reported, "We didn't see nothing 'cept spiders and a rat."

We continued on the straightaway, marking the walls with orange Xs every five minutes and loudly singing the Beatles songs, hoping to attract the attention of Jude should he be within hearing range. At the next three intersections we did the same break-off and turning left or right. We saw a few people and several dwellings, but nobody acknowledged recognizing Jude when they were presented with his photo. After two hours we were at an exit, so we climbed up out of the tunnel into the fresh air and stripped off the jackets, headlamps, and facemasks, and after checking thoroughly for stowaway spiders, we stuffed all of the gear into our backpacks.

When we climbed up to street level, we saw that we were on Reno Avenue; the Tropicana and Luxor casinos were nearby.

Exhausted, we weren't looking forward to the trek back to the RV. Salli suggested, "Why don't you all get comfortable in the garden by the pool at the Tropicana? I'll get a ride down to the RV and drive it back up to you."

Graham said, "That's actually a good idea, but I'll go get the RV. You worked all night long; you must be exhausted. Why don't you lead the way out to the pool and I'll go hail a cab?"

The pool, surrounded by palm trees and tropical landscaping, was indeed relaxing. Under different circumstances it would have been quite awesome to sit in the sun and relax at the beautiful Las Vegas pool, complete with a waterfall. But since my son was still missing, I slumped down into a plush lounge chair and put my arm up over my eyes to hide the tears that were brimming, ready to spill out with frustration. Nobody was talking; there was really nothing to say. My boy was still lost and possibly in danger. We all were relieved to be out of the tunnel, but we knew we'd have to go back down after a bit of a break.

After about ten minutes of silence, Unger started to tell us a story. "Do you all know the story of Gideon in the Bible? He was an underdog, but he ended up as a warrior who was empowered with the spirit of God. He did not fear anyone or anything, and with only three hundred men he was able to defeat over a hundred thousand Midianites who had overtaken Israel. It reminds me that with the Holy Spirit empowering us, we are undefeatable. We will not allow demons or evil spirits to keep your son trapped underneath the earth. We are very few compared to the half million people who call Las Vegas home, but we must all have faith that God will lead us to Jude, and there is no need to worry."

Unger's story made us all sit up and take notice. It energized me; I jumped from my lounge chair, hugged Unger, and did a few stretches, waking up my tired, aching body. I hadn't slept much the night before, even though the room was very comfortable, especially with Jedidiah sleeping peacefully next to me.

My energy seemed to seep to the whole group, and when Graham returned, he found us doing calisthenics. I declared,

"Let's go get something to eat, and then we're going back down there, and we won't stop until we find Jude!"

LUCY

That afternoon we must have sang through the two Beatles tunes a hundred times each down in the tunnels, but other than about a half dozen stoned old women and men, we saw nothing that would lead us to Jude.

Late in the afternoon, we decided that maybe going into the tunnels was the wrong plan. We had broken into our separate teams of three and four, and after only five minutes we heard screaming and a lot of commotion coming from the direction where Salli had led Unger and Nester. We quickly retreated to see what had happened and found Nester quite shaken up. He had accidentally knocked down a large web and had a couple of monstrous black widow spiders crawling on him. Salli assured him that he was quite safe, but nevertheless, both he and Unger were very overwrought. We soon found an exit and left the tunnel.

After a short break in the fresh air, we decided to break up into two teams again and watch the entrances to see who went in and out, hoping to talk to the tunnel residents. Maybe they would lead us to a clue. Salli had suggested a couple entrances then went home to sleep, so we were down to a six-member team. She warned us to steer clear of the entrance near the Hard Rock Café; it was known to be a very dangerous underground neighborhood.

Graham, Jade, and Nester were with the RV at the north end of the strip near Circus Circus, while Unger, Jedidiah, and I were near the Rio on the west side. Salli had reported that there were four policemen stationed at four other tunnel entrances, doing much the same as we were. We didn't want to intimidate any of the people; we just wanted some answers. Sadly, we didn't get what we wanted, and at seven o'clock we gave up for the day. Graham picked us up in the RV and we returned to the Alexis.

Despite Unger's earlier Gideon-inspired pep talk, the group was depressed. Thanksgiving was only a few hours away, and it wasn't looking like we would have Jude back in our midst for the holiday.

After a hot shower and donning a new sweatshirt and sweatpants, Wal-Mart specials, I called Lael to report in, letting her know that it didn't look like we'd be home for the holiday. I also asked her to check on my cat; no doubt Jethro would be hungry and in need of a litter box cleaning.

Next, I called my mother; I'd called her earlier in the day, but I needed to let her know that nothing had changed. We had planned to have a huge family dinner at the inn, but it had to be cancelled. Funny how somehow the inn and the whole wedding business seemed so unimportant now; without my son, I wasn't sure what to feel.

Jude had been geographically distant from me for several years, but he was a huge presence in my life. There had been a time when he was mad at me for trying to convince him to seek a safer way of spreading the Word of God, but even then he was my little boy. I couldn't imagine living without him. I tried not to dwell on the possible dangers that he could be enduring, and I really did not want to think about Jude not being able to survive.

Jade saw me sitting alone on the balcony at our suite and came out to join me. She leaned over and gave me a long hug. "Mom, he's all right. I can just feel it. He's my twin, Mom. I would know if he was hurt. He'll be okay."

"I know you are probably right, but until I see him, I'll worry. I'm a mom; that's what moms do. I don't think you realize just how much I miss you two when you're gone. I've always known, of course, that you would grow up and move away, or at least move out, so I'm not saying I wanted you to never grow up. I am saying, though, that I love you both so much and I'm trying to have faith that God will reunite us soon."

Unger and Nester had walked to a neighborhood Chinese restaurant and picked up several servings of take-out. When they returned with the food and a couple bottles of wine, Jedidiah poked his head out the door and announced that the food was ready. Jade jumped up energetically and almost flirtatiously strolled through the open balcony door and centered her attention on the young man with brown curls who was relaxing on the leather couch. "Come on, Graham, let's get some food." She reached for his hand and pulled him up, lighthearted and giggling.

Graham echoed her joy, evident that he too felt that we were gaining ground. "Looks like you're feeling pretty good, aren't you?" he inquired of my daughter.

"Yes, I've been praying and listening to God out there on the balcony. I am confident that we are going to find him very soon!"

I was pleased that Jade was feeling optimistic, but I still had trepidations. I drank a couple of glasses of wine, ate an egg roll, and a few bites of beef lo mein. The wine made me very sleepy, so I was the first to bed. I decided I may as well sleep while I had a case of the drowsies. I hadn't slept much the night before, and I was really dragging.

Several hours later, I woke up and sat in a brocaded slipper chair near the window, looking out at the full moon shining through the upper half of the window, trying to not disturb Jedidiah, who was sleeping soundly, snoring lightly.

I prayed silently to God, asking him for the safe return of my son. After a few minutes, I decided I'd go check on Jade. Opening my bedroom door quietly, I saw that the balcony doors were wide open, and I could hear someone talking on the balcony. The digital clock was displaying three o'clock; I was a little alarmed. Edging closer to the open balcony door, I realized that it was Jade and Graham whom I'd heard. Clearing my throat to catch their attention, I said, "Aren't you two going to sleep?"

Graham answered, "I'm sorry, Lucy. I hope we didn't disturb you. We did sleep about four or five hours, but we both woke up and wandered onto our own balconies at the same time."

Jade continued the explanation, "Yeah, Mom. I knew you'd be freakin' if you woke up and couldn't find me, so I asked him to come over to my balcony when we decided we both couldn't sleep anymore. We've just been getting to know each other better."

"That's okay," I said. "You didn't wake me, but I think maybe you should try to get some more sleep. Tomorrow could be another very long day. And if we do find Jude, Graham's going to need to be well rested to fly us all home."

He conceded, "You are right. Jade is positive that we will be finding your son today, Lucy, so I probably should try to get some more sleep. I know you will be anxious to get back to Kansas City when you're all back together, and my fatigue should not be a reason for you to have to be away from home any longer than necessary." He rose up from the patio chair, and after saying a quick good night, he returned to his suite across the hall.

I said, "I think that since I'm up, I'm going to give Salli a call. She's working the night desk at the police station again, and I think I'll sleep better after getting an update from her."

Jade sat down on the opposite end of the couch where I sat dialing the phone. Shortly, I heard Salli's voice on the other end of the phone, "Las Vegas Police Department; how can I help you?"

"Salli, it's Lucy. Do you have any news?"

Before I finished asking my question, Salli interrupted boisterously, and if she wasn't working, I may have thought she was drunk, her enthusiasm was so outrageous. "Lucy, oh my God, I was just getting ready to call you!"

Confused, I asked, "You were going to call me, why?"

"Lucy, your boy is here! Long story, but he was just brought in a few minutes ago!"

Suddenly elated and frightened at the same time, I asked, "Is he all right? Can I talk to him?"

"He's fine, but he's giving his statement to the sergeant right now. I think you'd better wake up everybody and head down here. I told Jude that you were in town and had been looking for him. He wants to see you right away!"

"Salli, oh, Salli, we'll be right there! Thank you!"

Jade and I were jumping, hugging, and yelping loudly. Jedidiah heard the commotion and came to see what the excitement was all about. "He's fine; Salli says he's at the station. Will you go wake up the guys?" He pulled me into a very emotion-driven hug and a quick kiss before he raced out the door and pounded on the door cross the hall.

LUCY

Less than thirty minutes later we were all bustling into the Las Vegas PD. Salli had been watching for us at the inner doors, and after a quick hug, she immediately took us through to a conference room where my son was waiting for us.

"Jude!" I said loudly and with glee. "Oh thank God you are all right! You are really okay, aren't you?" I was hugging him closely, tears flowing down my face. I hadn't taken time to put on any makeup, so at least I didn't need to worry about my mascara weeping.

"Yes, Mom, I'm fine," he answered. "But truthfully, I am very glad to see you and my sister. All of you really," he said, suddenly noting that the room was full of people coming forward to hug him or to shake his hand. "I'm sorry if I gave you a scare; I guess I never dreamed that you would come all the way to Vegas for me when I missed my flight."

"Son, I would go anywhere for you to make sure you're safe. Don't you know that?" I asked.

Nester was at my side, reaching out to hug Jude, and said, "Boy, you nearly scared your mama to death, and the rest of us too. What happened to you?"

Jedidiah was next. He also hugged Jude, and said, "It's great to see you, Jude. Are you sure you're all right?"

"Hey, there Jed! Thanks for coming, dude!"

"We're all just happy to have you safe. And when you've had a chance to get cleaned up, you can tell us all what happened, but there's plenty of time for explanations later. Let's get you out of here."

Salli opened the door, calling out enthusiastically, "There is a large RV parked illegally out front. Can I talk you all into leaving?" She was smiling and attempting to push us out the door. She looked at me and said, "Lucy Golden, it has been wonderful getting to know you. People like you and your family are the reason I wanted to be a cop. Give me a call sometime, and maybe we will meet up together again in the future."

"Salli, I'm so very thankful to you. I hate to think how our search in the tunnels would have been without you leading the way. You are such a good person; Las Vegas is lucky to have you on the force." We hugged, and I followed the rest of my family to the RV.

On the way back to the hotel, Jude asked, "Did you guys really go down in the tunnel yesterday?"

Unger answered, "Yesterday, and the day before too. That's got to be the scariest thing I've ever done in my life. I hate spiders and I'm claustrophobic, so I hope you appreciate the trauma that we all suffered." He had a jovial attitude with his lament, but I know he indeed had been frightened. He had not wanted to appear weak or useless, so he had fought his fears.

I looked at Unger, sitting close to Nester on the sofa in the RV, and said to him, "Unger, I know we all appreciate the fortitude that pushed you through. Please, relax now. Thank you, everybody, for helping with the search. It is a day to be very thankful, and since today is Thanksgiving, what better way to celebrate than to all be together. I feel like you are all my family now. Nester, Unger, and Graham, you all three will always hold a special place in my heart. I don't know how to thank you."

Nester and Unger both said that no thanks were needed; they were happy to help.

Graham announced, "Here we are, back at the hotel, but before we get out, may I say something?"

He proceeded, "Even though I'm in the business of rescuing people, I don't often meet up with such friendly, gracious, generous people as yourselves. Don't get me wrong, there are good people everywhere, but I don't often feel so welcomed into the flock so quickly. I have to thank you for a good experience.

"Now, let's get inside so this boy can get cleaned up. I think we are all anxious to hear his story."

Before allowing Jude to shower, Graham asked us to make a decision about when to return home. It was decided to go out to eat a large breakfast and then fly home, aiming to leave Las Vegas by ten o'clock. With the flight time and driving time from Kansas City, we could still make it home to have a family Thanksgiving dinner together. While Jude showered, I called my family, and Unger made phone calls to Gianna and Bea. Jedidiah also called his family, and together a plan was formulated for a dinner to be ready for us when we got back to the inn.

We ate breakfast at a nearby restaurant, helping ourselves to their all-you-can-eat buffet. Jude, always good-humored, was truly enjoying being the center of attention. He hadn't yet explained his disappearance, but he did tell us that he was starving; he hadn't had much to eat in the last two days. I watched him put away a large stack of pancakes, about a dozen strips of bacon, half that many sausage patties, and a huge bowl of oatmeal topped with blueberries and whipped cream. Upon finishing that, he declared it was time for dessert, and he returned to the breakfast buffet to get two large cinnamon rolls and a glass of milk.

Unger good-naturedly kidded him, saying, "Jude, if you eat that much all the time, we're going to have to increase our food budget at the inn."

That's when I remembered something that Tom Southwick had said. "Jude," I asked my son across the table, "Tom said you were getting rid of all of your things because you were leaving Las Vegas. What's going on?"

"Well, Mom, I had wanted to surprise you with this, but I guess sometimes surprises don't turn out so good.

"You see, a couple of years ago I got hooked up with a church who wanted to be my benefactor, I guess you'd call it. They wanted to help me finish my degree and then start me in the seminary to become a pastor. So anyway, I took some online classes and finished my BA degree and have been doing the seminary thing too. The agreement was that once I had two years finished I'd move to the town where the church is and become their part-time youth pastor while finishing the seminary.

"So that's what I'm doing, Mom. I know you always wanted me to be a pastor, and as it turns out, you were right. That is where God has called me to be, so once I finish at seminary, I'll be able to take on the roll of the head pastorship at the church after their current one moves on."

"So Jude, where is this church?"

"Manhattan, Kansas, Mom. I'm going to be just down the road from where you live now. Isn't that something? It's pretty cool how God stretches out his hand and draws people together. He has wonderful plans for us, Mom, and I'm so happy to be coming back home!"

"Oh, Jude, that is the best news I've heard, second only to Salli telling me that you were found this morning. So you've been planning this for over two years? And you didn't tell me, why?"

"Mom, I didn't want to disappoint you if it didn't work out. Especially after you moved to Whitney, I knew you would be heartbroken if I told you I was coming to Manhattan and then it fell through."

I could feel my face stretched into a huge smile, and then Jude added another bit of news. "I'm even ordained already, in fact. One of my online courses offered an ordination package, so I paid the small fee, and I'm ordained now to perform weddings and funerals in several states, including Kansas!"

"Well, that is good news," I said. "That's kind of amazing that you can do that on the Internet. I might even have a job for you if you are interested. We have a few weddings booked at the inn, but as of yet we haven't been able to make final arrangements for a minister to perform the ceremonies."

"I'd be glad to help you out, Mom. Just give me the times and dates, and I'll see if they will work with my schedule."

Jedidiah nudged me, and, leaning close to my ear, he whispered, "Maybe he'll be able to perform our wedding too!"

I whispered back to him, acknowledging that I liked his idea.

Jude playfully said, "No secrets! What are you two up to?"

Jedidiah answered, "You'll find out soon enough."

Finally, when we were safely aboard Graham's Lear jet, Jude told us his story, explaining to us why he had disappeared.

JUDE

"On Sunday morning, I packed up all of my stuff and sorted out a few things I wanted to keep. I crammed everything else into an old duffel bag, and balancing it on my back like a pack, I rode my bicycle over to see a couple of my friends, Juan and Juliette. We ended up going out to Red Rocks and doing some rock climbing. We stayed out there till dark, and then we went back to their place and had some steaks and baked potatoes. I crashed on their couch, and the next morning we slept kind of late. When Juan had to leave to go to work at one thirty, I left too and rode my bike over to the tunnel entrance under the Caesar's Palace parking lot.

"I did some painting on the 'Jesus Loves You' mural until the people started coming into the tunnel. While I was cleaning out my brushes, a couple of them walked by me and just ignored me; they wouldn't even look at me when they walked by.

"A short little guy, looked kind of like an Indian came in, and I got his attention. I asked him if he'd want a bicycle. Initially, he was all jittery and said, 'No, I can't afford that.' But when I told him I wanted to give it away, he latched onto it real quick. He was happy to have it.

"Shortly after he rode into the tunnel on my old tiger-striped bike, this black guy with long black dreadlocks come walking up to the entrance, carrying a big wooden pallet, kind of strapped onto his back. I called out to him and asked him if he wanted my pup tent and sleeping bag. He said, 'Yeah, sure, I'd love to have a tent and bag, but I got my hands full.'

"I told him I'd wait right there at the entrance and he could have them when he came back, but he begged and pleaded with me to just follow him in the tunnel. He said he was getting a blister and really didn't want to do anymore walking than he had to. Long story short, he talked me into following him into the tunnel."

"Oh, son," my mom said. "You could have been killed!"

"It's okay, Mom. I just had a feeling that I needed to help this guy. I had a first-aid kit in my pack, so if nothing else I could give him a Band-aid for his blister. He didn't look very big or mean, so I thought I'd be fine. I would just give him the tent, bag, and a couple of Band-Aids, and get back out.

"Unfortunately, it didn't work quite like that. When we got to his crib, he needed help getting the pallet untied from his back, and then he wanted me to help him move his bookshelf so that it was up on top of a stack of pallets. He was telling me that he's the librarian of the tunnel. He collects books and people pay him a quarter to borrow a book. But he wanted to protect the books, get them up off the floor of the tunnel so if a little water flowed in the tunnel they wouldn't get wet.

"He also had some more pallets stacked together with a cot and a lounge chair up on top. We got to talking, and when he found out I was a missionary, he proclaimed that the whole Christian dogma was a farce. He said he'd read through the Bible three times but did not believe any of it. Penbroke, this tunnel guy, challenged me to try to convince him that God was real. I sat down and started telling him how Jesus had saved me and changed my life.

"I kept talking to him, quoting scriptures, and I even read from my Bible. It was pretty dark in there, but I had a couple of flashlights in my pack and some extra batteries, so even after it was nearly pitch dark down there I was able to keep reading the Bible to him.

"After about two or three hours, he started challenging me, pressing me to prove to him what my name was. I had my ID in my pocket, so when I pulled it out, he grabbed it, and that's when I noticed his terrarium. He opened up the glass lid of the terrarium and dropped my ID into the little glass box that was about a foot square.

"I said, 'Hey dude, what are you doing?' I shined my flashlight down into the terrarium and saw about a dozen black widow spiders in there closing in on my driver's license. That was when I first kind of felt like I might be in trouble."

My sister said, "You're crazy, Jude. You should have got out then."

"Yeah, maybe I am crazy," I agreed. "But I knew I wasn't going to be able to get on my flight on Tuesday without that ID, so I had to stick around and figure out a way to get Penbroke to give it back. He was acting a little crazy then, and when I asked him why he did that, he said that he was having a lot of fun talking to me. He didn't get many visitors, and he didn't want me to leave.

"He offered me some jerky and a banana that was black and mushy. I declined and pulled out a box of granola bars and a bottle of water. It wasn't much for supper, but it was better than nothing. He started unpacking his bedroll out of an old plastic trash bin that had a lid snapped on it. He told me to settle down and get comfortable; he wanted to have a slumber party!

"I still had my sleeping bag in my pack, and for once I was happy it was one of those mummy-style bags. It was getting pretty cold down there, and with those spiders I wanted to be as covered up as much as possible. So I crawled down into the bag, pulled it up tight and cinched it around my head like a hood, and kind of stretched out on the lawn chair that he offered to me. All this time he kept talking and asking me questions about Jesus; he never shut up. He just kept talking and talking!

"Then, all of a sudden he fell asleep and was snoring loudly. I sat in the chair, swaddled in my mummy bag, and waited probably ten minutes or so, listening to him sleep. I wasn't sure what to do, but I couldn't just leave my driver's license with the spiders. I had a feeling I knew where we were in the tunnel; the Hard Rock Café was directly above us, and there was another exit very near. I had a buddy who worked nights in the Hard Rock, and he had told me if I ever needed a place to crash to just help myself; he showed me where he hid his key. I figured I could sneak out of the tunnel, go sleep there a little while, and then maybe come back with some help.

"I stuffed all of my stuff back into my pack; it seemed like I had to keep everything with me to survive right now. I snuck out and made my way to my buddy Ray's place, found the key, and before falling asleep on his futon, I set the alarm clock so I'd get up really early and hopefully get back before Penbroke woke up. I'd still have time to make my flight.

"The next morning I took a quick shower and went back to the tunnel. Penbroke was just waking up and didn't seem to realize that I'd left. That was when it dawned on me that I should have looked for a tongs or pliers or anything to use to get into that terrarium and reach my ID without getting bit. I was pretty mad at myself for being so stupid, and when Penbroke started challenging me again about Christianity I decided that God must have wanted me to spend another day with the guy; maybe I could save his soul. I figured I'd just have to get a later flight.

"All day Tuesday I prayed with him and tried to convince him that God is real, that he should open up his heart to just believe. He was a tough one, though, and I figured out that he was also an addict. I didn't know yet what his drug of choice was, though. He hadn't done anything in front of me, but he was pretty off the wall, crazy, and flying high sometimes. He almost passed out a couple times, but then he'd just pop back up and go wild again.

"I tried to get him to talk about the spiders and how he planned to get my ID back out. He told me that he'd named every one of his pet spiders, and he told me some pretty farfetched fantastical stories about his eight-legged beasts. He was pretty proud of them and said he'd find a male once in a while and put him in the terrarium. Then he'd watch them while they bred, and then cheer on the female while she ate the male.

"There were a couple of women that dropped by and looked through his books. They were truly creepy, with lots of tattoos and piercings, and they smelled real bad. If they'd been more normal I might have tried to get them to help me, but they scared me even more than Penbroke did.

"It was kind of hard to keep track of time in the tunnel, and before you know it, it was pitch dark again. I really didn't want to spend another night down there, and I knew I had to get my ID out soon.

"Then I watched Penbroke crush up a couple little white pills, and he sniffed them through a straw. I asked, 'Hey, dude, what are you doing?'

"He thought I wanted to try it out and he told me it was oxycotton—the really good stuff, according to Penbroke. I asked him why he did that. I told him that God could give him a natural high, but then he really started acting crazy. I thought maybe he was going to have a heart attack or something. He was sweating, clutching his chest, and then he just kind of passed out on his cot.

"I was scared and I didn't want to leave him to die, but I thought I'd better get my ID somehow. I kind of panicked and decided I'd go back to Ray's apartment again and get some tools or help to put this horrible experience behind me.

"By the time I got my stuff all packed up again, I could see that Penbroke was stirring a little. I kind of ran out of there and rushed to Ray's apartment. I searched through his kitchen and came up with a pair of tongs and some oven mitts. I made my way back to Penbroke, and he was gone. So was the spider terrarium and my ID.

"I searched around the tunnel a little and asked a couple of guys if they'd seen Penbroke the librarian leaving. But when I asked about Penbroke, I saw fear in their faces. None of them seemed very anxious to see or talk about the guy.

"I was finally nearly ready to give it up when I spied him. He was just leaving the tunnel and had the spider terrarium fastened onto the back of a bicycle with ropes. He was swaying quite a bit, and I was a little afraid that he'd fall, break the glass box, and the spiders would get out and bite people. He was weaving in and around a bunch of people by the casinos and yelling crazy stuff like, 'I'm Spiderman, make way for Spiderman!'

"He was causing quite a stir, and I was chasing him. By the time I finally caught up to him, he had stopped at the park by the Flamingo and was untying the terrarium. He spied me running toward him and he started yelling, saying stuff like, 'Stop that guy. He's trying to steal my spiders.'

"People weren't really paying much attention to him; well, they weren't coming to help him out or to stop me anyway. They were backing away and giving him space. One guy came close enough to see what he had in the terrarium, and he ran away screaming that there were big black widow spiders in the glass box. He got the crowd kind of riled up then. A security guard came out, and together we backed Penbroke into a corner. That's when he opened up the box; he unfastened the latch on the lid while holding the box close to his chest.

"He threw the lid back and shoved his free hand inside. He had my ID in his hand and he started screaming! He screamed that he'd been bit. He dropped the terrarium and the spiders started going everywhere! The guard and I started stomping on the spiders and Penbroke was screaming and wailing, carrying on about being bitten and people killing his babies.

"Suddenly, there were EMT's showing up and some cops. They took hold of Penbroke; he was fighting them all so they had to restrain him with cuffs. They took him away and then the EMTs insisted that I go with them too. They thought I might have been bitten too, so they wanted to make sure I was going to be okay. At the hospital, they checked me over real good; I had a couple mosquito bites, and they found a new bite on my hand that they thought might be a spider bite.

"After they decided I'd be fine, they called the cops to see if they wanted a statement from me. They sent a squad car for me and gave me a ride to the cop shop. When I walked in, the redheaded lady cop at the front desk got all keyed up when she found out who I was. She told me that my family had been looking for me and she was all eager to give you a call. The sergeant made her wait, though, until I told them what had happened."

"So were you bit by a black widow or not?" my mom asked.

"Yeah, I think I must have been. But they gave me a shot and cleaned the wound up. People don't usually react much, let alone die from a black widow bite, despite the terror they seem to cause. I had been scared, but the doctor assured me that I'd be all right."

By the time I answered everybody's questions about my ordeal and repeatedly assured my mom that I was all right, I was exhausted and asked if I could take a nap. I stretched out on the comfy leather couch, and when I woke up we were setting down in Kansas City. Graham was a very good pilot; it had been a very smooth flight and landing. I was surprised to find out that Jade had invited him to go to Whitney for our Thanksgiving dinner; she seemed pretty smitten with the guy.

LUCY

After Jude finished with his tale of the tunnel and the spider man, he took a nap on the airplane. Jade gave up her seat next to him on the leather couch so he could stretch out, and she went to the cockpit, sitting with Graham for the rest of the flight. I couldn't hear what they were saying, but they seemed to be having a fun, lively conversation.

When we landed in Kansas City, Jade said she had invited Graham to join us for dinner at the inn and she would wait with him while he took care of getting the plane fueled and stored in a hangar. I agreed that he was very welcome to join us, and I asked if he had a car at the airport. He said he had called ahead and made arrangements to rent one. We offered to let them use one of ours; we could all ride home together in the PT Cruiser and leave them Unger's catering van, but Graham insisted that he'd rather have his own wheels.

Shortly after hugging my daughter and her new friend good-bye, the five of us were on the road toward Whitney, Jude riding with Jedidiah and me. Thankfully, the roads were clear and dry and the sun was warming the air to a beautiful fifty-degree Thanksgiving Day. We stopped in Topeka and did some quick wardrobe shopping for Jude since he only had the clothes on his back. We had stopped at YWAM before leaving Vegas and retrieved his guitar and Bible. But everything that had been in his duffel bag had disappeared when he'd been taken to the hospital by the EMTs. We made good time and were back at the inn long before dark.

Even though it was late November, there was still a lot of color in the landscape. The inn stood as a massive splendor, the exterior lights shining and picking out the flecks of quartz in the stones. The inn seemed to sparkle. All of the lights were on to welcome us home.

We parked in front near the double-arched stone stairways that stood as parentheses—like sentries around the stone fountain. As we climbed the stone staircase, the ornate carved doors were opened by Mrs. Butler. She said, "Glad you are here; now the Thanksgiving celebration can truly begin. Come in, come in!" She joyfully hugged us as we entered.

The entry and ballroom with the ten-foot ceilings were lit by the beautiful, bright chandeliers, accented with hundreds of dangling and dazzling crystal teardrop shapes. Centered in the ballroom were several oblong tables lined up end to end, covered in a shimmering golden linen tablecloth and decorated with gorgeous floral arrangements in fall tones and pewter candelabras holding tall ivory candlesticks. Quickly, Jude was the center of attention, milling in the throng and calling out to my brothers, Perry and Tommy, who stood near the stone fireplace. A fire was burning, and Jude began telling his story to his uncles, who were soon joined by Jedidiah's brothers Elijah and Darwin.

I slipped behind the marble-topped registration desk where my dad was pouring drinks. I opened the locked drawer where we kept the guest room keys to get a key for my son so he could use one of the guest rooms to change clothes. I noticed that the keys to several of the rooms were missing, so I thought I'd better check the reservation book quickly to see if other rooms were booked too. In the book I saw that number 2 was booked for Mr. and

Mrs. Kermit Weed through the weekend. I was curious; maybe they wanted a second honeymoon. Four of the other rooms were booked as well—all of Gianna's four sisters and their families were staying in guest rooms. I wrote Jude's name in the book for room 7, collected the key, and went to find him. Jedidiah followed with the bag of clothes from our shopping spree. I found my son and urged him to go change into some new clothes. He was wearing a Harley Davidson T-shirt and blue Royals shorts. Jedidiah and I followed Jude and gave him the key to the guestroom and his bags of clothes. I told him to go take a quick shower and change.

Jedidiah and I also left to run home for a quick change. Just as we both returned, Jude was bounding down the stairs after his shower, and his sister and Graham followed us through the front doors. Noticing his twin sister, his face beamed with genuine pleasure, and he hurried toward her. "Sis and Graham, you're finally here! Now the party can begin!"

"You look good, Jude," she said. "Where'd you get the clothes?"

"We stopped in Topeka, and Mom bought me several outfits. She was in her element; do you remember when she used to buy me outfits of clothes? I think she always wanted me to be preppy, no offense, Graham."

"Jude," Jade said with a note of caution in her voice and a tilt of her head, with an expression that said, *Watch it*. "You could use a little improvement in your style. I know your favorite places to shop are thrift stores, but seventies plaid pants and polyester golf shirts really are not a good look on you."

"Yeah, I know, you've always had more class than me, sis. But can you juggle?" Comically, he picked up three wooden blocks from the mantle, part of a Thanksgiving decoration. He started tossing them in the air and did a fine job of juggling them.

Laughing at him, Jade said, "Okay, bro, you win. I guess that clown collection you used to have gave you an edge on juggling skills and bold clothing combinations. Whatever you choose to wear, I'm just glad that you're okay and you are here!" She plucked one of his blocks out of the air, and, ducking another, she moved in for a hug! "I need to introduce Graham to the others, so I'll see you later."

Jade quickly introduced Graham to Tommy, Perry, Wes, Elijah, and Darwin, and then she took him to meet Grandpa and Grandma Goldensmythe. Grandpa was playing the part of bartender, mixing drinks near the entrance. As they approached, he was popping the cork off a bottle of champagne and chuckling when the bottle spewed the bubbly. He quickly maneuvered the overflowing bottle so that the liquid was pouring into champagne flutes that were lined up on a tray.

"Hey there, Grandpa," Jade said gleefully. "Looks like you are having a good time."

"Hi there, pumpkin! This must be the indispensible Graham Sealove!" Putting down the wine bottle and wiping his hands on a towel that hung from his belt, he reached toward Graham. He shook Graham's hand, holding Graham's hand in both of his. Grandpa had a glorious grin, showing his perfect (false) teeth. "Thank you, thank you, son! Without your help, my grandson may still be with that horrible spider man!" The story of Jude's ordeal had quickly circulated among the family.

Jade made the introductions. "This is my Grandpa, Bob Goldensmythe." And to her grandpa, she said, "Yes, this is Graham Sealove."

Suddenly there sounded a loud gong, and after the crowd hushed, Unger announced, "Five minutes until we are ready for dinner seating."

I watched from the west end of the ballroom near the doorway to the dance circle as my family and new friends dashed here and there, finding their partners or rounding up their children. Jedidiah approached me and circled around behind, wrapping me in a bear hug, holding my back to his front in a tender, loving embrace. Whispering in my ear, he said, "My love, are you ready? Ready for us to share our engagement?"

I purred contentedly and said softly in reply, "Oh yes, what a wonderful new life we will have together. Look at this magnificent family that is gathered, our family. Did you ever think that together we could be a part of such a huge family? Even though we never had our own child together, we have so much more!" There were over seventy people gathered at the inn for the Thanksgiving dinner.

Jedidiah and I walked hand in hand to the head of the long table. Continuing our private whispered conversation, I asked, "When do you want to make the announcement?"

"How about right away? Unger and Gianna have all of the food set up buffet style, so before we go get our food, I'll ask Jude to say a prayer. After the amen, we can stand and make the announcement together, okay?"

I nodded my agreement and watched as people folded in, scooting back chairs, and boisterously finding a place at the table. I slipped the diamond engagement ring out of my pocket and onto my finger. At the far end of the long table were our fathers, cornered by our mothers at their sides. The Jordans and Goldensmythes were intermixed here and there with the Goldstone Inn family. Bambi Bellingham and Simon were seated next to Charlie, joined by a woman I guessed to be Bambi's aunt Willow. All of Bea Butler's family was present, including her daughters, their husbands and children, and Kermie and Kitty Weed. Holly and her grandmother were seated across from Ingrid and Bjorn Johansson. Lael and J.J. Jones were next to Shelby, her brother and sister, and my sister Bryn, with Frank. Nester was next, with an empty seat aside him for Unger, who was still busy in the kitchen.

Shortly, Unger and Gianna appeared, ringing the gong again for attention. Everyone quieted and Jedidiah said, "We are fortunate enough to have an ordained minister with us now. Jude, would you care to say a prayer please?"

Jude stood, and, joining hands with Jade seated to his right and me on his left, everyone followed suit by standing and joining hands. Jude began, "Please bow your heads. Father God, thank you for all of the blessings you have bestowed upon us. You are a great and wonderful Father. Help us to emulate you in all of our decisions. Give us the strength to forgive others and to live our lives focused on helping other people. On this day of thanksgiving, help us to remember that the greatest treasures we have to be thankful for are your grace, mercy, and love, given to us by you with the death on the cross of your only son. Bless the hands that prepared this food, and bless each of these wonderful people gathered here today to celebrate. Help us all to truly have the spirit of thanksgiving and to know the joy and peace of your great love. Amen."

A chorus of amens followed, and Jedidiah quickly interceded by saying, "Before you get in the chow line, Lucy and I have something we'd like to announce. Please be seated."

Giggles and the low hum of murmurings broke the silence, but Jedidiah quickly quieted the group. "At every place setting there is a wine glass filled with sparkling cider. Please join me in toasting to Lucy." He tenderly held my hand and pulled me close to his side. "This beautiful, lavender-eyed woman is the love of my life, and even though we lost each other for nearly a quarter of a century, we never lost the love we had for one another. The Goldstone Celebration Inn has brought us all together on this joyous Thanksgiving Day, and today we are officially announcing our engagement! Lucy has agreed to marry me in five weeks, on December thirtieth. Salute to Lucy Golden!" He raised his glass to tap mine and several of the other flutes raised nearby, and together we drank our bubbly.

Our family burst out with whoops and congratulations, applause and good wishes. Jude said, "Wow, Jed, that's wonderful news! Welcome to the family!" Jade had a huge smile on her face and tears of happiness streaming down her cheeks.

I answered back his toast, with a short response, "I'm very happy! Thank you all for coming! Jedidiah means the world to me, and I'm thankful to God for bringing us back together. Now, before I start crying, I think it is time to eat. Unger, Gianna, our mothers, and a lot of you have worked hard to cook this feast, so before it gets cold, let's fill our plates. Please allow our parents to have the place of honor of starting and then join in!"

But before I was seated, Kermie Weed stood up and cleared his throat loudly. "Can I make a toast before we start too?"

I said, "Kermie, you are most welcome to say anything you want."

Kermie stood tall, wearing a brown, polyester, knit, leisure suit that was surely at least thirty years old. His gray hair was slicked back with hair oil, and he wore a huge smile. The people were craning their necks to see Kermie as he stood to speak. He began, "My Kitty and I want to thank all of you wonderful people for sharing this day with us. We usually have a quiet Thanksgiving alone since our only daughter lives way out in California, but suddenly this year we seem to have become part of a larger family. And I hope I'm not stepping on any toes by saying this, but we've been given the privilege of staying here in the honeymoon suite while the Jordan and Braun boys paint the inside of our house for us."

Jedidiah and I exchanged glances, mine questioning, and his seeming to say, *I'll explain soon.*

Kermie continued with his toast, "I can't tell you how much it means to be part of such a kind and generous community. We are truly thankful to you all and to God! Now, drink up and let's party!"

The room exploded in applause and laughter. Chairs were rolled back and people took their plates to fill at the buffet.

Jedidiah and I stayed seated, and, disappearing into each other's eyes, we kissed, cuddled, and giggled like teenagers. I asked him if he knew about the boys' plan to help out the Weeds with their painting project. He quickly told me that all he had done was mention to his boys that someday we should help them get their house painted and they had taken it from there, deciding to do it for free and to pay for their room at the inn as a bonus.

We were oblivious to the commotion around us, dreaming about the future that was starting that very day, commencing that clear November day with the official announcement that we were to be wed.